SANTA FE NOIR

EDITED BY ARIEL GORE

BROOKLYN, NEW YORK, USA
BALLYDEHOB, CO. CORK, IRELAND

Published by Akashic Books
©2020 Akashic Books

Series concept by Tim McLoughlin and Johnny Temple
Santa Fe map by Sohrab Habibion

ISBN: 978-1-61775-722-8
Library of Congress Control Number: 2019935264

Akashic Books
Brooklyn, New York, USA
Ballydehob, Co. Cork, Ireland
Twitter: @AkashicBooks
Facebook: AkashicBooks
E-mail: info@akashicbooks.com
Website: www.akashicbooks.com

ALSO IN THE AKASHIC NOIR SERIES

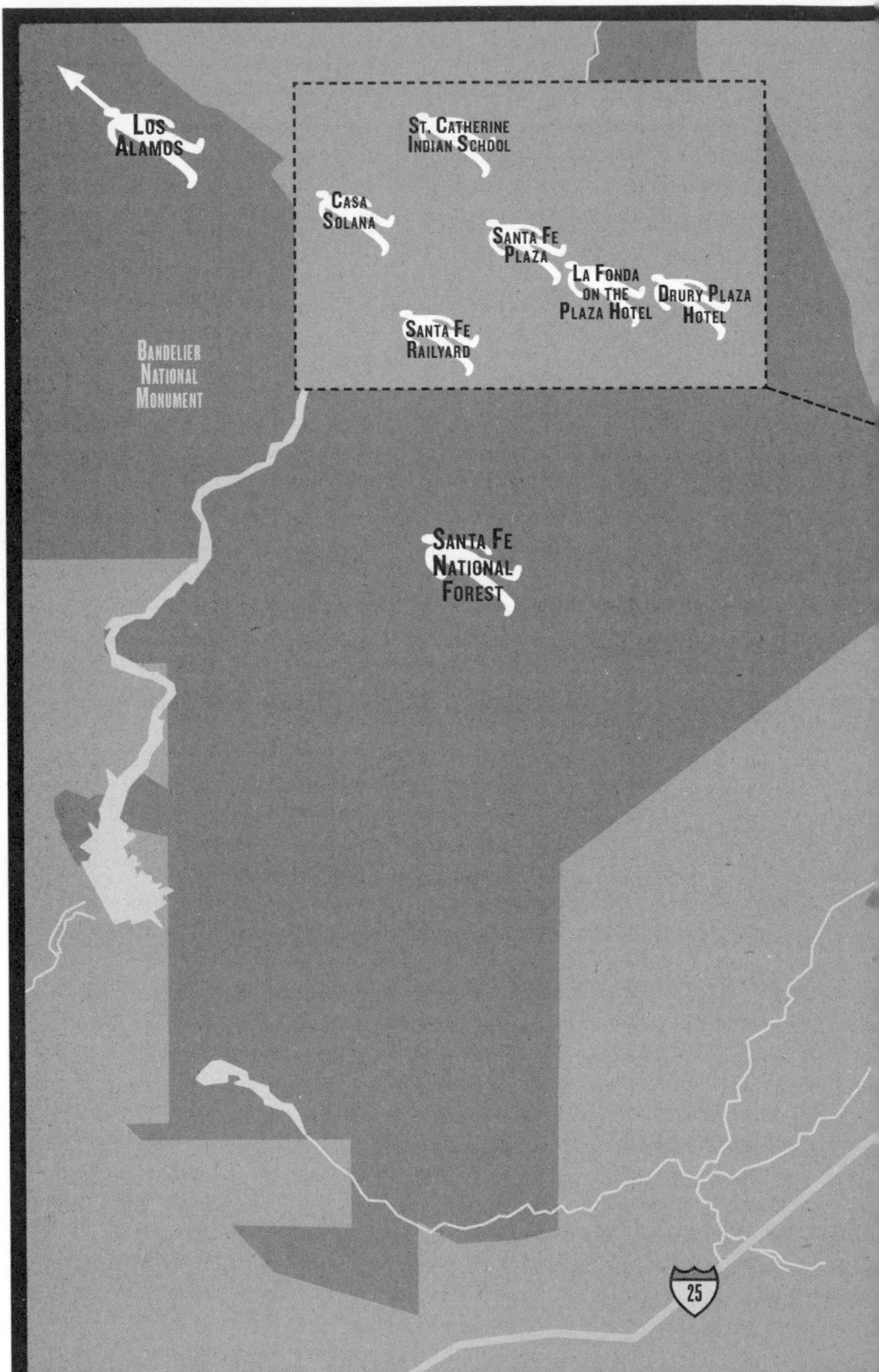
Los Alamos
St. Catherine Indian School
Casa Solana
Santa Fe Plaza
La Fonda on the Plaza Hotel
Drury Plaza Hotel
Santa Fe Railyard
Bandelier National Monument
Santa Fe National Forest
25

SANTA FE

ASPEN VISTA

SANGRE DE CRISTO MOUNTAINS

TEN THOUSAND WAVES

SANTA FE RIVER

PACHECO STREET

CASA ALEGRE

CERRILLOS ROAD

SOUTHSIDE

RANCHO VIEJO

ELDORADO

It would be fine to see you in Santa Fe & if you possibly change your mind, address is: Hotel La Fonda, Santa Fe, New Mex. for the next two weeks at least. I keep thinking about that idea we had for a couple of murders.

—Patricia Highsmith, *Strangers on a Train*

TABLE OF CONTENTS

PART III: WHAT IT FEELS LIKE TO BE HAUNTED

PART IV: WHAT WE DO WITH THE BODIES

INTRODUCTION
Sub Rosa

One way of looking at the plot of the typical film noir is to see it as a
struggle between different voices for control over the telling of the story.
—Christin Gledhill, *Women in Film Noir*

I n 1993, a Santa Fe man named Bill Faurot started to
transplant a rosebush that was dying. All the other rosebushes in his backyard seemed to thrive.

He sunk his shovel deeper and struck what he thought
was a rock, but dug up a human skull.

Local lore says he figured the thing was too ancient to have
kin. After all, finding bodies isn't uncommon here. New Mexico
is the only state in the union that actually requires we bury our
dead the proverbial six feet under, but there's a risk any time we
take shovel to ground: the other bodies could be anywhere.

We might discover someone else's dead when we're trying
to bury our own.

One block of homes near Fort Marcy Park was built right
over a nineteenth-century Spanish-Indian community graveyard. Archeologists say an unknown number of bodies are still
piled, one on top of the next, under those homes.

Faurot set the skull he'd found on a shelf as a bookend.

In 2009, my mother came to Santa Fe to die.

I followed her out of my own sense of love and duty.

I'd spent time in this mountain town before—when the sunsets painted the Sangre de Cristo Range bloodred, I felt that magical *Land of Enchantment* vibe the tourism board slogan promised.

But as soon as I parked my trailer here for real, my neighbors warned me: *Land of Entrapment, more like it. You'll never escape.*

This caution intrigued me.

Maybe it should have terrified me.

A city older than the United States, founded long before any pilgrims ever washed up at Plymouth Rock, Santa Fe has its secrets—its revolts and its hangings, its witch trials and its hauntings, its Indian school of forced assimilation and its Japanese internment camp.

The stories in this collection reflect a fundamental truth about this city: history depends on who's telling it. Too often the story of Santa Fe has been told only by the conquerors and the tourism PR firms. In *Santa Fe Noir*, you will hear the voices of the others: locals and Native people, unemployed veterans and queer transplants, the homeless and the paroled-to-here. When I asked the contributors you'll read in these pages if they had a Santa Fe story to tell, they invariably shrugged and said something to the effect of, "Oh, I've got a story all right. But it might not fit the image of Santa Fe you're looking for."

I said, "Try me."

They came back with the stories that never make the glossy tour brochures: the working class and the underground, the decolonized and the ever-haunted; the Santa Fe only *we* know. Like crows, the stories in this volume begin by circling the city—Eldorado, Aspen Vista, Los Alamos. And then we come in for the kill.

Conquered and reconquered, colonized and commodified, Santa Fe understands—from historical genocide to the murders of family members—the intimacy of violence.

Even the city's breathtaking beauty is a femme fatale: droughts come like stalkers. At night, temperatures can drop fast and deadly.

For some, it's a transient place: Your peyote trip ends here, or your last espionage assignment. You were an anchor baby born in a sanctuary city, or your car broke down near the Saint Francis exit. Your ancestral land was sold out from under you, or you followed your dying mother.

You're broke now.

You just hope your bad luck has saved you from worse.

You're a noir story embodied.

My own first touchstones for noir were film and life—not literature.

Christmases when I was a kid, we went to see *Sunset Boulevard* or *What Ever Happened to Baby Jane?* in some beatnik theater.

My mother used to wake me in the middle of the night to reenact the wire-hanger scene from *Mommy Dearest*—just for laughs.

She taught art on death row at San Quentin and was, for a half dozen years when I was a teenager and young adult, engaged to marry a man incarcerated there.

I spent many adolescent days in the death row visiting room. It was the first time in my previously hippie upbringing that my mother herself allowed me to eat candy bars from vending machines.

While she and her boyfriend whispered to each other and giggled, a Snickers bar on the table between them, I smoked cigarettes in the corner with various serial killers. Men convicted of rape and mutilation joked about the food in the cafeteria. I laughed. But I couldn't square anything in my mind.

I still sometimes think about the way the Night Stalker's hand grazed mine as he took a nonfilter from my pack. The way he stared at my chest, scrutinized my neck, and then, as if only as an afterthought, locked eyes with me. After I read about the children and women he'd killed, I couldn't help but imagine what it would feel like to die, his gaze the last one you'd ever see.

I blew smoke rings to distract myself from that gaze.

I applied lipstick, and looked away.

But when the Night Stalker tapped me on the shoulder and asked me for another cigarette, I demurred.

I couldn't afford therapy, so I turned to noir.

Because all violence—from child abuse to genocide—is confounding without the context of a noir philosophy.

The genre comes to us from the WWII-era realization that people are not, in fact, basically good, but rather easily overcome by their base impulses—or they want to be good, but they're swamped by outside forces. They're drawn into bad things, and they can't figure a way out. People betrayed their own neighbors and lovers to the Nazis, after all—that's the dystopian reality that gave rise to noir.

Not that the Nazis were the first.

People immigrated to lands they had no claim to, demonized those who already lived here, drew borders to suit their own business deals, and amassed armies of mothers' sons to stop uprisings and coming caravans—that's the dystopian reality that gave rise to contemporary Santa Fe.

Bill Faurot kept digging under that rosebush.

Next he found a black garbage bag that contained a decomposing torso.

* * *

I wrote my first noir tale back in Portland—editor Kevin Sampsell dared me. When I started writing, I had no idea *whodunit*. But as I delved into the history of the genre, I had this harshly shadowed lightbulb moment: the narrator in noir has her own agenda.

The victim has agency in noir as well. Morality—and immorality—exist outside the law. Women and outsiders have real power. Like punk rock, noir owns the dystopian now and allows nihilism to meet camp. Like postcolonialism, noir speaks to the human consequences of external control and economic exploitation.

After he found the torso in the black garbage bag under the rosebush, Bill Faurot called the police.

It was a new body, that was for sure. Buried in the last couple of decades, anyway. Medical examiners ruled the remains were those of a female who died from a skull fracture that was probably caused by a gunshot. Her body parts bore markings similar to those made by a saw.

But there were no officially missing persons to connect the remains with.

A few years after *Portland Noir* was published with my story in it, I was down in Santa Cruz reminiscing about my ill-spent youth hitchhiking through redwoods. *Santa Cruz Noir* editor Susie Bright double-dared me. Would I write another?

Why, yes. I wanted to return to this idea of the shady narrator.

I wanted to understand the history of the West.

I wanted to explore why humans prey on those more vulnerable. It goes against all ethical doctrines, but it's as if we can't stop ourselves. We seem to hate being reminded of our own weakness so much that we'll even murder that which is vulnerable within ourselves.

* * *

In Santa Fe, evidence pointed to Doug Foote, a real-estate appraiser from Oklahoma who'd lived with his mother in that house with all those rosebushes.

Where was Donna Foote now? Doug Foote's story seemed questionable. He said she'd moved to Maryland. But DNA evidence said the body under the rosebush was hers. Doug told investigators he'd been taking a lot of hallucinogenic drugs in the 1970s. He could only remember that "something bad" had happened in Santa Fe.

The jury never saw that part of the video—where he talks about the hallucinogens.

Doug Foote was acquitted in 2003.

The Night Stalker died of natural causes in 2013.

Noir affirms our experience: Humans aren't ethical. The good guys don't win. Violence impacts. The bodies don't go anywhere. But lipstick looks good. And people still smoke cigarettes. No, they really do. They still smoke cigarettes.

After my mother died, I left Santa Fe. But just as my neighbors had warned me, Santa Fe would soon lure me back.

All of life, maybe, is a struggle between different voices for control over the telling.

Something bad happened in Santa Fe.

A pretty mouth whispers: *Believe the more vulnerable.*

Ariel Gore
Santa Fe, New Mexico
November 2019

PART I

A Land of Entrapment

THE SANDBOX STORY

BY CANDACE WALSH

Eldorado

> *"Over the Mountains*
> *Of the Moon,*
> *Down the Valley of the Shadow,*
> *Ride, boldly ride,"*
> *The shade replied,—*
> *"If you seek for Eldorado!"*

—"Eldorado," Edgar Allan Poe, 1849

I work at home, but my office has its own entrance, even its own can. When I bought the place, the office was kitted out like an artist's studio—easel, palette, the works. I saw a half-finished painting of an adobe wall below one of those iridescent salmon-streaked sunsets, the kind that makes tourists cream their panties. *Go ahead, finish the picture.* How many people get in car crashes while snapping sunset pictures, I don't want to know.

I tossed that crap in the trash right after they handed me the keys. I know, I could have left it with the local school. Shoot me.

I had an hour to read the paper before my first client, Sam. I was soon shaking my head about a Good Samaritan— on his way to get married—who got killed helping some jackass without AAA change a tire on I-25.

How often do you accidentally find that you've veered onto the shoulder of the interstate when you're driving somewhere? Never, right? So you're gonna wait until there's an El Camino stacked with ratty furniture and boxes, some guy sweating in the sun as he jacks it up, and that's when you swerve to the right?

My office doorbell went off with the staccato of a vintage telephone. It needs replacing. I did get rid of the cast-iron green-chile door knocker that felt like palming a choad. *Why is Sam so early?*

I opened the door to a stranger. Cropped hair, windblown, dark. Tanned skin with constellations of dots across her nose and cheeks. A red mouth.

"You're not Sam," I said.

"No, I'm Delphine," the woman said. "Delphine Hathaway."

Hathaway: you see that name around here. Above the brokerage, the wine shop, and on the nicer mailboxes, on the most tucked-away cul-de-sacs. I've only been here a few years, but long enough to know the taxonomy.

The first time I visited Eldorado, I drove out to a dinner party at night. My hosts didn't warn me that community covenants forbade (among many other things) streetlights, to protect night sky viewing, and that the street signs are affixed to their poles above headlight level. Although I never did find my friends' house, I found Eldorado.

As I finally pulled over at the end of some dirt road, my headlights pierced the night, pressing their beams against a muscular darkness that pushed back harder. I walked out a few feet before sitting down in sandy dirt. Stars pulsed with an eerie tempo: dots and clusters, arcs and whorls.

When I returned in the daytime, I saw that these sand-colored houses sit on several acres each, oriented toward the sun and away from each other. Piñon trees, gold chamisa, and swarms of cholla cactus dot the land. Prickly pears mound and bristle below their fuchsia blooms. Wild grasses grow every which way: blue grama, sage, galleta. Mountain ranges hug the town; some round like bellies and breasts, others crepuscular, jagged.

The Hathaways bought one of the first houses here in 1972, on what used to be the old Simpson Ranch. They had an Irish amount of children, and all of them went back east to college, got married, and bought houses so tucked away here you could spend years without going down one of the long, groomed dirt roads from which their long, groomed gravel driveways branched. Except Delphine.

I have an ear for stupid gossip like that, overheard at the grocery store when matriarch Bonnie Hathaway was there selling Girl Scout cookies with her glossy, gap-toothed granddaughters.

"And how *is* Delphine?" asked some woman in ill-advised white capris.

"Delphine is Delphine," Bonnie sighed with stately resignation. "We got a postcard from Ibiza last month. She's been teaching flamenco dance on a cruise ship."

"She was always . . . different," White Capris tittered.

Different.

"Are you going to ask me in?" Delphine asked, stepping forward in a fawn-leather Cuban-heeled shoe.

"I don't know you," I said, as I opened the screen door.

"Don't you know who I am?" she vamped with a throaty chuckle. "The black sheep of the Hathaway clan." She headed toward the black leather Eames lounge chair, trailing tuberose.

"Nope," I said. "Mine." I pointed toward the sofa. "So when you're on the cruise ship," I asked, "do you always drop by the shrink's without calling first?"

"The *cruise ship*," she said. "Is that what Mother's telling people these days?"

"What's the truth?" I asked.

"Nope," she said. "For that, I'll have to pay *you* a pretty penny." She smiled with a squint. "I will lose my mind staying here. I already know that. But I can delay it with a therapist. One I can walk to. Who doesn't know my family. Which narrows it down to you."

"You don't drive?"

"I'd like to see you three times a week," she said. "I'll pay cash. Tomorrow at eleven works for me."

I looked at my book, furrowing my brow as if I were trying to spot an empty slot in a sea of clients. But she was halfway out the door. A moment later, a car rumbled out of my driveway. I walked outside and watched the low, sun-sucking, gray-primed Trans Am drive too fast toward Impulveda Road, dust plume behind it like a squirrel tail. A family of quails skittered across the dirt road in their wake. Someone else was behind the wheel.

I had enough time before Sam's scheduled arrival to indulge in two guilty pleasures: a breakfast beer and NabeWatch Eldorado, the local message board where people posted:

Need a Plumber; Near Car Crash at 285 and Vista Grande; Lost Parrot; U-Haul Trucks Now for Rent at Hardware Store; Keep Your Dogs from Pooping in My Yard; Free Yoga Classes; Red Pickup Truck Speeding near School; Farmers Market Friday; Police Cars at Cleofas Court; HUGE Bull Snake in My Garden; U-Haul Trucks in Parking Lot an Eyesore; Dog Poop . . . AGAIN!; Fatal Crash at 285 and Vista Grande; Beware This Plumber.

"I had another platypus dream," Sam said. He had so many platypus dreams that I'd gone to the trouble of looking up platypus animal medicine. I also had no therapy chemistry with Sam—really, I should have referred him to someone else, but I needed the money—so drew from the animal medicine suggestions when I came up blank.

"Tell me about it."

"I was with my ex-wife. We were making love." He stiffened. "Why did you cringe?"

Damn it.

"You thought I cringed," I said impassively. "Let's stay with your dream."

"So I was making love to her, but instead of putting my penis inside her vagina"—*oh dear God, neutral neutral neutral*—"I consummated the act by licking her clavicle."

Platypus females nurse their babies from mammary patches on their skin; they don't have teats. They also pee, poop, lay eggs, and have reproductive sex with the same hole, the cloaca. As opposed to recreational platypus sex? I stifled a smirk.

"But I couldn't make her come, and my mouth began to ache. I went to get a glass of water and when I came back, she had turned into a platypus."

"How did you know she hadn't been replaced with a platypus?"

"It had her distinctive birthmark," he said, "near its . . . cloaca."

If the platypus is your totem . . .

"Sam, in the next week, I'd like you to redirect yourself, when you find yourself ruminating, to the present moment. Come back with a few things you've noticed within this mindfulness practice that make you uncomfortable."

After Sam left, I headed to the hardware store to buy a new doorbell. I noticed the gray Trans Am parked beyond the blacktop in packed dirt. My pulse quickened as I wondered if

I'd bump into Delphine, and whether she'd want to say hello or pretend she didn't know me, something I tell clients I'm fine with. It still feels kind of shitty.

The store managed to recreate the dinge and chockablock of a Norman Rockwell–level hole-in-the-wall, but not picturesquely. Sometimes it took a few minutes to get help, because of the lip-smacking pleasure the two bearded old codgers behind the counter reveled in while jawing with each other. It was as if they were recording a podcast. One memorable topic: Eldorado's status as an enduring Black Death incubator.

"One thing people don't realize about the guy who died from the bubonic plague here is that he and his wife kept a pack rat as a pet. The *official* story is that they left their bathrobes out overnight by the hot tub, and that animals infected their robes. But I know friends of theirs who said that they *adopted* this pack rat, slept with it, dressed it up in costumes, crazy shit like that."

Pack rats have a habit of arranging dried dog poop logs and other detritus into pretty designs. I wondered if the pack rat decorated the inside of the victim's house this way.

Today a new guy approached me right away. He reminded me of my brother. Shaved head, pointed beard. His sinewy arms, exposed to the shoulder, jumped with crude tattoos.

"Hi, I'm Todd," he said, grinning. A couple of gray teeth, a couple of metal ones. After I got braces, my brother appreciated how much more it hurt when he punched me in the mouth. I ran my tongue against the crosshatched inside of my lower lip.

Toothless, the platypus uses gravel to masticate its food.

I told him I was looking for a new doorbell.

"Great! You've got your battery-operated, your hardwired, and these Internet gizmos. Or you could go the gong route." He held up a metal disk suspended from string, and struck it with a little mallet, loosing a deep, undulating timbre. "That's what *she* said," he called out, threw his head back, and laughed.

Delphine took off her trench coat and tossed it beside her on the couch, sat down. Her cream-and-black spectator pumps caught my attention like a toss of dominoes, and I raised my eyes to hers, conscious not to rain glances on her body. Still, I noticed: black wool slacks, pellucid silk blouse.

"Can I vape in here?" she asked.

"It's better if you don't," I said. "It can be a barrier to delving into your feelings."

"You think?" She kept it in her hand, rolled it across her palm. "How ever will I satisfy my oral fixation?"

I took a deep, grounding breath.

"I ran into someone at the supermarket yesterday. Jacob," she said. "We went to preschool together here. Jacob was bigger than all of us then. The one whose name all the parents said with a roll of the eyes and a sigh."

Like my brother.

"I was the smallest kid in the school. One day I got to play with 'the coveted'"—here she raised her fingers in scare quotes—"red shovel. Jacob grabbed it and tried to pull it away from me. I didn't let go. He pulled me. Across the sandbox. Over the wooden edge. Over the grass and gravel."

She exhaled.

"By the time the teachers noticed, I had bloody scrapes all over my legs. It ruined my favorite gingham romper . . . it had plastic ladybug buttons. Mother threw it out after that day. The teachers made Jacob help them wipe down my scrapes with peroxide and bandage me up. After that, Jacob followed me around like a puppy. He gave me half his snack, put away my blocks." She laughed. "Imagine. I bossed him around like a tiny fairy queen."

It must have come naturally. She was a Hathaway.

"But after two days I got bored of him, and I told him to leave me alone."

I felt a pang for Jacob. "How do you feel about it now?" I asked.

She looked down, smoothed her pants over her knees. I could not see her eyes.

"He got his revenge," she said. "Eventually."

If you never went to its one bar, you'd imagine Eldorado to be the way it looks from the outside: clean-cut retirees, families with school-age children, the occasional hippie woman with a truly impressive garden and a pack of rescue dogs. If Eldorado were a body, a healthy, rugged body wearing Tom's of Maine deodorant, the bar would be its navel. Filled with lint and sweat and dead skin cells, a pungent odor, nooks and crannies, hairy around its perimeter.

The only thing that bar had going for it was that the manager usually hired lesbians to bartend. I still miss Josie. She leavened the tavern's funk with her swagger, the twinkle in her hazel eyes. Before she moved back to Sacramento, we could expect the occasional free beer to slide into our progression of pints along with impromptu slam-style erotic poetry snippets. It says a lot that I still think of her so fondly, given that a few weeks after Josie left, my girlfriend Rose followed that dreadlocked, freckled, gap-toothed siren to the City of Trees. I didn't see it coming. Maybe the erotic poetry should have tipped me off.

The platypus bill contains electrosensors that guide it to its prey.
I still go there sometimes, when it's almost empty and al-

most quiet and I can claim a corner of the sofa and work on my session notes. My ears snag winsome lines from quiet conversations. *I'm just an old chunk of coal. Maybe I'll be a diamond soon. I hope before I die.* But most of the time, people are drunk, loud, grimy. Farmers and ranchers drive ten or more miles to kick it without having to shower and change like they would in Santa Fe. They talk with the shaky recent divorcée with the nerve jumping around in her left eyelid, or the grimly proud Los Alamos scientist with the old Spanish family name, or the tall, courtly horseman who you'll later recognize on the documentary series about weird shit in the USA, episode topic: gay rodeos.

But if people are spilling out onto the front patio, if half the barstools are taken, if someone ordered pizzas, fuzzy-faced denizens will be rooting for the wrong team on the TV, and I just keep driving.

"I told you about Edward, who helped me study for my CPA exam," said Karen, my client who most needs to take a turn in a movie about moms behaving badly.

I nodded. She'd been guiltily titillated by his math-nerd passion, how nice he smelled, his penchant for suits and ties in this denim land.

"When my daughter needed a math tutor, I thought of Edward. And part of it was that I wanted to see him again. You know, I'm happy with my husband."

I'd been a therapist long enough to know that didn't matter.

"I knew he was good, and I'd vetted him myself."

"Your daughter's . . ." I looked down at my file.

"Fifteen. Her grades *did* go up." Her eyes welled with tears. She hesitated. "I read in the paper this morning that he was arrested because he'd been having sex with not one, but two different fourteen-year-old girls."

I handed her the tissue box.

"How could I not know? How could I have felt so safe with him? How could I have *liked* him? I thought I was a good judge of character."

"Is your daughter—"

"Fine. Nothing happened. I think she might be a little insulted that he didn't put the moves on her." She barked a laugh. "I told her that she was too old for him."

"And how does that make you feel?"

"Ancient," she said. "I primped for him. He must have looked at me and seen Minnie Pearl."

"But you were around the same age. What upsets you about it the most?"

"She formed a relationship, however innocent, with Edward, because of me. I don't trust myself anymore."

The female platypus holds her incubating eggs against her body with her tail.

I glanced at the clock. Delphine was my next client. Time for my summing-up bromide.

"The thing that stands out to me, apart from this sordid business, is how the infatuation with Edward used to make you feel. Where else can you find that in your life?"

Delphine breezed in, smelling of lily of the valley.

"Last time you were here, you mentioned that Jacob got even with you somehow. Do you want to talk about it?"

"Oh, that," Delphine said. "I don't know."

"Let's try."

She kicked off her red crushed-velvet ballet flats and tucked her feet beneath her. Her hair fell across her cheek, shielding her eyes. I saw her take a steadying breath, as if she were waiting in the wings to perform. The late-morning light slipped through the heavy wooden blinds, casting stripes across her white boatneck sweater.

Then she cried out in pain.

"What's wrong?"

"Leg cramp." She bent over her knees. "*Leg cramp.* Help me." She tried to pull her feet out from under her.

I grasped her calf, and gently unbent her knee. She wiggled her hips to release the other ankle, grunting softly.

"Punch it," she said.

"What?"

"My calf muscle. To stop the cramping. I can't . . ."

I formed a fist, tapped her spasming muscle.

"No, goddamnit, *hard.*" She arched her back. "It's going up my leg!"

I lifted her foot to my shoulder and whacked her calf muscle once, twice.

Delphine went soft with relief, her leg sliding down the front of me. She sat up, smoothed her hair. "I should go," she said.

"Stay," I said. I sat down and crossed my legs, which released a surprising, silent peal of pleasure. "That was one of the most intense cases of resistance I've ever noticed in a client. You were about to tell me about Jacob."

She rolled her eyes, paused. "When we were in high school, Jacob and I bumped into each other. He seemed friendly. I hadn't seen him in years—we went to different schools—but I had just passed my road test. My friends couldn't celebrate with me until that night. I was itching for something to do. He invited me over. I thought his parents would be home, or his sister, but the house was empty. He offered me a beer and I accepted it. We went out to the back patio. He pulled out two pills.

"*Valium?* he asked. They looked different, but he told me

one was generic. I popped it. When the pill hit, I felt a delicious calm descend. We just stared at the clouds. Then a ladybug landed on my wrist and it tickled. When I tried to raise my arm, I couldn't. So I tried to wiggle my toes. I could do that, just a little bit.

"*Have more beer*, Jacob said, holding up the can. I tried to raise my other hand. I couldn't move that either. He smiled and made a sound—*ding*—like a kitchen timer going off. And he stood over me, taking off my clothes while I watched, straining against my stilled body. I told him to stop. He just kept going. When he was raping me, he said, *You want me to leave you alone now?* And I told him yes, and he said, *Say it.* That's when he came, when I said it."

She raked the tissue across her eyes with trembling fingers. "I can't help thinking that if I'd said no to the pill, which had to be an animal tranquilizer, I would have been okay."

"It wasn't your fault, Delphine."

"I was so fucking stupid. I had no reason to trust him."

"We often learn these lessons the hard way. That doesn't make you stupid."

"And now . . ." She bent over, her shoulders convulsing.

I wanted so badly to place my hand on her arm, to soothe her. Some therapists did, some didn't. But after our innocent yet intense physical interaction earlier, it seemed innocuous enough.

I placed my hand on her shoulder.

She looked at me, tears streaming. "He just moved in next door to my parents' house! I have to move. Either out of Eldorado or back to Europe."

Her words licked through me like a flame. I would miss her so.

"What's holding you here?"

"You." She smiled crookedly.

A plume of warmth filled my aching chest.

"I want to get over this. I've never told anyone about Jacob before. I have only told the sandbox story."

"The sandbox story shows how tenacious you are. You're still that strong and determined."

She looked up at me through damp eyelashes. "A friend of mine wants me to take over his lease, because he can't afford the rent. But I have to do it tomorrow. My parents won't be home then. I've never told them what happened, and they would just blame me if I did."

"So it's always been a secret between you."

"Yeah, I left pretty quickly after that to go to Simon's Rock, at Bard, where you can start college as a high school student."

"Didn't they find that to be odd?"

"My mother went there, so not really. I thought I could always come home again. But I never felt comfortable here after that. So when my best friend from college's father fell in love with me, I traveled the world with him. When we broke up a few years later, one of his clients picked me up. It's been like that ever since. Except it appears I'm aging out of this line of work. And I'm tired of it. I want to fall in love with someone real. Is it too late?"

"No," I said vehemently.

She nodded. "But I need your help."

"My help?" To fall in love? My heart juddered.

"I know this is ridiculous, you're my therapist, but I don't know who else to ask. My friend has to work. Will you rent a U-Haul truck for me? I can give you all of the money. I just don't have a license. I can hire laborers, my friend knows some."

"That's a tough one, Delphine. You're asking me to cross a therapist/client boundary."

She looked crestfallen.

I thought of picking up the truck, entering the Hathaway compound, being useful. Delphine offering me a cold beer at the end of a long day. A stupid rule could keep Delphine trapped near Jacob. He could strike again. She could disappear from the Hathaway house, Eldorado, my practice, and my life.

"Then again, *not* helping you, knowing what I know about Jacob, seems even worse. Why don't you have a driver's license?"

"After the . . . you know, the thing with Jacob, everything seemed overwhelming. I never followed up with the paperwork."

We made plans to meet at the hardware store the following morning at eight.

The next morning, I showed up in my best yard-work clothes. Todd of the pointed beard walked us out to the U-Haul cluster. Delphine's clogs clonked against the macadam.

"That one," Delphine said, pointing to a fifteen-footer.

I gave him my driver's license.

He looked at Delphine's credit card and my license and shook his bald head. "The credit card's gotta match the driver's license name."

"Oh!" she said.

He stuck his pen in his mouth and worked it like a cigar. "Yeah, you know, we just gotta have these rules because people have all sorts of tricks up their sleeves, and it's not fair but life ain't fair, and these rules are here to protect all of us even if it isn't always the most convenient thing . . ."

Unable to bear his pompous bloviating for one more second, I handed him my credit card. "Delphine, you can reimburse me. Not a problem."

"Oh, thank you," she said, and threw her arms around me. I gave her back a horridly proper psychologist pat, when I wanted to pull her even closer. Then I noticed Todd leering at us. He ran his stubby fingertips over his chest and cackled.

"Little Todd wants a hug too," he said.

Delphine and I jumped apart. She turned toward the truck as I mutely signed the rental form, cheeks burning.

I slid my license and credit card back into my wallet and wondered, as we climbed into the truck that smelled of stale farts and coffee, how she'd gotten to the hardware store. Maybe she walked. I should have offered to give her a ride.

Delphine seemed somber as we carried boxes into the truck. The laborers handled her furniture. But the truck soon proved bigger than the job required. I was going to mention it, but she beat me to it.

"I'm pretty spatially challenged for a dancer," she said. "We could have gotten away with the next size down."

She told me her new place was down a long dirt road on the other side of 285. Most homes there were of the mobile variety, with appliances rusting out front, and adobe shacks with none of the grace of the houses of Eldorado. I suddenly appreciated the numerous covenants that ruled that land.

Delphine directed me to stop at a tall ranch gate crowned with an iron longhorn design. She hopped out, fiddled with the lock, and swung the gate wide open. I drove through, followed by the laborers in their ancient pickup truck, onto a rutted road. Horses grazed, alfalfa swayed.

After about a mile, she pointed to a tidy log cabin with a front porch.

"It used to be a ranch-hand cabin."

We parked and carried the first load of boxes inside. Two

old wooden built-in bunk beds barnacled the far wall. A small kitchen, potbellied stove, a flagstone floor.

"Home sweet home," she said.

As I trudged back and forth with Delphine's things in my arms, I felt a contentment I barely remembered. In sessions, I helped people, but I did it while sitting still. This was therapy too.

I wouldn't tell my supervisor about it, because he was hidebound to traditional rules. Even if he did understand, he really couldn't say so.

I swept out the truck and closed it up.

"If you leave now," Delphine said, "you won't get charged for another hour."

"Are you sure you don't want help unpacking?" I asked. "I don't care about the money."

"I care about the money. I insist on paying you back. You've done too much as it is."

"Okay," I said, deflated. I nodded to her, and she nodded back. "You have cell phone service out here? And the door has a lock?"

"The door has a lock, and if all else fails, there's always this." She lifted her jeans cuff, flashing a mother-of-pearl-handled gun strapped to her ankle.

The male platypus has a venomous spur in his right leg.

She kissed her fingertips and placed them against my cheek. "Thank you," she said.

In the truck's mirror, a few yards down the road, I saw the red lipstick her fingertips had imparted. I raised my finger to the smear and rubbed it, then drew it roughly back and forth across my lips.

Todd walked the perimeter of the truck and shined a flashlight around the inside. It reminded me of the time that I rented a car from the Santa Fe airport, and they charged me for a broken windshield even though I had returned it undamaged.

"I'll be right back," he said.

While I waited, I took photos of the unscathed outside of the truck, and the cab.

At the bar, the conditions were good. Just a few people smoking illegally on the front patio, most of the barstools free, quiet conversations among friends, and on TV, two of my favorite sports teams mopping the floor with their opponents. After a couple of hours, I was too drunk to care about the people spilling out onto the front patio, all of the barstools taken by people eating pizzas, fuzzy-faced denizens rooting for the wrong team on the TV. I remember dancing to AC/DC at some point, with other revelers. But after that, I went dark.

I don't remember how I got home. I woke up in my moving clothes, smelling of smoke and stale beer. My car was in the driveway, parked askew. The driver's-side mirror dangled from a wire, and I wondered which whimsically painted Eldorado mailbox I had clipped.

Wallet: check. All contents accounted for, except for the cash. I'd have to see how much I abused my debit card by looking online, but not yet. I'd make a big, slutty, greasy breakfast first, take a bath, smoke some weed, and watch old movies for the rest of the day.

Delphine didn't show up for her Monday appointment. Then again, she didn't have a car and she lived in the middle of nowhere. At a quarter past the hour, the new doorbell rang. *Bing-bong.* Silly of me to assume so fast. She'd made it.

I opened the door to two strangers. Dressed in blue.

"I'm Officer Valdez and this is Officer French. Mind if we ask you a few questions?"

"Come on in," I answered. "Please, sit down."

"Did you rent a U-Haul truck Saturday?"

"Yes, to help my friend—um, client—move."

My stuttering did not escape them.

"Well, that same U-Haul truck was involved in a robbery early yesterday morning, about four a.m. Right here in Eldorado, at the jewelry shop."

"There must be some misunderstanding," I said. "I returned it Saturday."

"According to the hardware store, you did not. They reported it as stolen at around five p.m."

"What happened?"

The cops looked at each other. Valdez nodded to French.

"An individual backed into the front of the jewelry shop with the truck, breaking the window," French monotoned. "The jeweler reported $100,000 worth of gold jewelry stolen. Todd Lapidus reported the truck stolen, and you're the last one who rented it."

"*That* guy," I said. "He checked the truck back in himself."

"Do you have an alibi?" Valdez asked.

I was at the bar! What a relief. Those new best friends whose names I couldn't remember would vouch for me. But then there was my blackout. The cops would have a lot easier time pinning something on me if they knew about it.

"No. I live alone." Goddamn Josie the erotic slam poet. Thanks for stealing my alibi along with my girlfriend. "You should probably speak with my attorney," I said. "Just to be prudent." I rifled through my Rolodex and handed them her card.

"Thank you for your cooperation. We'll be in touch."

Todd. He stole the jewelry, but tried to frame me. Just my luck to be the one he decided to nail. Delphine was my only client that day. *Delphine.* I hoped she was okay. I called her cell phone, but she didn't pick up. I'd drive over and check on her before I called my lawyer.

About three-quarters of the way down her road, I realized that the gate would be locked. I couldn't make a U-turn on the narrow road, so I steered into the next driveway. I saw a flash of telltale orange behind the neighboring house. It looked like a U-Haul truck.

I began to back out of the driveway, braking when I heard an approaching car. The gray-primed Trans Am rumbled by. In my rearview mirror, I glimpsed Delphine's profile framed by the passenger window, wind lifting her hair from the side of her face like a bird's wing, flash of gold at her ear.

The car turned into the next driveway and parked in the back. I parked my car behind a low cluster of piñon trees, and crept through the bushes and trees between the two hovels. I saw Delphine pull a burlap sack from the car, heard her curse as a small rain of mannequin hands spilled onto the ground. The driver's door opened, and out stepped Todd.

Todd.

He laughed, picked up a plaster hand, rubbed it against his chest. "Oh yeah," he said.

She took the hand from him and tossed it in the bag, then put her own hand on his chest. They kissed. I thought of his gray and metal teeth.

"Tonight, Joe will drive the truck out to his junkyard in Chupadero and blow it up," he said. "When he's done, it'll blend right in with the rest of those fucked-up carcasses. Get it? *Car*-casses . . ." He guffawed. My brother had that stupid sense of humor too. And yeah, we had the same taste in women.

I pulled my phone out of my pocket and clicked on the camera app, noting that the last photos I took were of the U-Haul truck as I returned it. Relief. I had *proof*. I snapped more photos of Todd and Delphine near the truck.

I was almost to my car when my phone rang. Loudly.

"Hey, what the fuck?" Todd yelled.

It continued as I broke into a run and slid into my car, dropping the keys on the floor after I hit the lock button. My hands scrambled blindly for those keys as Todd's meat hooks slapped against the windshield. Delphine ran up behind him, gun in hand. I rammed the key in the ignition and floored the gas pedal, knocking Todd into the ditch. As I hugged the curve, a bullet took out my right-side mirror. It would only be a matter of time before Todd's Trans Am caught up to my old shitbox Corolla. I turned left on 285, and blazed through a yellow light at the Vista Grande intersection, going 85 in a 50.

Delphine knew where I lived. I couldn't go home. Was she even a Hathaway? Was her name really Delphine?

Sirens. I saw a cop car's blazing cherry in my rearview mirror. Thank God.

"You again," Officer Valdez said, perhaps unnerved by my thank-you-savior smile. "Do you know how many people get killed at that intersection? We were getting ready to arrest you anyway. This saves us the trouble."

"Please do," I said. "Put me in your squad car, fast, and then look at these photos on my phone." I pointed to the cell on the passenger seat.

As I stepped out of the car, I heard the Trans Am in the distance. It crossed 285 and kept going. Were they thinking they'd head me off on my way home?

I sat in the back of the squad car, handcuffed, while Valdez completed mysterious and prolonged tasks on his tablet. The minutes ticked by.

I looked out the back window, saw Valdez lob my phone into the tall grasses. What the . . .

A giant truck hauling hundreds of hay bales barreled toward us, from the look of it fixing to blow the 285/Vista Grande light. That's the problem with that intersection—trucks fresh off the interstate off-ramp don't start slowing down in time, and then they can't stop, and some mildly distracted driver in a Saab or a Subaru hits the gas when their light turns green.

cTodd must have braked too late. The car slid under the truck, tires squealing. Its roof lodged against the bottom, as the truck's back wheels punched through its side.

I take little comfort in knowing that it was Todd's side the wheels chewed up and spit out, as seconds later, flames engulfed his corroded whip. They licked around the top and set the hay ablaze, torching the stacked golden bricks. Thick dark smoke billowed upward into the sky. Miles away, people wondered which forest was on fire. As everyone else looked up, my eyes stayed trained downward through the back window of the squad car, toward the crumpled and blackened Trans Am, hoping that Delphine's end was as merciful as she deserved. Strike that. As merciful as her tenacity was strong.

Later, most people agreed that the conflagration helped paint the sky with one of the most beautiful sunsets anyone could recall.

Platypus venom is nonlethal to humans. However, those punctured will find any kind of subsequent pain to be more intense for months to come.

ALL EYES

BY KATIE JOHNSON
Aspen Vista

The feeling that you're being watched is a common one. How often is it comforting?

Having grown up in a claustrophobic major city on the West Coast, I was relieved, as a young adult, to call Santa Fe home—a small city with miles of desert in every direction. As a child, I'd dreamed of Salvador Dalí dreamscapes. Now I lived in one. A perfect escapist fantasy. The people in Santa Fe were introverted, and if you wanted to get away from the adobe buildings that never rose above three stories (to preserve the view of the mountains), all you had to do was drive twenty minutes and you'd be in desert so desolate, it'd take months to find your body.

Surrounding the city were the Sangre de Cristo Mountains, Spanish for the *Blood of Christ*. Watch one sunset and you'll know why they named them that. The way the massive clouds, like parade floats, turn hot pink, reflecting crimson red on the mountains below, while the whole city turns gold. Callie and I watched a lot of sunsets against those mountains, never realizing how blood-soaked they really were.

Santa Fe is full of paradoxes—the high desert is like that. In any direction you can escape into vast desert, nothing but your body and junipers and piñons against the horizon. But if you go into the mountains—there is a whole kingdom of trees, peaks, and valleys in which to hide or get lost. If you crave the exposure of the desert, it is there ready to hold you like a heart on a platter. But if you want to be swallowed up for good, the mountains wait, ready to consume you in their dark folds.

"Danny? Danny, I think I'm lost. I need you to come into the woods and find me."

I'd been getting calls like that for weeks from Callie's phone. I thought about calling the police the first time it happened, but I wrote it off as an acid flashback or some lucid dream. I don't know why I kept picking up, maybe I was hoping she'd say something different, or just say goodbye. But she kept calling me into the woods. Acid flashbacks don't last this long. I hadn't gone to Aspen Vista since they found Callie's body up there in the fall.

Callie used to roll down the windows and let her hair curl on the wind as I zoomed up the winding mountain roads. Many trails etch off from the main road, but Aspen Vista was our favorite. Thirty minutes from the plaza—Santa Fe warps space like that. Some call it a vortex. One moment you're in the center of downtown, half an hour later you're walking on a dirt forest path, damp leaves underfoot, and all the aspens watching.

They found her body during the most beautiful time of year. In the fall, the aspen leaves turn bright yellow. The forest is gold and the paths seem littered with coins. Who says money doesn't grow on trees? But I would hardly call the aspens trees now; they watch with their eyes like people.

The last time we went up there began like any other. It was the end of summer. We veered off the main path to sneak away into a section of forest littered with huts. We'd come here with a blanket to make love or get high. The aspens are so skinny that with a little help you can pile the dead trunks into conical teepees. Who knows who started these things. College kids, or witches—it's all the same in this city. Among armies of trees and green grass, these huts inhabit the side of the mountain. The deeper you go into the woods, the more impressive the huts become, like real homes with thick walls and nearby campfires.

"This one is my house!" Callie gestured to a hut with a beautiful view of the opposing peak—a sea of pines and aspens, the wind swimming through them like an invisible entity.

"It's a fine one, babe." I cracked open a beer, handed it to her, and sat on a log in front of the hut's opening, an imaginary porch.

"Can't you see waking up to this view every morning?" Her smile was like the sunrise—sacred and intangible.

"Say the word, and we'll be bums, babe. I've got a cold sleeping bag and warm beer. Let's be homeless together."

I joked about hopping trains or living out of a car, but I never meant it. And anyway, our parents had put too much into our college tuitions for us to throw it all away and quit our paycheck-to-paycheck lifestyles. Callie leaned in to kiss me. Most days she was round-freckled cheeks and optimism. Other days she was tired. Not tired like I've ever been exhausted—from a long day of making coffee for strangers. Tired in the way that buildings and cars and a life that circles without a destination makes you tired.

"It would be so much simpler—if we just lived in the woods. It's all wrong, Danny. This idea of civilization is wrong. The cities and the minimum wage and the technology, it's not how we're meant to live. They think it's progress, their organized governments and electricity, but we never should have left the woods." Callie stood and grabbed the white trunk of an aspen in her palm. "This—this is what's real. The woods are the real world."

I could see her eyes glistening with tears. She looked away and hugged the aspen, its black eyes rubbing against her belly. When Callie got tired she cried often. And I couldn't fix it, not with beer, or weed, or my love. I stared out at the sea of pines and aspens, my hand over my mouth, as Callie sobbed into the nearby tree.

Sometimes I'd think, *Why do I have to love this crazy bitch so much?*

Later, when they found her body, littered with leaves like gold coins inside the farthest hut, I thought, *Why didn't I stay with her?*

Twenty minutes passed and Callie was still crying against that same damn tree.

I got up, walked off to have a smoke. When I came back, I pulled at her arm, said, "Callie, let's go. Let's go back to my place, I'll make you spaghetti. Come on."

Without saying anything, she bundled up the blanket we'd brought, and followed me through the forest to the main path. We stepped over fallen trees, and walked passed trunks with carved names and dates. The aspens followed us with their numerous eyes. Their green leaves fluttered, waving after us. The sun began to set and the curtain of trees looked like a veil. A shadowy golden world, so separate from the homes and businesses at the bottom of the mountain.

Halfway to the main path, Callie stopped.

"Come on, babe. The sun is going down." I always had a

feeling about those woods at night. Like we shouldn't be there past dark, like it wasn't wise. "Callie, come on!"

But she just stood, looking behind us at the trees we'd left.

"They want me to stay, Danny. They said it's okay."

"Who, babe?"

"The aspens, Danny. I can see it in their eyes."

"Honey, you know that sounds crazy, right?"

"It's the spirits of the woods. Every forest has them. They said it's okay if I sleep here tonight."

"I'm not letting you sleep out here alone." I stepped toward her.

"Then don't. Stay with us."

I looked to my left, at a tree with a face. Under two of the aspen eyes, someone had carved a jagged smile.

"Neither of us are staying here. You don't even have a tent, or food. Let's go home, and we'll plan to go camping soon, I promise."

"I don't want to go camping, Danny. I want to stay."

"Babe . . ."

"Do you ever think that if you stand in the same place long enough, the trees will believe you're one of them?"

I grabbed Callie by her arm, my fingers digging into her tighter than I'd ever gripped anyone. I dragged her behind me like a child, both of us tripping over dead trunks, and slipping on loose granite. She obeyed, fussing, for a few steps, before shoving me with her whole body, toppling me over. I smacked the side of my face on the base of an aspen, and the bark of its eye scraped my cheek. My face hot, and in pain, I yelled at her, "Fine, you want be a fucking tree! Grow roots and live here! I'm going back to town where people live and breathe!"

"The trees breathe—"

"You crazy bitch, look at me, I'm bleeding!"

Callie looked at my cheek with eyes like round leaves. She pointed to the tree I'd fallen against. Red sap leaked from the center of its eyes. "The trees bleed too."

The calls only came at night.

"Danny? I lost the trail. I thought I knew where it was, but I got turned around somehow. Danny, I need you to come get me, please." I never said anything back. Your parents don't teach you as a kid not to talk to ghosts, but somehow you know it's just something not to do.

Of course I went back for her after our fight. But after I left her in the woods that night, I let her be for a week or two. Then I started getting worried. I assumed she just needed to be up there. She'd be resourceful. Maybe she hitched a ride back home the next day and didn't want to talk to me. I figured we shouldn't talk for a while, and truth be told, I didn't want to talk to her. Yet after two weeks, with no word, I tried to call her, just to make sure she was okay. But her phone was dead, kept going to voice mail. After checking in with her parents and other close friends to no avail, I went back to the woods.

I found the blanket. That's when I filed the missing person report. A search party was sent out. They say the first forty-eight hours after a person goes missing are the most important. And if she went missing that night, or the day after, then I'd left her missing for a good 336 hours.

I could have walked that whole section of the woods before calling the authorities, but something in me knew. I didn't want to find her body, not alone, so I filed the report, let the rangers find it for me in the last hut at the end of the peak. This one was built with special care. Most of the huts lean against a living pine, which acts as a center beam, but this one was built so well it didn't need a pine on which to lean. The dead aspens crisscrossed each other, like a perfect thatched teepee. The walls were so thick you couldn't see through them. A perfect home.

The dogs smelled her first. The rangers called me over. Wind blew through the trees, and gold leaves fell on my head. Someone had built a tunnel out of small dead trunks to form an extended entrance to this hut. I watched a ranger get on his hands and knees, and disappear into the wooden tunnel. Indistinguishable runes were etched into the small dead sticks at the threshold.

As the ranger disappeared, I followed him in. Others in the search party objected, but the sound of the wind through the aspens' branches muted their voices into whispers.

The earth was pliant and damp beneath my palms. Grass didn't grow in this tunnel—as if it had been tread many times. The musk of rot overpowered the scent of earth. After a few feet of crawling, the tunnel opened into the hut. The ranger and I stood above her body. Only small beams of light penetrated the hut's thick walls, glinting on portions of Callie's stiff face, illuminating the many gold leaves scattered over her corpse. The hut's walls seemed to close in, the layers and layers of dead aspens, which crowded around her body, and us. The air was thin and dense at the same time. One of those impossible paradoxes that has to exist because it can't possibly be. A small beam of light shone on Callie's open eyes. I followed her gaze, up the aspen trunks. Their dark eyes looked back at me accusingly.

Disorientation and lack of food and water was what the medical investigator wrote in the report. But the last hut isn't even that far from the Aspen Vista trail. You can walk there and back in an hour. And the section of woods hosting these huts drops off into valleys, forming it into a neat triangle. If Callie got to the last hut, or even one of them, how could she not find the trail a half hour hike away?

She left me alone for a week after the funeral. But then she started calling. My phone ringing every evening, sometimes four times a night. Her voice crackling and distant through sounds of the wind. I wanted to believe it was sleep paralysis or the aftereffects of drug use, but when your deceased loved one calls you this fucking often, and you were at the funeral, and you know her phone is long gone and disconnected, and every day is a shallow shadow of the life you had since finding her body, well, you start to take these calls seriously.

"Danny? Danny, I miss you. I'm here, and I think I'm close to the path, but I'm not sure. Can you bring a flashlight? I know I fucked up, and I'm sorry. Please, just come get me. For the love of Christ, I need you to get me out of these woods. Please. I love you."

Holding the phone to my cheek, I began to cry into the receiver. She wouldn't let me mourn. She just wouldn't let me let her die.

"I love you too, babe. I'll be there soon."

It was so damn cold, my long-sleeve shirt and heavy winter jacket couldn't keep the dry wind from cutting into my bones. As I walked up the trail in the dark, the wind scratched at my face like precise little claws. I pulled my scarf tight around my mouth as I trudged up the snowy path. The aspens loomed over me, leafless and naked. When I got to the turn in the trail where the mountain stretches into the section of huts, I took a deep breath. I raised my flashlight higher, stepped off the trail, and headed into the woods where we'd found Callie.

Hiking in snow, my muscles stiffened, and my body grew heavy. I descended down the slope of the mountain, deeper and deeper. My calves burned, and the light I carried shook as my limbs tremored. The aspens grew denser as I maneuvered between their skeletal bodies. I came to the hut that Callie had called her "home." I looked out at the view from our make-believe porch, facing the opposing peak. The treetops were covered in snow. The wind hit my face too aggressively for me to register the view, or anything, as beautiful.

I looked behind me, into the doorway of the hut. I thought of going inside to rest, to cry, to gather myself from the abrasive wind, and maybe just let Callie's death hit me for a moment as real, but as I looked, the darkness seemed to move within.

I didn't feel afraid. I watched it for a moment, though I didn't raise my flashlight to it. The shadows seemed to curl in on themselves. They looked . . . cozy.

I decided not to disturb them, whatever they were—these hallucinations that felt familiar, like friends I hadn't seen for a very long time. I continued on. Through snow, and over fallen trunks, past the aspen with a carved smile. I stopped and gave it a wink. I thought maybe its smile grew, and I laughed at the trunk. I looked down at my boots. A sob choked in my throat, and a few tears rolled down my cheek, hot, then turned into cold trails where they'd slid.

"I miss her so much, you know?" I said to the face. "I didn't mean to—you know? I didn't mean for this—damn!" My teeth grinding against each other, I stared hard at the face in the tree. Its trunk was blunt white, the eyes dark, but somehow soft.

I began to sob, and stumbled toward it. I dropped the flashlight, wrapped my arms around the aspen, and pressed my face into its smooth bark. I held onto it tight, a poor substitute for holding her, but the only one I had. These trees were the only ones to witness my utter breakdown, to support me as I processed her death. My sobs built, then crescendoed, and as they diminished into heavy breaths, I pulled away from the aspen, keeping my open palms at its sides and my forehead pressed against its eyes.

The wind died down. The woods maintained an eerie silence, emphasized by the snow, like the silence of many people holding their tongues. I looked up at the aspen. Red sap leaked from the corners of its eyes. I chuckled, then kept walking.

I didn't pick up the flashlight. I decided the light from the sliver of moon reflecting off the snow was enough. I stepped over fallen trunks without looking at them, as if I knew where each part of the forest was placed. I walked and walked. I passed hut after hut. An hour must have passed, then another, and another. The section of forest I knew so well in the day didn't seem to have an end to it now. But I felt, in some way, that I knew it better than before. The darkness folded in on itself, the aspens tripled and multiplied. Their eyes followed. I never grew tired. The night fragmented and stretched. Their eyes anticipated. I was no longer cold.

I came to the last hut, but I knew it wasn't the last. It was the first, and forever. My future and past. I kneeled at the entrance, drew in a breath. I fingered the small dead trunks that formed the threshold. The aspens held their breath. The wood held a carved heart. Within the jagged lines of the heart, *Callie + Danny.*

All eyes drew on me. I knew I was not alone. And I felt comfort. They held me in their vision. I crawled into the tunnel. All eyes watched as I disappeared.

THE CASK OF LOS ALAMOS

BY CORNELIA READ

Los Alamos

> *As the orange and yellow fireball stretched up and spread, a second*
> *column, narrower than the first, rose and flattened into a mush-*
> *room shape, thus providing the atomic age with a visual image that*
> *has become imprinted on the human consciousness as a symbol of*
> *power and awesome destruction.*
>
> —"The Manhattan Project: Making
> the Atomic Bomb," atomicarchive.com

The thousand injuries of Richard Feynman I had borne as best I could, but when he ventured upon insult, I vowed revenge.

You will understand that I never so much as *insinuated* a threat. No, my vengeance would be played as the most patient of games, precluding even the faintest perfume of risk.

Feynman should suffer; I would not.

Equally, it was imperative he understand both that his slighting of me had precipitated this result, and that I was the sole author—indeed, the virtuoso—of his final comeuppance.

I therefore gave him no reason to doubt my friendship. I continued to clasp his hand with patrician bonhomie should we chance to meet, to exude amusement whenever subjected to his ceaseless onslaught of tics, prinks, and pranks. I refused to allow the merest glimmer of my distaste to show, whether he was breaking into locked file cabinets, "improving" upon the carefully sequenced cards as they coursed through the IBM machines, or shouting down Niels Bohr.

He saw me as merely a lesser chum amid the tittering audience he garnered with such compulsion, a negligible layer in the dull impasto against which he believed his own strokes of wit and genius might glitter by uplifted contrast.

The man had no inkling that my chuckles were ever more sincere, arising as they now did from my increasingly detailed and heartwarming plans for his imminent demise.

The fatal day, Monday, July 16, 1945, began as nearly any other in our part of New Mexico. There was the same chill of predawn as we rose in darkness from our plebeian bunks in various raw Quonset huts, or the old dormitories of the boys' school that had once graced this plateau.

I will say our usual chatter over the shared sinks was muted, and few if any seemed interested in breaking the night's fast.

There was good reason for this. I'd scheduled my private fête for Dickie Boy to coincide with the first test of our "gadget": Trinity, that grand *instrument du mort* toward the parturition of which we'd all labored during every conscious moment for the last four years.

The powers that be had ferried our plutonium core to the test site in an army sedan on Thursday, July 12, 1945.

One minute into Friday the thirteenth, the nonnuclear components had followed, to be assembled over the course of that day at the old McDonald ranch house.

By five p.m. on the fifteenth, the device was complete, awaiting detonation at the apex of a one-hundred-foot steel tower.

We'd begun moving onto the buses at two a.m. on the

sixteenth, shuffling through frigid lashings of rain. The test was slated to commence at four a.m., but soon the gossip began, mutterings from seat to high-backed seat on every bus:

Oppenheimer will ignore the rain . . .

No, he'll postpone while the skies clear.

Groves will call a halt to the proceedings to ensure the hoped-for blast can be filmed for the government, and posterity . . .

Chadwick will insist we go forward on schedule . . .

I ignored this pointless chatter, wiping away the condensation to peer out my rearmost seat's window.

I'd made sure of a place for myself aboard the very bus to which Feynman had been assigned. But though I had full view of my fellow passengers, I couldn't locate his absurdly large head atop that scrawny body anywhere between my seat and that of the vehicle's army-issue driver.

I well knew I could not inquire of my seatmates whether they had any clue as to the smirking jester's whereabouts. They must not link the pair of us in any memory of the splendid and awe-filled day sure to come.

The bus's engine rumbled alive, making droplets of rain skitter faster down the window glass.

And then, pelting toward us, came Feynman at last. He sprinted through the rain like an awkwardly malnourished cricket, waving his skinny arms as he clambered onto our bus, just as the driver grasped the chrome handle to clap its hinged doors shut.

"About time, Dick!" yelled some wag from the front seats.

"Wouldn't've missed it for the world," replied my nemesis, his nasal Borough-of-Queens honk forcing that final word to rhyme with *soiled*.

Feynman's lovely wife Arline had died of tuberculosis only one month earlier, yet he seemed to have a grin or a joke ready for every man he passed while slouching down the aisle.

I'd heard that his MIT professors had begged Princeton to take him on as a graduate student despite the all-too-necessary quotas, writing that their prodigy "isn't like other Jews."

In that they were correct: he was worse.

Thankfully, I was a Yale man myself, and so had not had to suffer the displeasure of his company until we'd been marooned together here by the war effort.

Small mercies.

Feynman continued down the aisle, until at last he stood, hunched and dripping wet, directly before me.

"How's it going, Thurston old pal?" he asked, looking me in the eye with his typical horrid leer.

Too late, I realized that the only unclaimed seat was the one beside my own.

"Dick!" I stuck out my hand, grinning for all I was worth. "All's well that ends well, eh?"

Our group was dropped off exactly twenty miles out from the blast site.

I'd climbed up behind the wheel of an empty old army truck, hoping for a better view. The radios were on the fritz, so we had little idea when, or even *whether*, the test might be conducted.

Finally, I heard a crackle from the set a few feet away, nestled against the rib cage of an NCO who was lying facedown on the ground with his arms crossed over his helmet.

A distant voice broke through the static, intoning ". . . *twenty seconds* . . ."

I put on the pair of dark glasses I'd been issued to protect my eyes from the flash.

At that moment, Feynman leaped up onto the bench seat

beside me. The man was a veritable leech, shoving me over with a sharp elbow and then sliding in even closer.

"Don't be an idiot, Thirsty," he cackled, lips smacking. "The only thing that can hurt your eyes is ultraviolet light. The windshield'll block that."

And just as he'd finished uttering those boastful words, the flash came.

Despite his bravado, Feynman flinched and ducked his head below the dashboard, screwing his eyes shut before muttering, "*That's* not it, *that's* the afterimage . . ." He sat up straight once more, jostling me.

Not to be outdone, I removed my own glasses.

The white light changed to yellow, then to orange.

Clouds formed and disappeared again.

Compression and expansion.

The ball of orange grew, rising and billowing. Its edges turned black, and soon we could see that it was a ball of smoke, flashing inside with lightning as it became ever larger.

This went on for sixty seconds . . . seventy . . . eighty . . . and at a minute and a half the shock wave finally reached us: the heart-stopping *BOOOOOM*, followed by an unearthly, thunderous rumble.

"What's *that?*" asked some journalist fellow, standing just outside the truck.

Feynman snorted, amused. "That was The Bomb."

I glanced at my watch. Five thirty-one a.m., with the second hand just passing thirty.

What remained of the day was pandemonium, and well-earned.

We'd done it! All of us!

The years of labor, the horrid meals and the never-enough

sleep, the thin mattresses on creaking wire! We'd overcome all exhaustion, dismay, and discouragement to produce this glorious feat, this magnificent engine which would now save the lives of tens of thousands of Our Boys in the Pacific.

The detonation of Trinity had rekindled us all, pumped the lifeblood of esprit de corps back into every last resident of Los Alamos.

We couldn't congratulate one another heartily enough. Army men danced drunken jigs with physicists. Comely secretaries do-si-doed with apple-cheeked calculator girls. Chemists clapped engineers on the back and were nearly knocked down by their brethren's returned clouts of joyous camaraderie.

Even Oppenheimer, who had lately come to resemble a wraithlike mere shadow of his former mere shadow, was pink in the face and light on his feet, head thrown back with laughter every time I glanced his way.

It was pure carnival as the high-desert night came on, the sizzle and spark of Eros ignited by the Promethean gift of Thanatos we had just bestowed to all the world beyond our gates.

And I was undoubtedly the calmest man for miles around.

Never doubt that I toasted and boasted with the rest of the fellows, the very picture of a hail fellow well met. But I savored the knowledge of how vastly *my* evening's denouement would eclipse our communal high spirits, in the afterglow of Trinity's climax.

My pleasure lacked but one ingredient to ring down the curtain: Feynman himself.

Pretending to swig from yet another proffered fifth of rationed rotgut, I spotted my prey at long last.

He sat cross-legged on the hood of a jeep, pounding away

on his bongo drums like a cheap wind-up tin monkey. I shuddered when I drew close enough to realize he was shoeless, the soles of his feet encrusted with filth.

"A good evening to you, sir!" I cried out, giving him the benefit of my broadest grin.

He turned toward me, the rictus of his own smile rendered even more sinister by the nearest bonfire's shifting flames.

"Thirsty!" Feynman's bongo-playing ceased. "That was something today, huh?"

"It certainly was something, all right!" I nodded in idiotic concurrence. "It certainly was!"

"Want a drink?" Feynman produced a steel flask from some unseen pocket.

"Damn right I do, pal." I reached for it and unscrewed the cap.

I put the neck to my lips and tilted my head back, taking a real gulp to put him at ease. The harsh liquor made me cough and sputter.

"Not the quality you're used to, I *suppose*," he said, lifting a pinky finger while pretending to sip daintily from an invisible cup of tea.

"Whatever the hell you poured into this thing," I replied, handing it back, "tastes like God's own liquefied *shit*."

My unexpected profanity made him guffaw.

I could tell, then, just how very drunk he was, and I was ready to take my chance.

Turning the flask upside down, I poured the rest of his revolting lighter fluid onto the hard-packed ground.

"Just a cotton-picking minute, there!" Feynman leaped down off the jeep, lurching to grab at his now-emptied vessel.

"*You* don't need to drink this crap, old pal," I said, presenting it to him with a grand flourish. I threw an arm across his upper back. "I've got something far more special to share with you. Been saving it up for just such a celebratory occasion . . ."

The vile little troll had the audacity to wink at me. "You don't say!"

"Shhh! Mum's the word . . ." I leaned in, my lips close to his ear. "You were my partner in crime today. Let's down the reward all by our lonesomes."

He laughed again, leaning into my armpit. "Guess you're earning that nickname, Thirsty."

"Well, what the hell, Dick. We both know you've been the *real* genius of this entire operation from the *get*-go . . ."

The man literally giggled, emitting the sort of high-pitched, grating feminine squeals I hadn't heard since being forced to attend dancing school as a child.

I rapped a knuckle gently against the side of his forehead. "If *this* old noggin doesn't deserve to be toasted with the finest of seventy-five-year-old whiskeys," I whispered, "well, then, I don't know what *does*, after today's performance!"

I had him hooked then, reeling him in with the sort of finesse I usually reserved for killing large salmon on Restigouche River.

He growled into my ear, wetting it with flecks of spittle, "Got a bottle hidden under your bunk?"

"Don't be ridiculous, old man!" I whispered back, gesturing at the crowds around us with my free arm. "Leave my cask of grandfather's single malt within reach of *this* pack of thieves?"

"*Cask?*"

"I'm sure you've seen one in the funny papers," I said. "A little wooden barrel, the equivalent of six bottles, and all for us!"

"Lead on, Mac . . . Duffy." Feynman belched, tugging at my sleeve.

I decided to return his wink, with interest. "At your service, *mon frère*."

I switched a dim flashlight on, once we were beyond the sightline of our fellow revelers. By this point I knew I could count on Feynman's inebriation to get him good and lost in the dark as I circled and wove the pair of us around endless spindly pines and piles of rock.

In the utter boredom we'd all endured during our spare moments, nearly every one of us had explored the old Indian caves surrounding our workaday environs.

The cave I'd chosen was a small one, of very little interest.

For my purposes, it had the advantage of a shallow alcove to the rear, just out of sight of the main entrance. Most grown men could only just squeeze into this through a narrow split in the rock. There was no true egress out the back wall—just a far skinnier crack that only the most malnourished of children might have wriggled through, though it did allow a slight zephyr to blow in, occasionally, from beyond the cave itself.

I desired that Feynman should die, but would never voluntarily grant him the satisfaction of rapid suffocation.

When he began to complain of the distance we'd traveled, I produced a flask of my own. It was filled to the brim with a pint of the same fine Scotch whiskey I'd promised him.

He took a gulp and mellowed considerably.

I patted him on the back. "Good, isn't it?"

Feynman raised the flask toward me. "Here's to your generosity, old pal," he said, before taking another hearty swig.

I took it to raise toward him in turn. "And to *your* long life, my friend."

"The hell are we?"

"Almost there." I handed the flask back. "Drink up."

He laughed, taking my direction to heart.

"Lots more where that came from," I assured him. "And we're so very close . . ."

I left the flask with him, knowing he'd drink himself even more insensible.

"Ah!" I cried. "We've reached the promised land!"

I played the flashlight quickly across the cave's entrance, then bowed him inside.

Once I'd stepped in behind him, I reached for an actual pitch-covered torch I'd constructed, lighting it up with my Zippo.

The warmth of its flickering light seemed only to inflame his thirst.

"Where is it?" he demanded, weaving. "Where's a whiskey at?"

I jammed my flambeau into a crotch of rock and pointed toward the curve in the cave wall. "Why, just back there, old buddy, old pal. *Right* around that corner."

He almost tripped over the large heap of bones at the center of the cave's floor: ribs and jaws of smallish animals, mostly.

"Yale man?" asked Feynman, eyeing the pile before he looked up at me with reddened eyes.

I sighed. "Bulldog, Bulldog."

"Skull and Bones!" he shrieked, laughing, his voice echoing loudly in our tiny crypt.

"Now, now," I said, waggling a finger at him, "you won't catch me out with that old saw! Go get your whiskey, man! You've earned it!"

He lurched around the corner and readied himself to slip through the crack in the rock beyond, just as I clocked him across the back of the head with the shovel I'd secreted beneath all those little skeletons.

Feynman dropped like a rucksack of bricks.

I worked him into the alcove and wrapped the chain inside twice around his waist, then pulled it even tighter and padlocked both ends to the heavy grommet I'd cemented into the rock wall several months earlier.

I spun the lock's dial, then made sure it was well up behind his back, though I doubted he'd come to before I'd finished my night's happy toil.

After withdrawing, satisfied, from his tiny new domicile, I raked all those little bones off my neatly piled stack of bricks and mixed myself up a good sloppy pail of mortar.

I laid the first course in the crack of his cell, then the second. Third, fourth, fifth . . . the work went well and I didn't hear a peep out of him, save his occasional rasping breath.

As I placed the eighth row's first brick, I heard him moan.

I smiled, reaching for another brick. Three narrow courses to go, and he'd be sealed in for good!

"Whaddaya . . ." he said, his voice no more than a croak. "Thirsty?"

"Why, hello there, Feynman," I answered with great cheer.

I heard the chains rattle against stone. He must have been trying to stand up.

"What gives?" he asked.

"I'm tucking you in for the night, old sport—a nice long rest."

The chains clanked again, but he said nothing more for a moment.

I loaded up another brick with a slap of mortar from my trowel.

Then, of all things, Feynman began to laugh. Hearty, joyful laughter—I might go so far as to say the man guffawed.

"Oh, you've done it, Thurston!" he said, wheezing a bit before he began to chortle again. "You've played the best joke of all! Damn it, I thought I was the master, but haven't you just gone and kicked my sorry ass with superior wit!"

"Now that you mention it, I will indeed have the last laugh, Feynman."

"Won't the boys crack up when they hear, back at the mess hall!"

"Funny," I said, "I don't think they'll hear a thing."

I was about to place the very last brick when he began keening, screaming at the top of his lungs, rattling the chains and wrestling against them with all his might, by the sound of it.

I knew well that no sound carried back to our so-called bit of civilization from this carefully chosen spot, so I began to scream along with him: yelling, baying, howling at full tilt.

And then I took my own turn at laughing, louder and louder, my glee echoing back from every stone, every last brick.

I had never felt such joy, such sheer and utter happiness, in all my days.

I laughed until I could barely breathe, and was about to double over when I heard Feynman's voice behind me.

"Go fuck yourself, Thurston," he said calmly.

He cracked me in the back of the skull with my own shovel before I could so much as turn my head in response.

I'd awakened to find myself trussed in chains, lying on my side along the ground, ankles bound to my wrists behind my back.

He'd rebuilt two-thirds of my wall.

"There's a good fellow, Feynman," I said. "All in fun, what?"

I tried to laugh but we both knew he wasn't to be jollied

out of putting his own finishing touches on my cherished blueprint of vengeance.

He stopped for only a moment then, leaning over his neat masonry to look me dead in the eye. "Should you *ever* get to use a padlock again," he said, "which I must admit I doubt highly, you may want to change the combination from its factory setting."

"For God's sake, man . . ."

"25-10-25," he muttered, rolling his eyes. "What a *moron*."

It's rather dark in here, now that Feynman's placed the final brick.

Fiat lux.

THE HOMELESS DETECTIVE

BY DARRYL LORENZO WELLINGTON

Cerrillos Road

Camo beer. Camo beer. Falling asleep on the streets was hard. Passing out a helluva lot easier. Five Camos in a pack. Three to knock him out. Two waitin' for him in the morning, 'cept on mornings when he couldn't make it back home. *Back home* was euphemistic. *Back home* was a ramshackle box trailer in an empty tract near the city dump.

Leo Malley had convinced himself five years ago: He wasn't a human being no more. He was a bum. Difference was no less than between house cats and alley cats. Human beings lived at known addresses. Human beings relied on street signs, the fire department, or the cops. He learned from his lessons panhandling well enough to appreciate that house cats believed his stripe solely deserved leftovers. He wasn't terribly impressed with dem goddamn house cats—whether they shared their small morsels of tuna. Okay, he liked the gals that worked at the Wendy's burger joint. Connie always handed him a free coffee. Finishing it, maybe he could have a shot at reorganizing himself.

He lifted his shaky hand, the skin prematurely flabby and spotted. Leo looked like he hadn't bathed sometimes, whether or not he showered at the Interfaith Community Shelter. He was a body of shakes.

A cold front had surreptitiously hit Santa Fe the night

before. He limped this morning; his socks must have swollen three sizes larger. Lucky he had a couple of Camos. His Camo pain medicines helped him bicycle to town. He couldn't find a reason to still bike to the park where truckers picked up migrant laborers. He rarely secured money panhandling, surly as he looked holding his *Help Me* sign. He should head over to the joint where the "good people of Santa Fe" served the homeless.

Got my coffee. Grab me some food.

Five in a pack.

I wanna see what nuclear war looks like.

Freaky. The racing thoughts began drum-drum-drumming in the back of his skull, like timpanis. The crush of confused thoughts began when Connie shouted, "Hey Leo, want another coffee?" And slipped Leo a newspaper alongside it.

His eyes fell on a headline describing United States military tensions with North Korea. "US and Korea Escalate Nuclear Arsenal Conflict." Thoughts began running amok. Cramming his limited space for 20/20 foresight. Leo's brain. Like a light switch. On again. Off again. Sometimes his smallest thoughts barely permeated his verbal consciousness, while his frustrated mind ran the gamut of brutal associations. It took that kind of insistent repetition to cut through his psychological welter sometimes.

He thought: *Nothing. Nothing to live for no way. I would like to see a nuclear blast. Hope Korea drops the bomb. Be a motherfucker.* People with limbs frayed. People with skin falling off, like slabs of meat and flesh in the butcher shop. People goddamn glowing green. Zombies. Radioactive sewer rats. Probably resembled the lives of homeless sewer rats all the world over.

Memories haloed Leo's skull by then, sometimes sort of happy.

Memory was a disingenuous pastime; sure, sometimes he thought maybe everybody's memories dematerialized to tears and fears, like a balancing act in the long run. He had seen plenty of both back when he lived in regular houses. Back until his late forties, he had been a truck driver. He had been a cabman. Picked up whores. Picked up druggies. Picked up Muhammad Ali one time. Picked up Bruce Springsteen. Springsteen was a short guy. Whiny. Whined about his motel room, his food, his fans.

Bruce Springsteen. Narcissistic little bastard.

These days, Leo welcomed a catastrophe. He had spent half of his life drinking too heavily, Lord knows, still managing at the edges of the rental world. Since then. The same song. The same pictures played in his dreams, churning alongside his daylight frustrations. Lucky he was a big guy. Kept moving. Kept living. Problem though was when he slept, or lightly dozed, he started twitching. He noticed that about the others. Most times when he saw a bunch of alley cats passed out, or sleeping, they were twitching in their sleep. Like him.

The problem with memory was that he always returned to the worst. He returned to the question of whether the hypothetical holocausts in the newspapers resembled the conflagration he personally witnessed, or erstwhile lived. Trapped in a house fire. Five years ago. So what if he could have died? Forget about that past life. Ya mangy alley cat. Keep living like a zombie. Burned-out.

Tough luck.

Paula shouted, "Hey Leo, want a coffee to go?" He limped to his bicycle. Leo got irony. Maybe he *only* got irony; sometimes every *blah blah blah* in his head sounded like sarcasm. And he didn't know whether to laugh or cry when he remembered he officially got listed on the homeless statistics a few years back when the half-decent apartment he lived inside burned to the ground. A wayward life. A few drunken decades. A house fire. "Hey, be careful," he heard as he hit the curb.

He realized, before he'd bicycled halfway to the Interfaith Community Shelter, that he'd begun the morning badly. The house fire was a ticket to panic. He couldn't handle rehashing the memory without believing his vascular system imploded inside his rib cage. He might hit his zero/void, the point where he blanked out. *Hey, stupid, stupid*, he thought, *why can't ya forget to start remembering?*

It may have already begun. The street traffic surrounded him like swarms of locusts. The cars blazed like flashlights inside a pinball machine. He bounced here, there, and back and forth, a pinball surrounded by sounds, *brrnnngs*. The flippers whacked him. Again. Again. They whacked. They hurt him like salt to his wounds. And like a wound that was too painful to touch, he couldn't remember much without retreating to the safety of knowing he could never live like the house cats again.

Doubted it. He zero/voided too often. He *blanked*. The *blankness* where his fragile self-identity broke into a thousand reflections. But he couldn't bring himself to look at one of them, the edges singed by chiaroscuro reflections of himself going up in smoke. He was belligerent, unresponsive, or unpredictable when he was stuck inside it.

The bell rang when Leo entered Kelly Liquor Barn, fingering two dollars in his pocket. "Hey, how about I buy one beer in a five-pack? Come on. I've been a good customer. When all the other bums see me buying here, they buy too. Call me the Pied Piper, right?"

The Kelly clerk straightened his shoulders, then arched his

eyebrows, making Leo wait while he helped other customers. The average bum couldn't wait patiently three minutes, so Leo beat the odds, unfolding his *Santa Fe New Mexican*. Remember the headline: "US and Korea Escalate Nuclear Arsenal Conflict." Coupons. Advertising. A local news story on water-rights disputes.

The subsequent story involved a cold case. A *cold case?* Sounded to him like a frozen-dinner package. Leo paused to glance impatiently at the store clerk, while he impatiently skimmed the newspaper. And?

He had a hard time following the text. The photo was conventional. The cold case suspect (roughly answering to Leo's size, age, and height statistics) was a mangy white guy. Second-class citizen. Reported to have been homeless for stretches in the 1990s. He had been incarcerated in 2003. And? He escaped in 2011.

So was this news, or old news?

The next paragraph clarified that *the escapee might be involved in several recent homicides.* Police investigations saw *signature evidence fitting a pattern.* Circumstantial evidence led the police to investigate the *possibility the suspect was behind the recent deaths of Lisa Marie Bennett by fisticuffs and strangulation, and the death of Marie-Jose Jaramillo by bludgeoning and strangulation. He is considered violent so the police ask that people do not approach him if they do see him.*

Leaving Kelly Liquor Barn, Leo squatted on the steps, his hands still stuck in his pockets. No luck scoring a Camo. His hands slowly ungripped, and reached for the newspaper stuffed inside his armpits. Yep, he wanted to read the article again. He couldn't say why he recorded the victims' names, *Lisa Marie Bennett, Marie-Jose Jaramillo.* The suspected cold case killer's name slipped his mind.

* * *

Leo visited the Santa Fe Interfaith Community Shelter twice a week.

The real name for the shelter was Pete's Place, by the way. Leo visited when he needed basic necessities. He grabbed a shower. Swallowed a hot lunch. He never spent the night. Tensions lingered whenever he ran into that short guy, the in-house manager. The in-house manager, Schroeder, still shot him nervous looks. Funny, back when he was a cabbie, Leo remembered believing Santa Fe didn't look like a town with many indigents. Santa Fe belonged to cultural sophisticates. But there were indeed a few poor places—barrios—on the outskirts of this fancy town for folks with second homes and favorite pets.

The building that housed the shelter had formerly been a pet store. Local citizens of this "cultural mecca" had shown their humanitarianism—their truly "impeccable refinement"—and converted the pet shop into storage space for humans beings.

Alley cats still called the shelter by the former pet store name, Pete's Place. Yep, per usual, Leo got the irony.

'Cause an animal shelter was an animal shelter

Leo got Pete's Place better than he got the designation *shelter.* Somebody was always ready to steal your bike, skim your small change. The guests included: Dope fiends. Alcohol fiends. Clowns with all kinds of maniac lunacy. *Me. Me included.* 'Cause *sometimes I pull crap like the incident with Schroeder.*

Needing a drink, Leo cut a path behind the Allsup's; blankets and bottles littered the asphalt nooks. He checked the empties. No luck. Then he spotted Kasey and MaryAnn—a couple of sewer rats so addled and addicted they wore tatters—

doing what alley cats do. Howling, while nursing Smirnoff vodka.

Leo thought, *I could ask for a shot, or stick around, wait for them to start carping.* Soon enough, Kasey accused MaryAnn of seeing somebody.

MaryAnn spat, "You jerk."

Leo played dumb. Okay, he added fuel to the fire, and disingenuously mentioned he thought she knew so-and-so, or he thought he'd seen her hanging at such-and-such. Misery loves company.

Alley cats drew blood.

Kasey reeled back and swung.

MaryAnn sobbed, caterwauled.

While they screamed, Leo nonchalantly fingered the bottle; snagged it; stuck it in his backpack. He didn't see any point in wasting it. He biked away. Telling himself he needed it, he really needed extra alcohol before he entered Pete's Place.

Planning on paying Kasey and MaryAnn back or something? You're a sorry excuse—his bad conscience began picking at him. He biked to a marginal grassy area; he ducked low beneath a fence, sulking, hiding.

The Smirnoff vodka was hot on his tongue. Rather than making him slow down, the firewater sting encouraged him to gulp. And gulp. He accidentally dropped his *Santa Fe New Mexican.* Wiping it, he stained the newspaper worse. Too bad, because he wanted to reread the Santa Fe killings story. A homeless killer, huh? Leo wondered: *Is he still on the streets?* The next vodka shots began stinging in an unpleasant way. He flashed back to how his sores stung, his skin pores ached for weeks following the house fire. *The house fire. Still can't stand remembering it.* He climbed on his bike; within minutes, nearing Pete's Place, Schroeder's name popped back into his mind. The in-house manager there still blamed him because his stay at the shelter had been a big unapologetic disaster. *Forget about it. Screw it. Never apologize. Never apologize to them. Big Deal*, he thought.

Big deal, huh. Things could be a bit easier. If at least ya stayed at the shelter. What happened?

Pete Place's in-house manager, Schroeder, was a fidgety, slightly bowlegged little guy. His slightly condescending smile consumed his body. He dissolved into his twin-peaked lips. The bums who knew the score liked to claim he received $200,000 a year for marginally feeding the homeless. His manner was vaguely priestly, so his nickname was Saint Peter. Nightly, he welcomed the shelter rats. Meeting them at the end of the corridor, right before they entered heaven, he reminded the filthy masses that getting into Pete's Place had protocols, rules, regulations. First of all: put your personal items, small change, keys (keys?) down here. Leo still heard his tiny, wheezing voice:

Please empty your pockets, please place your belongings in the tray.

Please turn around.

Do you have any drugs, or knives, or concealed weapons on you?

Is that everything? Your items will be returned to you after we see them.

Saint Peter explained the preliminary frisks, when challenged. Policy required it for "clients" and "residents" planning to stay overnight. Funny, when the late-night legions gathered, smelling worse than a bucket of worms, then the big iron entryway opened, and then the crowd filed inside one by one, the brightness inside the corridor making it feel like ascending into heavenly light. The bottom line remained that every night guest performed Schroeder's instructions: *Empty your pockets. Spread your arms. Hands up. Arms out. Pull up your shirt. Let's see your waistline. Guys, let's get this done.* Saint Peter would stretch his purgatorial hands. It got done.

Leo began feeling crowded, flinching inside his clothes. He couldn't stand Schroeder's hands, nor the way his face appeared out of the nowhere wearing a smile so wan it self-imploded like Silly Putty. And he couldn't sleep in the shelter bunk beds, other bums in the room. The communal bedding brought back memories of his weeks hospitalized, weeks he couldn't stop coughing, and then nights recuperating in a motel that some medical program subsidized before he hit Pete's Place where each evening Schroeder jangled a little metal tray. He survived. But his feelings hardened. He weathered it, bridging the gap between fear, fantasy, and the zero/void.

Don't be a crybaby, he told himself; but he was the same Leo Malley who blanked. He was the same Leo Malley who zero/voided. The ledge creeping closer, closer. The zero/void wasn't a place of complete unconsciousness. The zero/void was like a film watched in a stormy theater where the projector frequently jammed; sections were omitted; the final showing resembled a camera obscura viewing.

No, he told himself, less convincingly. *No* couldn't stymie something from happening. The hands became snakes; tiny serpents; cinematic adversaries. He believed, maybe on a blind, tactile level, he believed on that evening that Schroeder's fingers brushed him someplace questionable. He shoved back, shouting, "Can I get a special shower? Are you trying to pull a rabbit out of my pants or something?" He stuffed his shirttails back inside his jeans.

Personnel filed inside. "Get the cops," somebody cried, like the way they spur dogs to *sic 'em, sic 'em.* In Leo's state of mind, it looked like three-dimensional shadows and murky shapes wearing Santa Fe Interfaith Community Shelter name tags surrounded him.

He brayed, "I'm calling this bs. Where you touched me is out of line, motherfucker!" He hoped the sound waves dispersed the threatening shadows. And although he was a sad, sad, paranoid piece of work, while he zero/voided in his semiconsciousness he appreciated getting a chance to assume a chest-thumping fight stance, while he spewed "bullshit" and "faggot" right in the faces of the house cats. He spun until his energy tapped. He woke up sunken and limp, like a wrung towel; his arm hung in a blood-pressure cuff.

Schroeder insisted to the Pete's Place personnel—"This man has to go."

Other people argued. Vis-à-vis his medical records. A notation following the house fire. *Post-traumatic stress.* Stress which could lead to *personal-space issues.*

Schroeder shot back that he was fine with Leo applying for Social Security disability because the staff could help him with the applications; nevertheless, *faggot* and crude language wasn't—

Leo lost the next few sentences. He heard a heavy, heavy sigh, a protracted pause, sensed a signature moment, and by hook, or crook, the staff let him stay. One more night. Didn't matter anyway. His bad conscience caught up with him, *Ya blew it. 'Cept if ya apologize,* wrestling with his zero/void angels. He wasn't arguing that he *shouldn't* apologize. He couldn't. He couldn't apologize *because the house fire, and the cops and the hands; the hands; the hands inside the zero/void contrived to steal his last vestiges, the vestiges of his memories. And scraps*

Things got better.

Leo happened to find an abandoned trailer near the city

dump. He didn't have to worry about personal space out there, except when the cops showed up—rainbow-colored lights freaking him out because officialdom had to know who was squatting. He avoided strangers. He biked to Pete's Place twice a week, and said, *Hello, cruel, cruel world.* And consumed hot snacks. And news. And newspapers. Today's news. A premonition. Somebody was going to ask him about the headline. *Lisa Marie Bennett,* or *Marie-Jose Jaramillo.* Headline: "Killings in Santa Fe."

Leo Malley snapped out of his reverie, back into the moment.

Pete's Place. Big crowd. Outside: Bums shoeless, sockless. Belongings crammed in shopping carts. Inside: Alley cat heaven. Feed me. Feed us.

"No bread," Leo sullenly told the server.

The wrinkly faced woman's demeanor epitomized the same-old-tired-same-old. She neither had much of an individualized face nor recognized individual faces. Proof: Missus Wrinkly Face responded by staring right at him sans comprehension.

She piled his plate with extra bread.

Leo sarcastically flashed a thumbs-up.

Mrs. Wrinkly Face responded belatedly, looking peeved.

The blackboard read:

TODAY'S LUNCH
Sloppy Joes
String beans
Broccoli salad
Ice cream
Bread

Food was memory. The good ones. The crappy ones. Hot tamales. Mashed potatoes. Vegetables assorted. Bread. Day-old bread. Chef's salad. Lunch: a beet salad and a bologna sandwich. Funny spaghetti combinations. Spaghetti with turkey. Spaghetti with ham. Corn beef. Enchiladas. Guacamole. Chicken legs. Bisque and pork 'n' beans. Straight out the cans. Good. Bad. Crap. A stingy church group strictly served chef's salads. Loaves sans fishes. Bums pretended it was okay. Remember that Giggles liked to say: "Santa Fe food is mush. Santa Fe style: sweet, sour, and sordid. Try swilling it all without getting sick." Remember the lunch when a volunteer group served filet mignon? Gotta love it. Hope springs eternal.

"Did I eat all that? Don't remember. I suck it down," he grumbled, when Giggles finished her recitation of past meals.

He noticed that the woman across from him at the shelter table weighed maybe three hundred pounds. Blind. Near-blind. Handicapped. Homeless. She dipped her Sloppy Joe into her chocolate ice cream, then spilled her water cup into her broccoli salad. She swallowed without hesitating.

Giggles meanwhile shuffled her bare feet in and out of her goofy slippers, her bottoms still her pink pajamas from a night spent at the shelter.

"Do I mutter? This is what I got when I said, *No bread*."

"Guess she didn't hear you," Giggles replied, pointing at his plate. She cupped her ear. "Watcha say?" She studied his plate colors: the blues, the greens, the juices bleeding into themselves.

In Leo's mind images flashed: blue police car lights.

"Least at the county jail they give you plates with dividers," a particularly well-dressed man with an accent argued.

"He's Total Texas," Giggles shot back, pointing at his cowboy hat.

The Texan smiled, tipping it.

Leo heard an edge in her voice. Funny, sometimes. Like Giggles's humor. Nobody knew her real name. She slept at the shelter because she somehow knew a way to keep a penknife wrapped inside her favorite blanket.

Other voices swarmed the tables: *President knows what he's doing. He's gonna screw Korea. It's like when two mad dogs face off. There won't be any World War III. Tall tales. Rumors. Lost-my-car-title blues. All I regret about my last stint is that my daughter died. A stroke. I dunno. I think they might have took her out just to hurt me again. Seems they'll do anything to hurt prisoners*

Hey. My lease is up this month. The real reason I'm splitting is it's past time to join up with cousin. My cousin? Remember. He's in a militia in Oregon—

It's a crock.

Listen. Not to Giggles. Giggles snarling. Is he hot shit in Texas?

Listen. He didn't escape from prison. He escaped while he was on work detail.

Right under their noses. Part of what this manhunt is about is they're embarrassed.

Next. Helicopters. Manhunts.

Leo remembered he still had the latest *Santa Fe New Mexican*. Stained: foodstuff all over the front-page photo. Greens, blues, ketchup. Colors of police sirens and, yeech, blood. He waited to hear the victims' names. *Lisa Marie Bennett*. Or *Marie-Jose Jaramillo*. When he stood, he got up to stuff the *Santa Fe New Mexican* in the trash.

Red alert.

Schroeder approached. Since Leo didn't want to engage, he split toward the exit. Bums bowed and blanketed in tableau along the walkways resembled a refugee camp. He heard rain.

Storm rumblings. Nobody who changed shirts, shoes, and socks sparingly appreciated rain. The murkiness oozed lava lamp–like into the shadowless horizon. He backtracked. He spoke inexpressively to the lunch-line server: "Can I have a second plate?"

"Pardon me. Everybody gets two plates. You've already had your two."

In the background he heard Giggles snapping that she wasn't a cigarette bank. Bums and winos should scalp smokes at the Santa Fe Cigar Shop.

"This is my second plate."

"I've seen you in line twice. I'll have to ask Schroeder if we can let someone have three plates."

"Don't ask Schroeder nothing. Okay. Okay?"

The lunch-line lady signaled Schroeder.

Leo began walking toward the exit. Shadows filled the distance. And he knew what all the bums were thinking: *How hard, how bad*. Then he realized the soiled newspaper was still in his hands. He folded the paper at a point that cut the suspect's eyes, while he lifted the garbage top.

Giggles at that precise moment asked him to see his *New Mexican*. "Crazy shit," she said. "I knew her," she added, less ambiguously, since the other headline threatened nuclear war.

"Lisa Marie Bennett?"

"No."

Names stuck in his head. "Marie-Jose Jaramillo?"

"How's everything going? How are we feeling?" Schroeder asked.

"No trouble here." Giggles intuited that Leo didn't want to answer.

Schroeder recorded infractions.

"Wait a sec. Should you be here? Didn't I say you were on suspension?"

"That was way, way back," Leo mumbled.

"Oh. It's you. Leo. You're not on suspension."

Leo drawled his words out: "Good. Everybody talks. Nobody listens."

"Who did you think he was?" Giggles piped in.

Schroeder was conciliatory. "I'm listening. Seriously. Where do you stay? How have you been?"

Giggles pointed at the photo in the *Santa Fe New Mexican*. "That guy who broke loose?"

"The killer. He'll do it again. Sometime." Schroeder smiled, shrugged. Befuddled.

Leo thought: *Gimme*. And snatched the newspaper away. "I gotta use it for toilet paper." He tossed his hand like a salt pinch over his shoulder. He reread the section that stated the cops had *reasons to believe*—

Faces: while reading he saw prematurely wrinkled faces—faces regardless of chronological ages withered inside balls of flesh to the point that physical ailments and psychological tics appeared interchangeably sourceless. The bad skin. The cracked stare. Stringy, scraggly, silvery hair camouflaging a profile. *Looks like me, sure*. Photo looked like every white homeless guy who badly needed a shave.

He thought: *Me. Him. Just like the lady got me confused with somebody else*. He finger-drummed the newspaper photo. Wondered about it. *Wouldn't I be a wonder boy with a mirror and a comb?*

Been too long. Been too long.

Think happy thoughts. Flowers. Pastels. Big blooms. Day that me and Giggles panhandled. Giggles had the idea that selling some trinkets would be sweetest; when she returned thirty minutes later she pushed a shopping cart full of floral arrangements.

Q: How in the hell did she get them? The blooms?

A: Giggles—she of course giggled her rejoinder—rummaged the bins where they dumped the flowers after burying the stiffs.

That's bs.

Nope. Cute, right? Or irony. *Or irony?*

He had to pee. And shit. Port-o-lets outside. He wrested the handle. Oh, there she was, Giggles sat on the Port-o-let toilet hole, shooting up.

Before leaving, he remembered images, sounds, sensations from his hours at Pete's Place: Giggles shooting up on the toilet; heat, heat on his tongue; the storm raising up New Mexico dust; a woman crying, crying that she'd lost everything. Crying until he couldn't take it anymore. Crying until her sobs blurred with the rain: a perfect musical accompaniment. Rain, after all, was the sound of disappointment.

He waited too long before he started biking back to the trailer. His mistake was uncapping the Smirnoff. That vodka burned a hole in his shoes, worse than the holes in his memory. He finally began pedaling, pedaling harder, like he believed his velocity could retrieve the hours lost. A big downpour whistled his way. It surreptitiously caught him—he couldn't say *by surprise* given that he had taken a measured risk. Say: It hit. Like a feint. Like a fist. It sang its refrain of—

Disappointment. Disappointment. Disappointment.

His disappointment with himself, his bottle, or Giggles, her needle. He veered into the parking lot at Santa Fe Place mall, hung around beneath the walkway awnings, watching the storm transforming Southside Santa Fe into a vacant window. Picturing his "home" leaking. New leaks every big storm. Picturing Giggles's habit. He preferred not having to see it. He still imagined he could "get with" her. He suffered stupid dreams like that involving the few women (scratch, last human beings) he regularly communicated with.

Hey Leo. Paupers. Addicts. Lost souls. Ain't they your people?

Yeah. Alley cats were his people. The problem remained. The answers lay wrapped inside nuances as subtle as the rain—and hushed voices—because Leo rarely heard simple answers without hearing the contrariness wrapped inside them. The problem remained that his people stank. They couldn't help it. They stank perennially. It was bearable by himself, or maybe with two or three tired, woozy, and drunken others. But when they were crowded together in shelter spaces like at Pete's Place, the stink escalated beyond nausea. Rain, sludge, and rot worsened it.

They stank. They raged.

They raged because they'd been kicked out of homes; kicked out of apartments; kicked out of overpriced Motel 6s. They raged because they'd gone too long feeling threatened, solitary, going hungry, and then when they collected nickels and dimes they were still obstinately criticized; still hassled by business owners who controlled where they could and couldn't sit or sleep, and if they stuck around they got cuffed by the cops. They raged because at the shelter—in lieu of housing assistance, or small sums—they were given clothes, lots of hand-me-down coats, shawls, slacks; hey, somebody found a silk shirt inside the Pete's Place clothes donation closet. Then without other assistance they were told to do something—get a life—get a job—but the miscellany was invariably soiled; the personnel had forgotten how little good a new shirt had done them pursuing their own dreams.

Identify the strains: multiple, or simultaneous, voices of sympathy, cynicism and irony. Like listening to the counselors at Pete's Place proposing *plans, services, options.* They spoke with voices within voices—like suspiciously multivoiced instruments—and as you listened you repeatedly heard the words *forms, applications, time lines*, like sticks and stones battering within the windiness of storm and possibility. Chance, really. Listen, listen to contrapuntal rain voices: lullaby and lament told you what you should expect. Personal embarrassment. Failure. Grief.

Before he hit the road, he remembered. He unzipped his backpack. He pulled out a plastic throw-over. *Remember where you got that parka? From the clothes closet at Pete's Place? That ain't helped you none, Mr. Prick?* The point remained that the counselors at Pete's couldn't acknowledge the futility of goddamn everything. Homeless cats already with nothin' should expect no less than . . .

Disappointment. Disappointment. Disappointment.

Traffic began looking scary, so he set his teeth to the wind, and he couldn't stop when the *Santa Fe New Mexican* in his pocket billowed; the pages separated hitting the ground. He briefly tendered the thought of retrieving them as they tumbled windily away. He didn't need them to prove his point. The social workers dealt with facsimiles. Pitying the homeless. The mental illnesses. The addictions. The self-destructive behaviors. Nobody hoped to name the fuel to the fire. Rage. Homeless killer. Big deal. The real deal was homelessness, helplessness, and rage. He skidded.

He stymied the worst that could happen by flinging his foot down like an anchor. Thinking hurt. Thoughts like these exhausted him. *Damn. If the homeless rage ever cut loose, could be a bloodbath.* He muckily regrouped. But before he wobbled less than a mile—like a pilot in the mountains regaining his perspective above the view—he slipped again. The difficulty was partially the darkness, partially the rage that consumed him, past exhaustion. He lay watching his bike wheel spin, water filling his socks. He didn't recognize the first street sign: the second: the area: the neighborhood. Details missed the mark. He had no idea how long he had been oblivious, or biking the wrong way.

Damn residential neighborhoods.

Never been a problem in the past. He had the knack; he could fall asleep anywhere.

He huddled inside a stark alley facing a wall mural; winged angels; horny devils; a knight hoisting a sword; he couldn't tell for the life of him whether the mural was religious, facetious, or pornographic. *So, the psycho had been homeless, huh,* Leo's last thought, before blankness. He startled awake. He reconsidered: never lie down beneath angels and demons.

Spanish music wafted in the dark. Realized he was in the barrio somewhere. What happened? Rage wouldn't answer. He wasn't sure how he had ended up lost in the city where he used to hustle rides. He dreamed he was a taxi man again. The car radio kept playing the same song, "Fire and Rain," over and over. And wasn't this an irony? He'd been trapped in a house fire—how long ago now?—and since then he lived mostly in a leaky trailer. Get it? *Oh, I've seen fire / And I've seen rain.* And fire. And rain.

Bugs. Creepy crawlers sidled his clothes; his skin pores had begun itching like a virus spread over him. He shuffled, slow as Sisyphus. His rock was homelessness, drunkenness, rage; they dissipated; they left behind lethargy. He walked his bike across the street to the less residential area. Fast food palaces, convenience stores, and garbage dumpsters promised safety. He stumbled on a metal post. Past nights, he might have tied a string between the drive-in sign and his bike, so that somebody approaching with bad intentions carelessly tripped up. He was too tired, so he curled up. Worming, so to speak, becoming wormier, wormier, until he reached a place colder in his bones than his wet clothes. Then Giggles appeared, her apparition. An avatar. She pulled up her sleeve. He expected to see her needle marks; but instead she kept haranguing, *Something is wrong, Leo. Wake up, Leo. Something is really, really wrong*; and, at first, he wasn't sure whether he was hallucinating when a Honda pulled directly across from him; headlights illuminating the interior faces; a woman in the passenger seat screamed.

Bright lights. An open mouth. A flash of tongue. A smear of red lipstick. A scream.

Leo's mind rehearsed the elements before he rearranged them into patterns. From this point on, he could barely distinguish what he saw or heard. In the place where he went sounds became pictures; pictures screamed and choked.

Screams became unfathomable distances.

Followed by a tall, trampish man distinguished by a hairy mane who vaguely resembled Leo—ten years past—a woman scrambled from the beige car.

The objects described in the headlines. Did he see them? Or hear them? The blunt instruments. The knife. A broken shoe skittered across the sidewalk. Did he see it? Did the sounds create the pictures? Or the images redouble the sounds?

The woman lay strewn; the man had begun kicking her. The darkness leavened nearest the dead, dying, or damaged body.

Leo must have looked once. Or twice. Long enough to see the killer pull a set of cable wires. Darted a glance long enough to know not to look in that direction again.

Like a nightmare. Seventy-five percent of Americans have nightmares in bed. This guy Leo Malley can have 'em anywhere.

Terror. Moans. Silence. He had heard Spanish music all night. Then suddenly silence descended like a knife, and the aftermath was a dissipated revel. A beat party scene. Dreams were fragmented. His worst bad dreams invariably repeated. He relived them twice over, so he waited for the violence he had witnessed to replay. Distance, perspective, and contingent reality kept going. The forward-moving clock hands kept going. Like the Honda, riding on the brakes, rolling slowly, slowly away.

He climbed on his bike. He followed, pretending to be someplace else. Anyplace else. Pretending he was panhandling roses. And he made seventy-five cents. And Giggles made eight bucks. And he made three bucks. And Giggles made $23.68. And he scored forty-one dollars. Get real. He never scored forty-one dollars. He washed out. Giggles maxed out at sixty-five bucks. Leo Malley sold two roses. Net earnings. Net economic worth: $3.85. *Wake up, Leo,* he thought. The neighborhood was like a great big room that he could close his eyes inside, believing, with ease, all his problems, his helplessness, his homelessness, was stuff he could straighten out in the morning. The Honda rumbled, paused, swerved.

It swerved into the dead-end alley, wriggled, like a snake entering a hole. Leo paused at the very tip of the turning place, remembering the alley was blind. "I ain't gonna look," he muttered, like the moment in a dream when you promise yourself you won't look. You won't descend the staircase. You won't enter the cellar. You won't risk turning the corner. Nobody keeps the promise.

Nobody.

He saw the killer in tableau beneath the mural phantasmagoria.

He's bigger than me, Leo thought, studying him from the back. *He's got a decade on me. Stands straighter than me. He's a big mossy tree.* There was a mantra Leo used in past times when he needed to steel his nerves. There were times on the streets when the fear maximized: fear of strangers and gangs, fear of cops and business owners. His mantra was, *Fuck. Fuck. Fuck.* And occasionally varying *Fuck* with self-deprecations. *Leo Malley, white trash, $3.85 man.* Then varying those with raw epithets. *Bitch. Wets. Cunts. Niggers. Fuck. Fuck. Bitch. Wets. Cunts. Niggers. Bitch. Wets. Cunts. Niggers.* It wasn't a particularly noble mantra. Shameless. He couldn't mean the killer. Or why couldn't he? The fact that they were both white guys sharpened the edge. The repetition over and over in his head convinced him he was colder, less human, less vulnerable—since he was a crestfallen white guy, maybe he liked that type of language. He wasn't even sure whether he directed the disgusting epithets at himself. A distinct *zip* added insult to injury. A fly unzippering. He heard a sharp *zip* and a plunky trickle. The instant he heard the killer pissing, Leo picked up his bike. He charged.

He slammed the big mossy tree against the mural.

And slammed.

The big mossy tree crumpled.

The fallen big mossy tree moaned, weakly writhing on the ground. This way, that way, looking for anything, Leo recognized the habits of a compulsive hoarder. The Honda was crammed with bags, clothes, detritus. Leo began rummaging. Pulling stuff out of bags. Disgorging the automobile. A handful of objects he grazed inside the Honda were bloodstained. Clothes. Socks. Toolkits. Hammers. Rivets. Pipes. Gloves. Cable ties. Cable ties provided a way to bind the suspect's hands and feet. *Get outta here, fast, faster.* He realized his bicycle spokes were crushed anyway. He paused long enough to loop new knots, like a child playing Cat's Cradle. He redoubled the cords, finished the job, beginning to see the angels and demonic imagery—the derelict presences—on the mural wall were living, sentient, huh, realizing he was hallucinating, or spinning, confusing past, present, and future Armageddons, or he had been zero/voiding since this morning, Lord knows since when.

Yep, he always told Giggles, *I get irony.* The irony that he had not gone looking for the cops since he was nine years old. The irony that he left the killer tied up beneath satanic devils; yet the minute he left the scene he believed he stepped inside illustrated phantasmagorias: looking for the blue-capped creatures that frightened him no less than angels and devils.

Nuclear war? Naw. Funny, though, the long and the short of it is. Armageddon. Has. Come.

His tongue raw in his mouth, his mouth bruised. *And where am I? And how come my arms hang bloodless? My wrists sting, like I'm handcuffed? How much time has passed? None. Hours. Think back: think back to leaving the dead-end alley.* Nearly sleepwalking. Nearing familiar Santa Fe, he laid the bicycle down. The bike frame was broken, bent at a sharp angle; the spokes network mangled. He leaned on the spokes with his elbows. The spokes softly pinged, pinged, while he pressured them back into alignment. He still couldn't walk the bicycle much faster.

He had something to tell the cops. Damn straight. He had already begun disbelieving it. The story was factual: the imagery coloring his thoughts was semifactitious. But he seized phrases, *Dead body. Hope she isn't dead,* then, *The killer is in the alley.* A flashlight sprung on him, like a sword drawn slantways from the scabbard. At first, in his head, he heard the *ping ping*, like a Pavlovian bell. Then he heard Reginald Prescott. Prescott was one of the policemen who occasionally visited the city dump. *Step away from the curb.*

"Oh, you," Prescott said. He sounded disappointed, gesturing Leo away from the bike. Same guy that dropped by Leo's campsite. Per usual, Prescott wouldn't leave till he nudged the hibernating bear. "Had to be sure. You look like him. Go home. What am I saying—home? Say something."

Before Leo finished answering, Prescott interrupted: "Something I should know about? What happened to your bicycle? Go back to the dump. The trash can, where you stay. Like Oscar the Grouch."

Leo paid less and less attention to Prescott, barely listening—even when the man snickered—because when he tilted his head a certain way he heard *ping ping*; the sound when he slammed the bicycle; the sound when he laid the bicycle flat. *Ping ping*, like a triggering bell.

I don't look like him so much, up close. And he's down. And the ping ping *sound was right after the killer hit the wall. That's where I recognized the sound. I kinda think I know where he's tied up. Need help. Need help retracing my steps. It got scary right afterward when them pictures on the mural started moving, looked like they was moving, lucky I tied him down.* Leo believed he sensibly appended the right details; maybe he unspun the whole fucking story, like unwinding a ball of thread. Or maybe not.

Prescott frowned, gawked, and pursed his lips like an administrator. Looking vexed, he raised his palm, spat, then looked away. "Lotta nerve. Lotta nerve, Leo—"

"It's none of your business when we're gonna catch him. You got a lot of nerve asking me all of this. And you already see there's a police sweep in progress."

Prescott glanced at Leo reprovingly. "But maybe that's none of your business neither. Don't insult police work again." He began nodding his head stupidly, and he wouldn't leave until Leo copycatted the gesture, and began wagging in agreement. "Comprende? No comprende? Scram."

A police sweep? An unusually high number of police vehicles on the street? Definitely. Roadblocks. Cops checking civilian vans. Leo approached; red and blue lights spinning like shadowy genies escaping a million bottles.

"Sir. You have obviously been drinking. You either go someplace and have a coffee or I'm going to have to pull you in. I don't want to hear another word out of you."

An officer looking up from another driver's license inspection, "Sir! Is there something that you want? Need?" Leo got scared, stumbled away.

Slouching to his knees, too enervated to bother himself over the consequences, he stationed himself at the doorstep of the only diner left open this hour. Three police cars meanwhile ran up and down the Cerrillos neighborhood. *Lotta cops in the wrong location,* Leo mused, so drowsily that the thought mattered less than that the patrons entering and exiting Denny's politely sidestepped him. First piece of luck all day. He had raged all day long. Raged when he read the *Santa Fe New Mexican.* Raged when he read about the killer. Raged when he repeated his mantra. Raged until he couldn't—he had to let the bile seep out of him. Couldn't do anything about killers. They strike. They strike again. Killers kill. Drinkers drink. Just fall asleep here. 'Cause least people have the courtesy to sidestep me. Two of 'em. Blue devils. "It's the fucking level of unprofessionalism," one complained, entering Denny's.

The other cop stopped, tapped his shoe. "This is not the place to sleep."

A black cop gazed down at him. "Especially not tonight." He sounded like he had something special in mind. "Get it? You must have noticed the sweep? Have you seen anything unusual?"

Say: *I tackled the killer. And I tried to tell ya fellow officers. Can't talk with all the bullhorns and sirens.*

Say: *And I feel ashamed looking at ya, officer. I don't want to tell ya the crazy thoughts I was thinking.*

He prattled, maybe he sounded like a baby with stones in his mouth, maybe he raised his voice when he sounded slurpy in his own ears. He couldn't stop himself, still blathering while the shoes disappeared, seconds gone.

Leaving Leo babbling to thin air. *Huh?* The black cop returned. He held several pamphlets. The first pamphlets in the stack ubiquitously read, *Help for the needy,* or, *Social Resources.* The next set extolled church and Christianity with titles like, *The Lord Provides.* The black cop insisted, "Get off the street," intended in a different sort of way than the others.

Thanks. Thanks for your concern. Thanks for Jesus. Presences nudged him left, then right. Gently rocking waves, leading him, leading him along until the thought broke through: *Rage. I just got rage. But I ain't him. Me. Him. Me. Him. Nothing else matters. But at least the killer wasn't me. They might not know that. They gotta understand it wasn't me.*

Leo lumbered directly toward the blue, the red lights, converging at the street meridian. Everything shape-shifted. Cops, human figures emerged from the bulbous glow. A cop car tapped him, swinging open; he kicked back, like an emotional yo-yo.

The angriest cop, billy club in hand, stepped out of his car, still fuming, before he swung into Leo's mouth and belly like he was swinging a golf club.

And where was he? And who was speaking? Leo moaned lying facedown, handcuffed, pretty much welcoming the zero/void. Officer Prescott at last had something significant to say—"Let's drop the assaulting-an-officer charge, okay? Can you speed up, please? He's about to get sick back there."

The other cop in the front seat grumbled, hearing Leo retching up.

Prescott turned to the backseat and grumbled, "Damn, Leo. Sorry about this. Sorry this happened. But we're jittery tonight. You better sleep it off in the cell. We're looking for a real killer out here."

Officer Prescott may have been right. Maybe the county jail was the place to recover. The rainstorm was a precursor to two days of somber weather. Leo spent his brief jail stint lulled by the pitter-patter, sleeping in a warm, dry place, listening to the rain without hearing the old refrain: *Disappointment. Disappointment. Disappointment.*

He didn't bother pleading his case; his stomach panged. When he signed his release papers on the third day (guess the cops really had dropped the assaulting-an-officer charges), the jail officials at the desk handed him a list of fees and sums he owed the county—fees he would have to pay before he could have his bike returned. He thumbed a ride "home."

He recognized within a few hours that he was still sick. The hurt sustained layers down; down in the pit of his stomach where the billy club sucker-punched him. He took to his natty cot. Lying hours face upward. Dieted on bottled water and canned tuna. Nothing else left at the trailer. Not even a Camo.

He dreamed the same scenes, over and over. He revisited the house fire, less hysterically, in particular the moment which he usually couldn't stand revisiting when he put his hands over his eyes and (pretty bravely) leaped through the blazing door. He really did it. The dream paired with imagery of the killer? But had that really happened? Pictures of binding/ rebinding the Santa Fe killer but good. Brave, too, he supposed, assuming the imagery was real.

It wasn't worth believing in it. It wasn't worth revisiting his zero/voids. *Leo Malley. $3.85 man.* It sort of wasn't worth believing in himself.

He dreamed he told Giggles the whole story, before she collapsed into giggles. Or congealed like a pillar of salt. In any case, in his memorable moments, seconds, split seconds, he remembered his mantra, *Fuck. Fuck. Fuck. Racial epithet. Racial epithet.* And, rolling over, feeling self-disgust, he realized none of it could have happened anyway.

The next morning, he felt strong enough to hitchhike. *Hey Giggles, hey Paula at Wendy's, starting to miss me yet? Who misses me?*

Making his way into Santa Fe, he was halfway to the interior. A newspaper bin. *Lo, behold.* Sure, he prevaricated when he told Paula and Connie at Wendy's that he had gotten into a fight, sort of the truth. Connie slipped him a coffee and a *Santa Fe New Mexican.*

"*We don't really know what happened,*" read the official quote. Leo thought: *Who? How? Where?*

Suspect found in a Southside alley. "We really don't know what happened. We found him with his hands tied, his feet tied. He won't offer an explanation." The suspect is believed to have attempted a murder on that very evening, leaving Ms. Yevette Sandoval bruised and battered in a Burger King parking lot. The victim was discovered shortly before the suspect. The victim has been hospitalized and is expected to live.

The police detective hypothesized, "*Maybe he had a partner. Maybe they had an argument; something led to a falling out. But who knows? Maybe there's a civilian hero out there.*"

So, Leo liked the sound of it, *The police detective,* and the phrase played in his mind, *The police detective, The homeless detective, The police detective, The homeless detective, The homeless crime solver,* like he was a house cat in an office with *Private Eye* on his door tag. His secret weapon was—*Fuck. Fuck. Fuck. Racial epithet. Racial epithet. What kind of crime solver am I? What kind of human being am I? What kind of human being am I not?* He felt doubtful. He felt awkward. *Ha, maybe I shouldn't feel so scummy. 'Cause it worked, and the killer was a white guy, anyway.* He felt unheroic.

That night, back in his trailer, he zero/voided, and as the sickness, the strangeness, and the surreptitiousness of it all caught up with him, Leo Malley began laughing, laughter that pierced the dark, laughter that resembled breaking into midnight song. Disbelief ceded to astonishment. Astonishment ceded to ridiculousness. Lucky that he was going to be okay, by the sardonic laws of the heroic survival of the alcoholic fitless. Very, very lucky that his best gal at Wendy's slipped him twenty bucks. Lying bedded, he opened his palm in the darkness, and deftly unhooked a painkiller from his five-pack. The popped can went *psssst.* Camo beer. *Camo beer.*

SOS SEX

BY HIDA VILORIA

Casa Alegre

The place is silent as I walk through the open barbed-wire gate, down the driveway toward the new-looking Big Wheel I've seen sitting, unmoved, at least a dozen times from the safety of my passing car. It, and the toys beside it, seem like they were dropped by playing children unaware that they would never be returning to put them away. Or by someone who wanted to give the impression that kids live in the house. After weeks of watching it during daylight hours I'd still never seen any sign of kids. Or of anyone, for that matter.

I step as quickly and quietly as possible toward the back of the property. I made sure to park my car down the block, out of sight of the house, in case they have surveillance cameras. I'd also put on the long blond wig I bought as a disguise a few blocks before turning down the street and parking.

I'm 5'3" and skinny, which makes me little by American guy standards. I figure between that and the wig, as long as I keep my head down I'll look like a long-haired white guy (instead of a Latino guy with a short black fade) or possibly even a white girl. Which is good because if what I think is going on here really is, I definitely don't want the sick fuckers knowing who I am.

It all started with Erica. Well, to be fair, it was winter that started me down this path. I'd been looking for an escape from the lethargy that had descended upon me with the falling of the leaves. My motivation, my very life force, seemed buried, like the earth, and I'd sunken so deep into my subconscious that speaking to anyone other than my dog had become difficult.

Somehow driving made it better. It made me feel like I was going somewhere. Even though I was literally just spinning in circles, needlessly burning precious fossil fuels like a fucking moron.

Every morning I woke up to the Santa Fe sunshine and another promise of productivity. I had my morning coffee and toke to motivate the mind, and then whipped out the ol' laptop. Hell, sometimes I'd even bring it with me somewhere to make me feel like I was really working.

Most Monday mornings I'd end up at Betterday Coffee, the closest café to me. I'd plant myself with my laptop, notebook, breakfast burrito, and visions of lining up a week's worth of work. Over the years, I'd inadvertently learned enough carpentry to convince people I knew shit. That, along with my Dartmouth degree and my small size—ideal for getting into tight crawl spaces—had made it easy for me to find a steady flow of fairly well-paying work as a property appraiser.

It's not the worst job in the world, but it's nothing to write home about either, and it slows down drastically in the winter. So I often found myself distracted by one of my online addictions or the clientele. The Betterday crowd typically consisted of a surprising number of ethnically diverse, model-looking millennials among mostly retired, white, former hippies. Young and old, modern meets rustic—like Brooklyn hipsters practicing animal husbandry.

About a month ago, I was there hoping to feel inspired about follow-up e-mails and scheduling, but found myself immersed, instead, in real estate listings. They're one of my aforementioned online addictions, along with camper vans and tiny houses. That day's distraction: a reasonably priced three-bedroom, two bath on Hopi Road, with an open house.

I love open house days in Santa Fe because it's easy to hit a bunch of them. The city's actually not that small *geographically* speaking, clocking in around the same size as Manhattan, the stomping ground of my twenties and early thirties, but its population is tiny by comparison—just .12 percent of Manhattan's 1.66 million.

What you lose in anonymity you gain in the ability to get anywhere you want to go in twenty minutes or less.

The lack of traffic and gigantic sky had lured me back to the City Different six months ago. Five months later I met Erica at the Tuesday afternoon open house on Hopi Road.

I wasn't really interested in buying the house—didn't even have the money yet—but I was interested in *her* the moment I saw her. She was the definition of svelte in tight black Prince-style pants that flared a bit at the bottom and a black, semi-see-through lace top that showed off her long, lean figure. Her face resembled what a pretty female Cheshire cat might look like, with a wide smile, mischievous to the point of making one momentarily wary.

It was her sharp green eyes that most intrigued me. When she fixed them on me I got the strong impression she knew things. Mysterious things that evade most folks' perception.

I sensed this for a second and then it was gone, replaced by real estate banter. How long the place had been listed, what the owners were hoping to get for it, why it hadn't sold yet. That one was easy enough to answer. The layout was bizarre, including a grand staircase leading to a basement (a rarity in the Southwest), with two tiny, windowless rooms entirely carpeted from floor to ceiling.

Outside, there were decks off the dining room and master bedroom, but they were both covered with thin, worn Astro-turf. The yard was barren, with a very well-secured dog run in one corner—and, in the other, a concrete storage shed so short it looked like it had been made for little people. The padlock on the door was unlocked so Erica and I peered in. It was empty, and just tall enough to sit up or crawl around in.

"Guess that's the gnome hovel," I said to Erica, and she laughed.

We agreed it was weird and started to walk away when the graffiti visible directly above the shed, painted on the concrete wall of the taller shed on the neighbors' side of the fence, caught my eye. I walked back to make out the lettering.

SOS, it said, then below it, *Sex and ME_ _*. I couldn't make out the last two letters.

Whaaat?

"Oh my god, why does it say *SOS* and *Sex* on there?" I asked, no longer laughing. "That's so creepy! Do you think somebody was trying to let someone know about what was going on inside that shed?"

"Or the shed its spray-painted on?" Erica added.

I stepped on a rock to peer over the fence. There were two more sheds toward the other end of the neighbors' yard that looked like small houses, except the windows were all barred up and the doors were chained shut with thick padlocks. The shed directly in front of me, with the graffiti on it, had a small window facing me that had been barred up with some kind of industrial metal grate. As I looked closer, I could see a dim light on inside behind the ratty curtain covering the window.

I dropped down quickly, a cold sensation suddenly running

through my body. I'd been too afraid to scooch up higher to get a better look inside that window. Too afraid of what I might see. Or of getting seen by whoever was involved with whatever was going on back there.

I described it all to Erica and we were so freaked out that we hightailed it out of there. Then, with her following me, we drove around the block to get a look at the house on the other side of the fence. Unlike the quaint red-brown stucco houses on the block, with their nicely manicured or overgrown desert yards, this one was a newer manufactured model placed on a concrete covered front "yard" surrounded by an unusually tall chain-link fence with a big *Beware of Dog* sign mounted on it.

Oddly, given the sign, the gate to the driveway was wide open, and children's toys were strewn carelessly in front of the garage at the end of it. The storage sheds I'd just seen were completely obstructed from view by the house and garage.

Something about it seemed off, just like the house behind it. Enough that we decided to report it to the police upon parting ways. They'd called us each back to report that everything seemed fine. They'd gone over and spoken with the next-door neighbors, who'd said an elderly couple lived in the house and they'd never noticed anything unusual.

"Fine my ass," I'd said to Erica over a Manhattan at Tonic a few days later.

"Yeah, I guess we knew they weren't going to be able to go in there without a warrant or anything." She tucked her hair behind her ear.

"I know, but I'm still glad we called it in. Maybe if something else happens it'll give them enough to check it out. Honestly, maybe it's just me, but I got a really bad feeling from that place."

"Me too," Erica said, "and actually, I didn't tell you this

before because I didn't want to freak you out even more that day, but there was this house my company listed a few months ago, a foreclosure on Camino Monica . . ."

". . . a total fixer in Barrio la Canada, like three months ago? I remember that one."

"Yeah, that was it—when my coworkers first went to see it, they found all this weird, creepy shit in the basement. They showed me pictures they took."

"Another basement?"

"Right? And there was stuff spray-painted on the bedroom walls, like, *Satan Lives Here*, and a picture of a scary face saying, *God can't hear you crying*. And it gets worse . . ." She paused for a second. "In that basement, there were a bunch of old metal cots with handcuffs on them. Like they'd been keeping people locked up down there. It was *horrible*."

I felt my stomach drop the same way it had when I'd heard a news report about a sex-trafficking bust in Albuquerque. Apparently they'd found a bunch of mostly Native American preteen girls locked up in dog cages in various Motel 6 rooms. They'd been sold who knows how many times a day for sex before the bust.

It's something most people I know don't think about, or like to think about, but it happens everywhere. Sex trafficking is one of the largest growing "industries" in the world, and Native women make up about 40 percent of the victims despite being just a fraction of the population. I know all this because my own mother's twin sister, my Aunt Lupita, was kidnapped when they were ten and never seen again.

Their parents, my grandparents, had immigrated recently from Chile and were working heavy hours, so the girls had gone to the park one afternoon together, unsupervised. Lupita never returned after heading off to the public restroom.

The authorities suspected sex trafficking, and told my grandparents as much, so I'd grown up hearing about it. Hearing my mother's fearful warnings to my little sister about "bad men," and never going places by herself. I, in turn, was assigned her chaperone and told to protect her.

Despite all that, my awareness of this dark side of existence had, for the most part, faded conveniently into the background once I'd gotten out into the world on my own. Until now.

"Holy fucking shit," I said, "it sounds like the house was being used for sex trafficking. That shit is real."

I told her about the recent bust in Albuquerque, and my Aunt Lupita, as we gulped down the rest of our Manhattans. We talked about how fucked up it is that this shit goes on everywhere, right under people's noses, because people want to believe it's not happening. But even gleaming, tech-wealthy San Francisco is known to be one of the biggest sex-trafficking hubs in the world.

"Well, if the cops won't do anything, I guess I'm just gonna have to scope it out myself," I said to Erica before calling it a night.

Which is why I'm sneaking down this driveway right now after a couple of weeks of driving by at different hours, on the lookout for anything I can use to get the cops to go over there again.

I make it past the toys and around to the back of the house, out of view from the street. I take a second to catch my breath. I wait another to see if anyone has noticed my trespassing.

The house feels deserted. There's no sounds at all other than the singing of the birds in the trees. So I turn to the sheds in the backyard. The first in my line of sight are the two that look like little houses.

I head over to the first, stand by the front door as silently as humanly possible, and lean my ear in to listen for sounds of human life. Nothing. So I walk around to the side and try to peer in the window, but I can't see a thing behind the thick dark cloth on the other side.

I repeat my motions with the second shed, with the same results. This leaves only the concrete shed in the back corner. The one that had the light on inside.

I don't scare easily but I'm aware of my heart racing and pounding in my chest as I approach it. I stop for a second and reconsider. I've come this far unspotted, unhurt, and, most importantly, un-*traumatized*. Maybe I should cut my losses and leave now.

But I keep seeing *SOS Sex* in my mind. The place those words were scrawled on is right in front of me, and it might've just been teenagers being stupid, but it might not. I have to find out, because if it's as bad as I suspect it might be, I need to do something.

I walk over toward the concrete shed. It's about six feet by eight feet and there are no visible windows from this side except a small one in the rusty metal door. I walk over to the door and stop. I steady myself and wait for several minutes, listening intently. I remember that I might want a picture of what I see, and take my cell phone out of my pocket to be ready. Then I take a very deep breath, turn to face the window, and I look in.

The light's still on but it's dim and the window is dirty so it's a hard to make out anything at first. As my eyes begin adjusting, I see a small wooden chair next to a plastic folding table covered with alcohol bottles and other crap, and across from them: a metal cot.

My heart skips a beat. I quickly look away and glance

around me to make sure no one's there. I look over the fence at the house for sale on the other side. No one. I pull up camera mode on my phone and look back in.

The cot has a thin mattress and old pillow on it, and wait . . . there's something hanging from the metal frame. I squint, forcing my eyes to adjust further to make out the shape. It's a pair of handcuffs.

Holy shit.

I start backing away from the door reflexively but remember that I should take a picture to show the cops. I head reluctantly back to the door, point, zoom, press, then make for the back of the house without checking to make sure it came out okay.

I stop for a second to catch my breath before heading back down the driveway to the sidewalk. I look at the picture. You can't see them at first but when I zoom it in there they are: handcuffs on a metal cot.

I make it to my car and drive away, heart still racing. I don't know what feels weirder: what I saw, or the fact that it was right there, in this cute family-friendly neighborhood named, ironically, Casa Alegre. The minute I'm out of there, on Agua Fria, I pull over, take off the wig, and call Erica.

"Do you think we've stumbled upon some sick sex ring run by the same people at the house in Barrio la Canada?" I ask her over a sunset margarita at La Choza that night.

"Well," she nods, "they certainly have some similarities."

I drink enough to ensure that my head is spinning for some reason other than my messed-up discovery and the thoughts it has elicited, and Erica drives me home. Next day I wake up earlier than usual, as often happens when I've gone to bed piss drunk. The sun's just started rising but I take a Lyft over to my car.

I turn it on and find myself instinctively driving back to Casa Alegre. I've never driven by this early, I realize. I might see something new. I turn onto the street and park a few doors down, with a good view of the house.

I light up a cigarette to buffer me from this seediness, and have just exhaled my first disgusting six a.m. drag when I see a black Escalade with tinted windows pull into the house's driveway. I slide down my seat a bit. It's the first time I've ever seen any activity at the place.

The driver, a man, and the passenger, a woman, get out and head straight to the backyard with their heads down before I can get a good look at them. I suck my cigarette down in record time, sitting here wondering what's going on. I see them heading out carrying heavy-looking duffel bags as I'm about to snub it out. The woman drops hers when she opens the car door. There's a sound of clunking metal.

"Fuck!" I hear her mutter as she bends over to pick up the bag.

She leans out away from the car for a moment and I notice that she's sporting the longest French braid I've ever seen. It's so thick and long that it looks like a horse's tail, or mane, if it were braided, and the hair's laced with so much gray that it looks dusty. The woman's skin is aged and caramel-colored and her wrinkle-bordered eyes are dark brown and round.

She looks like a horse, I think. A mean, old, weathered horse.

Just then I feel my phone vibrate. I slink down farther into my seat to take a look. It's my mother.

The horse woman closes her door and the car backs out immediately and speeds down the block. I answer the phone.

"You should see my garden, Marcos, it's *beautiful,*" my mother launches in.

I don't know if it's because I'm still half asleep or because this kind of stuff, sadly, makes me think of her, but I tell her the whole story. At some point midway it hits me.

"Fuck, I didn't get a picture of the license plate number!" I yell into the phone, "Damn it!"

"That's fine, Marcos, it's okay, don't worry," my mother reassures me. "You shouldn't get this involved in all this stuff anyway. These are probably very bad people, and Santa Fe is a small city."

The Escalade is long gone by the time I get to the part about the horse woman, and when I do I hear her gasp a little on the other end.

"A long French braid?" she asks, sounding startled.

"Yeah, like really, unusually long. Why?"

"There was a girl that went to school with my sister and me who everyone thought was weird," my mom begins. "She almost never spoke and she looked nervous or sad most of the time. After my sister had been missing for a while and it looked like she might not be coming back, the school held a service for her, and the girl came with her mother.

"At some point I broke down sobbing, and when I looked up, her mother was staring right at me. You'd think she'd look sad or concerned or something, but no. It was the weirdest look on her face and I never forgot it—or her—because she had the longest French braid I'd ever seen."

"Oh my God. Are you saying you think—"

"I don't *think*," my mother cuts me off, "I *know*: that woman has to be one of the monsters who kidnapped my sister."

She hangs up before I can respond. I try back and it just rings. I leave her a message to call me back and drive home. When I get there I try her again and it goes straight to voice mail.

"Hello?" Erica answers, sounding a little sleepy.

"I'm so sorry to bother you but you're not going to believe this."

I relay the events quickly.

"So I'm worried about my mom," I say, wrapping it up. "She's not calling me back. I'm gonna head over to her place."

"Okay, but wait, wait—I may know something about how to find the woman with the French braid."

"What? How?"

"I remember an ex of mine from years ago and his buddies joking around about a woman they knew from work and, I *think*, if I'm remembering correctly, it had something to do with her having a French braid . . ."

"Oh my God, try to remember!"

"They used to joke about her braid being so long and thick that she used it to auto-erotically asphyxiate the men she slept with."

"Where did they work? Do you remember?"

"Fuck!" Erica shouts. "I can't! But I think I can get ahold of my ex and I bet he would remember."

"Okay, awesome, thanks. I'll check in with you later," I say. I pull onto my mom's block.

She's not home and I bet I know just where she is: looking for the horse woman. She'd been saying to my sister and me for years, once we were grown and out of the house, that if she ever found *el puta madre que me quitó a mi hermana,* she'd rip his penis off with her own hands and choke him with it as he stood there screaming.

She isn't the kind of person who typically says anything like that—she is *a lady,* as she always says. So I kind of believe her. And I don't want her to take the fall on account of those scumbags.

I want to do it. Do it for Aunt Lupita, and my grandparents, and my mom. Do it before my mom does so she won't spend the rest of her days locked up, away from her beloved garden.

Me, I don't have a garden. I don't have shit, come to think of it. Nothing that amounts to much anyway. I'll make the world a better place by offing these scumbags and spend the rest of my days reading in the prison library.

My phone rings. It's Erica.

"So I messaged him and he actually remembered her name!" she shouts.

"Oh my God."

"And get this," she continues, "I looked her up on the city records and I've got an address for her."

"That's amazing! I'll be at your office in like five."

Erica is kind of crazy, I guess, because she decides to go with me to check out that address and make sure my mother doesn't somehow beat me to it.

"Fuck, I'm out of cigarettes," I lament as we get into my car. "This shit's so fucking gruesome, smoking just seems to kind of go along with it these days."

"Well, do you want to stop at Owl's Liquors and get some?"

"No, it'll waste time."

"No," Erica suddenly announces as we near the turnoff on Agua Fria, squeezing my arm, "I want to stop at Owl's. We *have* to stop."

I look at her and she pierces me with those eyes. I miss the turn and pull into the Owl's Liquors parking lot a block later. I'm about to get out to get that pack when we hear screaming.

"It's all your fucking fault!" a man's voice is yelling. "If you'd have just gone to the store and bought some fucking paint and covered that shit up, like I told you to, none of this shit would be happening."

Erica and I look over to where the shouting is coming from. There she is, in the far corner of the parking lot: French braid.

My take on Erica was more spot-on than I'd even suspected—she knows things. I look back at her, shocked.

I slide my hand into my jacket pocket. My pocketknife is there, as expected. I'd grabbed it before running out to meet Erica.

"Sure, blame it on me," French Braid yells back at the guy, "that's been your plan all along, right?"

They're standing in the empty back corner of the large parking lot, away from the entrance to Owl's Liquors, by the same Escalade I saw in the driveway this morning.

". . . blackmail me after I found out your game and didn't turn you in," she continues shouting, "get me to do all your dirty work setting things up so you could always pin it on me if the shit went down!"

"That's bullshit!" he screams, but it sounds like he's lying, even to me.

I look at Erica. We watch him storm off into the store. French Braid, in turn, gets into the Escalade and screeches out of the parking lot.

It's dark now. This is my chance. To avenge my Aunt Lupita and all our family's suffering. To make sure this asshole can't handcuff anyone ever again. To finally do something with my life.

I reach into my coat pocket and feel the hefty pocketknife, which I've never seen used the way I'm going to except in the movies. I undo the lock feature. The guy comes out and heads toward where the Escalade was, mutters something under his breath, then lights up a smoke.

"The minute I get out of this car," I say to Erica, "drive

away and don't look back. Drive home. I'll get my car from you later."

"What?" I hear her say as I open the door.

"I *mean* it," I hiss.

"Hey, you got a smoke, man?" I say, walking toward the guy. "I'll pay you for it."

"Um," he says, looking over at me, "sure, okay."

He reaches into his pack. I reach into my pocket.

Three minutes later, he's slumping to the ground and I'm walking away, out of the parking lot onto Hickox Street. I pull some paper towels and a small bottle I'd filled with rubbing alcohol out of my other pocket and douse and clean the knife off as discreetly as possible as I go.

I walk several blocks to Tune-Up Café and walk inside. As I wait in line, I pull out my phone and check my e-mail. I order an Angry Orchard Hard Cider and find a seat on the outdoor patio. Someone wants an appraisal tomorrow at two; I press *Accept*, see a confirmation e-mail pop up.

I see a text come in from my mom: *Por fin, justicia por Lupita.*

I down my cider and order another.

PART II

THE CHILDREN OF WATER

TÁCHII'NII: RED RUNNING INTO THE WATER

BY BYRON F. ASPAAS

Pacheco Street

In my dream, I hear coyotes heckling from the darkened arroyo near my old apartment. Shadow puppets dance on the wall, illuminated by car headlights passing east and west on St. Francis Drive. The Sangre de Cristo Mountains loom over Santa Fe.

He lies next to me, snuggled in the pit of my arm, his left hand on my chest. *Who is this man?* The weight of his arm on my chest entraps me. The stranger opens his eyes and stares into me, delirious.

I woke to the howls of an oncoming train. I slouched on the wooden bench, my legs splayed, my leather bag anchored around my shoulder.

The person next to me smiled.

I wiped my mouth.

"Is this your train?" The blue in the stranger's eyes was daunting, the color of turquoise—like *his*, the stranger in my dream. His blond hair wasn't completely blond but held bits of gray around the temples.

I nodded.

"I figured the squeals of the train would wake you up," he said. "I wasn't staring, just so you know. Is this your normal train?"

I nodded again, silent.

It had been close to a year since I moved to Brooklyn from the Harlem projects. Before Brooklyn, I lived with a family of three, in a two-bedroom apartment, near my job—just over a year. Now, I took the R train each morning to meet the 2/3 train that transported me back into the neighborhood, where I was employed as a social worker.

"I've seen you before," the stranger said.

I smiled.

"You don't say much, do you?"

I pulled my bag closer to my side. The howl of the train came closer. I tilted my head to the left—no pop. I tilted my head to the right—two pops. I tilted my head to the left once more, rubbing the sore muscle between my neck and right shoulder. I winced.

"I'm guessing you didn't sleep well either?"

The R train squealed to a stop.

"Well, that's us," he said.

I stood, noticing the ache in my knees, and groaned. I stepped into the train and the door closed behind me. I took the first available seat.

My bench neighbor smiled from across the car, then surveyed the other passengers curiously.

Weekday trains were always stuffed with passengers heading into Manhattan from Brooklyn. For two years, I'd been erroring my way around this city, hoping to one day be able to navigate without the fear of getting lost. That day hadn't come. I still lost myself in the strangeness of New York. Sometimes I pondered why I left the desert—the harshness of the Southwest had nothing on the harshness of New York City. And the desert was my home. The desert knew me better than anyone else. I missed the desert now. I missed my home.

Here, I'd trained myself to keep my eyes down, to move steadily. I kept my cell phone fully charged and my earphones in my bag, so I'd have a soundtrack for my ride to Harlem. Sometimes I listened to music, sometimes to podcasts about finding true love or refocusing on the laws of attraction to center myself and gain a better understanding of the universe. Sometimes, too, I sat quietly and just watched the characters enter and leave the stage until the next intermission, which came every few blocks, but too often the voices began to speak inside me.

Alone in the throng of bodies, it felt as if I were the star of my own show. I was cast as the main character of this episode of *The New York City Subway*, baggage sponsored by Coach, who also supported the cast, which included the man with the blue eyes, the man with his hat out begging for money, the woman who talked to the empty seat beside her, and a car filled with extras.

I closed my eyes to the sounds of FKA Twigs. The voice of the woman soothed me. I loved this song—"Two Weeks."

The stranger's blue eyes hardened on me.

My last clinical placement before graduating from Smith College in Massachusetts was Santa Fe. That desert town had been my second choice, but I couldn't complain. Santa Fe was a reminder of my childhood—when my mom and dad packed us all up for family trips and we headed to Albuquerque, then Santa Fe, then Taos—that odd triangular circle through the northwestern part of New Mexico. I grew up in the Four Corners region, so this was home to me, but not quite home. Just close enough to *feel* at home.

From my apartment, I heard the occupants of the Arroyo de los Chamisos howl. After work, my ritual became a bottle of wine and a pack of American Spirits—the blue box. On my third-floor balcony, I faced west and took in the summer sunset. As darkness became tipped with orange, the wind nipped softly on my skin. Yes, I was home.

I hid my sexuality from my friends and family.

But, feeling frisky after the second glass of wine, I crept into the kitchen and read Craigslist ads on my laptop. At first, it was missed connections that I loved reading, but then my curiosity led me to casual encounters, then to men seeking men. I scrolled through the ads and only clicked posts that promised photos. In my darkened kitchen, I scanned dick pics from all sorts of men: cut, uncut, hairy, smooth, hung, bottoms. It was all there, online, and I was intrigued. I was horny. I was alone.

The train jumped and squealed to a halt, scraping metal against metal, forcing me to open my eyes to the new set of characters that filled the car while the old characters scurried off. The music vibrated thirst into my ears during this brief intermission. I was lonely in this city, and scared. I thought of those who might want me, but also might want to hurt me.

I was no one to this city. I was nothing to anyone near me.

Across the carriage, my bench neighbor squinted a smile with his turquoise eyes. The blondish stubble on his chin glimmered with age. He winked in my direction.

A part of me wanted to smile back, but I didn't. Instead, I shut my eyes and avoided a response. I fell into the music, and the darkness of the tunnel consumed me—"Child I Will Hurt You."

Down-to-Earth Guy—m4m 28 (Rodeo Road). Sane white guy here. Great smile, short black hair, moderately hairy,

blue eyes, athletic, looking for more than just a hookup.
Love to hike, run, bike, and soak in the New Mexico hot
springs. New to the area. Would like to explore the city
different as well as the desert. Get back at me. Versatile,
if it goes there.

With an alias and fake e-mail account, I e-mailed Down-to-Earth Guy. He responded quickly. His name was Jordan and it was past twelve when we began exchanging e-mails. With words, I flirted the best I could. He replied handsomely, in full sentences. It was well past one before I noticed the time and responded with one last e-mail. He sent a phone number. Without thinking, I texted him good night as my high wore down to a faint hum of sleepiness. I wasn't even sure if I was texting a landline or a cell phone, but my phone lit and rang. I was startled by the loudness, the brightness of Jordan's number flashing on the screen. The phone rang for a moment before I accepted the call—silence. Moments passed as I listened to the breathing on the other end, until finally, a raspy voice broke the awkwardness: "Hello?"

I lay in bed listening to Jordan talk. It took a few moments before I felt comfortable enough to speak. The night breeze brushed the curtains and swept across me.

"What are you doing?" his deep voice asked.

I replied shyly, describing the motion of my hand. Each finger surveyed the landscape of my body. His breath hardened on the phone as he exhaled deeper. My thumb pressed into the waistband of my boxers, exposing the hardness of my dick that throbbed with precum. His voice deepened as he continued to talk and described his own movements. I inched my way out of my boxers, kicking them to the edge of the bed, exposing my body wholly to the night. I lay upon the ghost sheets of his hands and wrapped myself within him. Satin licked my skin—my fingers crept down, touching the hairs of my thigh and pubic area. I let a gasp of excitement escape me.

"I want to fuck you," he said.

We talked in whispers, as if we were next to each other, our bodies melded harmoniously. I imagined his tongue deep in my mouth, pressed against my tongue, deep inside his mouth. The coyotes sang in the arroyo below. The hum of tires filled my room with light and the wind touched me.

I listened to his breaths. The excitement forced itself into his receiver—deeper, deeper, he moaned into the phone, into my earlobe, into my mind—until he groaned, and his voice quivered to a pause. "Oh. My. God."

For an hour, I lay naked with my cell phone pressed against the pillow, then the phone beeped. Now silence occurred in death—the death of my phone that needed charging. In my quiet room, I watched the shadows pass. The hum of St. Francis Drive and the laughter of the arroyo proceeded, and the Sangre de Cristos crested with white.

I had been up the whole night talking with Jordan. I thought about his silky body pressed against mine.

I held my breath as the train barreled under the East River. I often thought of the river swallowing the subway. It's been a fear of mine since childhood—the water—Tééhoołtsódii lived inside.

The water is not for the Dine'é, I was told, *we escaped it once.*

As a child, Tééhoołtsódii grabbed my legs and pulled me under Morgan Lake, the cooling pond for the power plant. It was my dad who saved me. He grabbed me from what held me under. I never knew what held onto my legs, but water filled my mouth and my throat and my chest. My mom was mad at my dad for taking me there. She yelled at him for allowing me to swim in that dirty water known for death. She reminded my dad of Tééhoołtsódii, the water monster who grabbed those who swam to his world and took them below.

I never swam again.

"Many of our ancestors died during the Long Walk," my mom said. "The Rio Grande is what swallowed them because the Diné were too cold and too tired, from walking, and could not swim in the winter's bitter cold water. The US soldiers didn't care. They proceeded forth to Santa Fe, on their horses, and left those to the water's hunger."

Hwéeldi is a haunted memory for the Dine'é.

A loud gasp for air escaped my chest when we reached the first station in Manhattan. The neighboring cast members in the car looked in my direction, as if I were one of the crazies. I closed me eyes again as the music submerged me back into its trance—"Ghost Lights" played.

Jordan showed up on my doorstep. We'd been talking for a few nights before I decided to give him my address. He stood at the opened door with a toothy grin, the same grin he displayed in the photos he texted. He wore that Western blue shirt I liked from his selfies, the one with the pearl-snapped buttons. His shirt was unbuttoned at the top and exposed the thick hairs of his chest. His eyes reflected the desert sky.

I hid behind the door, just a little, because I didn't want the sun to expose too much of me too soon.

"Oh my," he said. He leaned in for a hug and threw his arms around me. He smelled of musk, cologne, and coffee. The thickness of his arms wrapped around my back like a boa, bringing me into him. "You're fucking more beautiful in person than you were in photos," he said. "Jesus!"

We sat for hours, in the kitchen, chatting. We moved to the chaise longue and relaxed further. Jordan leaned against the armrest and used his hand as a headrest. Two darkened bands wrapped parallel around his forearm. He saw my eyes move in the direction of his headrest. "Youthful tattoo," he smiled. "For a minute, I was told I was part Indian."

I smiled.

"I know, I know," he said, "you're probably thinking Cherokee princess, right?"

I chuckled like the coyotes of the arroyo.

The sun through the window painted his body with evening light—brushstroked hairs thickened on his arms and the tuft of his chest was exposed. "Shall we move outside?" he asked.

I watched his silhouette darken against the dripping sun.

He opened the patio doors, where my pack of American Spirits rested on the small table. His arms rested on the low stucco wall. I rested mine next to his and we surveyed the land together. He was more beautiful than I could have imagined. He was the white knight we Indians yearned for. He was a trophy—a first-place trophy with blue eyes, blue ribbons. Jordan could be my winner, my prize to take home to my family. His eyes defined the desert sky.

He lit a cigarette from the box. "It's been years since I've smoked," he said. He closed his eyes as he took the first drag and the tobacco curled in embers. He tilted his head back, extending his throat. Smoke escaped his mouth and crept into his nostrils. "Oh god, I've missed this," he said. He opened his eyes and looked toward the fading sun, emptying his lungs.

Together, we blew clouds into the evening sky. The wind licked the dark hairs of his arms as the ash fluttered into the east, toward the arroyo, toward the ground, away from us.

"Let's go for a walk," Jordan whispered.

We walked the edge of Santa Fe High School, and along the Arroyo de los Chamisos Trail—a trail I knew from running daily.

My knees ached with memory.

"Do you know the story of this arroyo?" he asked.

I shook my head.

"La Llorona walks along this bed, they say, each night." Jordan placed his hands in mine. "They say she cries each night, howling with the guilt of drowning her own children. They say she caught her white husband with another woman; he had another family."

The sun sank farther behind the Jemez Mountains, and the night sky tipped itself with fire.

The story ran through my head as we walked through the arroyo. It reminded me of a story my dad shared with me once. The woman in my dad's story had no name, although she committed the same acts as the woman Jordan mentioned: she silenced her babies when she learned of her lover's betrayal— the Bilagáana, the Naakaii, the foreigner with bluish-green eyes who broke her heart, who walked eternally when she, too, was silenced by Tééhoołtsódii—the water monster.

Jordan laughed.

As we walked through the dim arroyo, Jordan nestled his head against my shoulder and the trees darkened around us. We turned around when finally the orange glow slipped into darkness. The wind sang softly around us, and leaves shuddered, as the ghost dance of night began.

At Times Square, I jumped off the R train to wait for the oncoming 2/3 train.

A voice teased from the crowd: "Are you following me?" It was the blond, who stood behind a woman, who stood next to me. "The 2/3 train," he said, "maybe we'll see each other again."

I shrugged.

The woman rolled her eyes.

The 2/3 train squealed and came to a halt. The doors hissed open. I squeezed into the subway car where passengers stood face-to-face, front-to-back, crotch-to-face, ass-to-ass, and my arms slunk into one of the straps dangling from above, while the blond disappeared into the jungle of bags and scarves and gloves—"Guilty Party."

I chose Northern Arizona University because it was within our Four Sacred Mountains of Diné Bíkeya. At the base of Dook'o'oosłííd, the sacred mountain of the West, I finished a bachelor's program and obtained a psychology degree. My parents were happy because I was the first in the family to get a college education. I was older than the other students, but I was glad I'd waited and decided on a career in mental health. My parents threw a big party when I returned to the northwestern part of the reservation.

For months, I looked for a job in my field, but nothing came up in Farmington. I waited tables at the local Applebee's until finally I got a call about a job at the recovery center. They hired me as a counselor's aide and I began to learn the stories of Shidine'é who'd succumb to their weaknesses for alcohol. I watched as Shidine'é admitted themselves or were forced to submit to mandatory recovery—many of those, my former customers at Applebee's, didn't look me in the eye. For months, I listened to the white practitioners talk among themselves about the abuse and neglect of the Diné Nation and their lack of support to help those walking the streets of

Farmington. It was embarrassing to hear them squabble and complain about people like me. Shidine'é were judged and mistreated by the educated white men of the recovery center. The ghosts of the addicted followed me home at night when I listened to their pain speak through my sleep. In secret, I cried with an ache of their trauma—it spoke to me. I felt them. I heard them.

I worked at the treatment center for a year before I had the gall to apply to grad school. My acceptance was to Smith, a private school in Massachusetts. I was nervous to leave the Southwest. I was nervous to be so far away from my family, so far from the land I knew as home. I was scared.

I mentioned the voices to my dad.

He suggested I needed a ceremony before leaving the Four Sacred Mountains. "It's something we do," he said, "especially if we leave our lands."

I laughed.

"Son," he said, "those voices will follow you if you don't take care of yourself."

I shrugged.

"You laugh now, son, but what you don't realize is that the pain of others will become a part of you. You need to see a medicine man."

I neglected my dad's advice and left for Massachusetts.

The voices followed.

I could hear them through my headphones even now. I could feel the pressure against my chest as the subway car began to sway. The woman next to me thought about her baby at home with the nanny. *Was the nanny the right choice?* she thought. *Was the iron left on?* I sensed the fear in her. She gripped the railing tighter. She closed her eyes in thought. The man asking for change was ex-military. He was discharged dishonorably because of misconduct with an officer who lied for his own self-promotion. The ex-military man was relieved of his duties before he could rescind his story. I felt his embarrassment. I felt the blond, somewhere. He was thinking about me—"Anyone's Ghost" played.

Jordan and I spent the rest of the monsoon season together, most nights at my apartment even though he lived just four miles away—off Governor Miles Road. On occasion, after one of my long runs, I'd find myself at his doorstep, dripping with sweat. I was a monsoon who trapped Jordan in my arms. We curled into his living room—sometimes near his bed, or in the hallway—never in the same place, and never in his bed because sweat dripped where it dripped, and we puddled upon one another and melted into our happiness.

As summer came to an end, our evenings began with Jordan and his bottle of wine. He knew I loved the reds—the dry ones because they echoed down my throat when I drank that dryness. We crumpled onto the floor before our evening light show. Each night, we awaited the Male Rain's arrival. With the apartment darkened, we watched the evening light muffled by clouds. Sipping our wine on the floor, we watched the Male Rain begin his dance with a crash of the drum. Silver-lined clouds sparked, and the scent of dirt loomed at the balcony door, whispering to be let in.

The Male Rain performed for an hour or so before the clouds cleared and the roads glimmered. The arroyo roared with rainwater, creating a chocolate river that ran from the Sangre de Cristos. We sipped wine and spent the night stretched out on my apartment floor, drenched in our own wetness, drenched in wine, drenched in each other.

* * *

Two months went by before Jordan and I had our first fight. I accused him of cheating, and he pulled a knife from the kitchen drawer and held it to his own neck. Maybe it was the red wine accusing Jordan, but I cried for him to stop and he got more wild when I called him crazy—*ayóó diigis*—and he pressed the knife deeper. It dimpled his pale skin just below his beard line.

"I would die for you!" he screamed.

I screamed louder, and the neighbor banged on the wall in annoyance.

When Jordan removed the knife, his neck was dotted red. I cried quietly.

"How can you blame me for something so stupid?" he said. The phone vibrated, again. "He's only visiting," he explained. "He's my ex; he's still my friend."

The snow came early in November. We watched the night flutter with white butterflies as Jordan held me in his arms. "I'm sorry, baby. I'm sorry I grabbed the knife," he whispered. "I don't know what came over me."

I nodded, but I knew what had come over him.

His phone vibrated. The message box appeared: *Are you home?* The ex's name popped up and Jordan grabbed his phone quickly. A dialogue of voices began speaking in my head. It was in a language I could not understand. I tried to make sense of the language—but the sight of the message kept reappearing in my head: *Are you home? Are you home? Are you home?*

Three weeks later, I went home to visit my family. I woke to texts from Jordan and went to bed with texts from Jordan. I'd planned to be gone for a week, and we spoke sparingly. In between family functions and trips to Farmington, I got texts with random time stamps. The voices spoke louder.

My phone jingled.

"Is that your girlfriend?" my mom whispered.

I smiled.

She seemed to understand my distance. My mind was elsewhere.

"Maybe you should leave early, son," she said. "Maybe you need to go home sooner than you thought. You should go before the snow hits—surprise her."

I left the next morning.

The snow was piled high in Cuba, but I pushed through and made it to San Ysidro. I could see the Sandias in the late-afternoon light—they were white and so was the land all around. The blanket thickened as the snow kept falling. The traffic snaked through the winding roads and what was supposed to be an hour's drive turned into the longest journey—from Farmington, from Dinétah, my homeland.

It was the worst storm to hit New Mexico that winter, and the traffic inched forward as darkness fell. I pressed on.

The City Different was muffled with snow. Mounds of adobe homes were covered in white and glimmered with evening piñon.

I pulled off the interstate at the Cerrillos exit, turned onto Governor Miles Road. I drove slowly through Jordan's neighborhood because the snow hid the roads. The houses gleamed with orange from the lampposts. The car parked in Jordan's driveway was not his and I slid to a stop when I noticed a stranger in his kitchen. Jordan appeared from behind, arms wrapped around the smiling stranger. He perched his head on the guy's shoulder and I drove away, crawling my way to my apartment.

I texted Jordan later that evening: *I'm home.*

The subway car veered right. I could feel its intense pull as it crawled uptown. I was used to the feeling of being tugged and knew pressing my body weight to the side would prevent me from faltering. I stumbled once, maybe twice, when I first made this trek up the island. I've watched many people stumble. I've watched it happen time and time again when people were jostled and pushed left, then right, by a ghost of the train who picked on those inexperienced.

The train neared my stopping point, 125th Street, where I would escape the jungle of bodies draped with scarves and gloves and the voices—"Everybody Gets High."

It was nearly ten in the evening when I heard the knock at my door. Jordan stood wrapped in the scarf I'd given him before I left to visit my family. He smiled his wide grin. "Why didn't you tell me you were coming home early?" He held a bottle of red wine and I smiled at the sight of it—the dryness in my throat needed to be quenched. We sat near the chaise longue and talked about my trip. We talked about the snowstorm, about my family.

"I would love to meet them one day," he said.

The looming memory of Jordan's face on the stranger's shoulder irked me. The voices spoke in that language I couldn't decipher. Bits and pieces were in English but remained blurred. The voices made no sense. There had been no shame in Jordan's movements when I saw him with the stranger. The moment reeled on repeat in my head—Jordan's smile planted on the stranger. Tears formed at the edge of my eyes.

"Baby, are you okay?" he asked.

I walked into the bathroom and ran the water in the tub. Water steamed hot. I added bath salts to soothe the stiff muscles of my back and thought about the ache in my knee from pressing the pedals on my drive from Dinétah to Santa Fe. I could hear Jordan in my head telling me it was nothing, it was my friend, he's only visiting, but the voices got louder and muffled Jordan's. The hammering, the memory, the splashing, the hurt all built up and pounded like monsoon thunder. The water bubbled as it filled the tub. Steam wafted against my skin and the mirrors fogged with moisture, fogging Jordan's reflection.

"Baby, are you going to talk to me?" he asked.

The pounding, the memory, the *bilagáana*, the splashing, Shidine'é, my long walk through the hurt which puddled and splashed in the water.

"Baby?"

Jordan's eyes remained blue as the sky when his pupils dilated and darkened below the water. A single bubble formed at the tip of his nose until it finally let go and surfaced and popped. His mouth remained open. His chest hairs reached for the air, but the water kept them silent. Jordan's arms went limp and I watched his fingers release the shirt he grabbed onto— mine—the tattooed bands of his arm exposed.

The water calmed before the voices stopped.

I have not returned home since the incident in Santa Fe.

My dad is worried about my well-being so far away, so far from the sacred mountains that protected our people from going crazy. My dad asks about the voices in my head. "Are they still talking?"

I tell him they're gone. I lie. The earphones are what muffle them, but the ghosts are still here.

The subway stops at 125th Street and I see the blond smile once more.

He holds a blue box in his hands, takes out a cigarette, and waves.

I smile and wave goodbye, but I don't think he catches my gesture.

He walks up the stairwell and into the light, his shouldered bag and a ghost-trail of smoke following behind him.

Each day, I make sure my phone is fully charged when I enter the subway stations of New York. Each day, I make sure to close my eyes and hold my breath when the train travels under the water. Each day, I walk with the guilt and grief of yesterday in hopes that music will muffle the memory of Jordan. I'm told I am a child of water. Both my parents' clans represent the redness and bitterness of a monster who lives deep inside me—that monster is filled with dryness and guilt, and a regret steeped in eternal shame.

WATERFALL

BY Elizabeth Lee
Ten Thousand Waves

T hey came for new bodies.
Droves of them from all over the world flooded the place every day, looking for salt scrubs, Japanese foot treatments, and hot herbal wraps that would make their bodies sweat and flush out all the toxic things that had been collecting on the inside. They wanted clean organs, clean blood, fresh polished skin. The chance to begin again. Afterward, they emptied into the steaming tubs and saunas, and laid their just-dunked bodies like soft noodles onto tatami mats in the relaxation room where, through heavy lids, they could look out giant circular windows and see the engraved wooden signposts over treatment rooms and private tubs called Cloud and Willow and Waterfall.

When they came to, they helped themselves to free goodies in the changing rooms: pine- and citrus-scented lotions and shampoos, facial mists and oils made out of tea tree, oregano, rosemary, and jojoba. And once all the body thirst was satiated, there was all that gorgeous nature of the mountainside to drink up too—soft, loving, and quietly wild. Amid the pine and juniper trees, deer and rabbits and coyotes and hummingbirds flapping around globes of sugar water. Thousands of black basalt stones piled up on rock walls were arranged in pretty swirling patterns along the footpath between the locker rooms and the main bathhouse, remnants of nearby volcanoes that had erupted millennia ago and had since been cooled and smoothed by streams and rivers into beautiful polished circles.

All the massage therapists at the spa knew the wild around the place was in check, just like they were, because while they were encouraged to use their intuition with clients, they were also instructed to use soft voices around all the poor frayed nerves coming at them, to wear black, and to move soundlessly among the guests. *Like ninjas*, Bella thought when she was given the details on "proper therapist behavior" by the spa director on her first day. It made sense that all those tired and healing bodies might need witnesses who touched and loved, but quietly; invisibly if possible.

She was the latest hire, and she kept quiet that first week. It had never been a problem for her to go deep inside herself, and to do what she did best, which was communicate in the nonverbal ways; the ways of the body. Each had its own special story and history where a person had lived hard or fractured something or ignored a pain for too long. She touched all those places—the rock-hard knots, lopsided backs, curved spines, faded tattoos, pale thick lines over wrists, star-shaped scars on shoulder blades and stretch marks along stomachs and thighs—with all the love she could muster. Loving strangers' bodies was the closest thing she felt to God. When she held a part of the body, it was the same to Bella as holding time and memory in her hands.

The man looked harmless enough. He was smoking a Camel nonfilter, the same kind Bella smoked by the dozen after her evening joint. They were sitting at different tables at a chocolate shop in town and she had been so engrossed in her elixir and the changing purples and reds of the sky that she was surprised to find she wasn't alone.

"Sky's emotional right now."

"Excuse me?"

"Locals call the sky New Mexico's version of the ocean since we don't have one. Others see God in it, magic, aliens, blah blah blah." The man took a long drag. "So the painters come, the artists come, all sorts of folks looking for healing, for hope. But I think mostly it's the crazies who come. And boy do they come and come and come." He looked up and shrugged. "Looks like plain old sky to me."

The man had that unkempt and dusty look to him like so many others in town. Bella figured it had something to do with the high winds and all that dry high desert going straight into people's clothing, hair, and skin. Maybe into their heads too, scrambling things lawful and logical up there, because it seemed to her in the three months she'd been in town that locals liked being uncivilized and a certain sort of dreamy. She wondered what else it might do to people to get all that dust and rock and time into their bodies and bones. And even older and wiser things. Dinosaurs. Volcanic dust. The sun, perhaps.

The stranger looked familiar. They must have met at that AA meeting she'd gone to the week before. Bella had heard that people in AA were worse than Jehovah's Witnesses, circling around newcomers and demanding phone numbers and commitments to attend more meetings. *"Don't stop until the miracle has happened*, they'll tell you," an old coworker warned, but Bella suspected he just wanted her to keep drinking so she would let him have sex with her whenever they got drunk after work. In reality, the experience hadn't been the worst thing in the world. The idea that addiction could be a disease comforted her somehow and she knew a part of her wanted it to be true. Still, all that talk of God and Surrender and Forgiveness was too much, and she decided not to go back.

"You don't have to do this alone!" the man had called out as she made her way down the stairs of the shop. "Let go and let God!"

You should mind your own business, you freak, she thought, getting into her car. She smiled and waved robotically as she drove past the man and turned out of the lot. The whole group seemed like some scary cult with everyone pushing God when she'd already had God stuffed down her throat when she was young and it had never done anything to protect her. Not when it had really mattered.

As she sped past Owl's Liquors, her forehead and chest blossomed with sweat. She hadn't had a drop of alcohol in three whole days, and that Want started to infect every space of her body again, showing her where she was empty, hungry, and in the deepest kind of pain. A pain older than anything in her life that could have mattered. "It's like coming in from an ice storm," a young blond lady had said to her after that same meeting. "You begin to thaw, and your feelings, your fears, all your old pain, numb and frozen—they start to move and all that moving hurts." Bella hurt all over, but her head hurt the most. She turned around, then pulled over in the parking lot at the local honey shop. All those needling questions were swarming around her head like tiny hummingbirds, sharp and picking her clean with their beaks. She pressed her forehead against the steering wheel until the bone couldn't take any more.

Signs of Dry were everywhere up in that high desert; the air was swimming with sunlight and juniper pollen and dust and microscopic things too small to see and name, too dense to ignore. The world of Dry had been getting into Bella's insides and her outsides and making her thirstier than going three days without booze already had. It was in the space between her eyeballs and her eyelids, wedging its way between layers of skin inside her chalky hands, getting into the long follicles of black hair, making them crackle like tiny, quiet wildfires; it was even creeping into the places in her body that were *supposed* to be wet: her lips, her tongue, down her dark pink throat, and then all the way up the other end of her, between her legs where pleasure, the very bud of her, still waited. Even her nipples were still tucked completely inside her chest, tiny and shelled, and so it made sense to Bella after three months of living in Santa Fe that she had once and for all found an earthscape where life was waiting beneath the surface of things, because it still waited inside of her.

What could that inside wetness feel like? How would it feel to be so wet you could finally orgasm? She had heard so many stories of what orgasms felt like from the women in her life. She wanted to know what it was like to feel those waves of hot move her toward that kind of bliss. Because that would feel entirely different to the burning feel of splintering rope moving in and outside of her every time she did have sex, like she was part of some stupid herd of cattle, taking turns, trudging forward and backward under a dark-gray sky.

She restarted the engine and sped through all the yellow lights down St. Francis Drive.

Carrie's house was a two-story gray adobe located in the north part of town, just off West Alameda and close to the small co-op and a coffee shop where hipsters hung out and wrote poetry and screenplays. As soon as Bella got out of her car, half a dozen black cats swarmed around her feet. "Oh, pardon me, excuse me!" she said, and laughed as they purred and rubbed against her calves.

"Well, hello there, stranger!" Carrie ignored Bella's hand and came in for a hard hug instead. It took Bella's breath away. "Nice hair. You look good." Carrie had makeup on and her hair was swept up in a tight bun, but her large brown eyes were the same. Large and full of gold and black specks.

"Oh, thank you. It needs a cut." Bella ran her fingers through it. It had never felt so dry.

"Well, I can see you've met the posse. Turns out the black cat superstition is especially strong in a town like Santa Fe. But it's not *their* fault how they look, is it?"

Bella looked down at a cat with different-colored eyes and decided he was the cutest of the bunch.

Carrie picked him up. "Well hello, Oscar!" she said into his face, before motioning Bella to follow her. "So," she called over her shoulder, "I guess you haven't lived here long enough to know you'll have to put gobs of coconut oil into your hair. It'll help with the dryness, I promise!"

Bella followed Carrie down the cool hallway and into a large kitchen with terra-cotta tile floors and a kiva fireplace in the corner of the room. The whole space was flooded with color. It was beautiful.

"Wow," Bella said, amazed. "I've never seen a fireplace inside a kitchen."

"Yeah, it's an old Santa Fe thing. You can have a fire while you're making a snack."

"My gosh, how nice."

"Yeah, it's a shame—most other houses around this area are like cinder-block dungeons. Made fast and cheap. Not with real wood ceilings or in the real adobe way. Come with me for a sec. I was just finishing up with something."

Outside the kitchen, three large black pots stood three feet from one another. Each had a different design of turquoise inlay. "I'm just getting ready to ship these to a gallery in Texas."

"Oh, are these yours? Amazing, Carrie! I had no idea." Bella came in for a closer look.

"Yeah, they're mine. Let me just finish this." Carrie began cutting large swaths of bubble wrap before wrapping each vessel.

The last time they'd seen each other they were fourteen and probably friends because they'd been the token ethnic kids at their Catholic boarding school in New Hampshire. They'd always been shocked by how much their classmates owned. Their rooms were full of down duvets, feather mattresses, velvet hair accessories, plush rugs, Beverly Hills creams, and French perfumes. Even Bella's and Carrie's mothers, who both worked in restaurants, wouldn't have been able to afford such fancy items. Bella did her homework in Carrie's room because of all the rooms at the dorm, she felt most comfortable there. It smelled like fast food and chips and the linoleum floor was bare like in her own room.

"So, what have you been up to?" Bella managed to smile, knowing how flat and stupid her question must have sounded.

Carrie cut a piece of packing tape and wound it around and around the bubble-wrapped vase. She draped a faded quilt over it and sat down with a sigh. "Geez, I don't know. It's been, what, twenty years?"

Bella nodded. She wanted some good news. Anything to get out of herself. The cold sweat covering her chest and back was giving her the chills.

"Well, I got married and divorced. Lost my parents. Worked as a waitress. Work as an aesthetician up at Ten Thousand Waves now." She winked. "I'm excited for us to be coworkers up there. Sort of like the old days."

"Oh. I'm sorry to hear about your parents."

"No, it's okay."

"Well, I see that you still don't go by Caroline."

"That's right, it's still Carrie." Her eyes brightened. "But now I introduce myself as, *I'm Carrie, like Stephen King's Carrie*, so there's that."

Bella smiled. "Yeah, true. That tells me something."

"Then I'll tell people something like, *But I don't seek revenge on young white girls I knew in high school*, because people around here might want to know that kind of thing. You know—with all the liberal white guilt and all." She laughed, and grabbed an orange from a bowl on the ground. "No, you and I both know those little bitches didn't know any better."

"And what about the Korean girls?"

Carrie snickered. "Of course not, I love you. I've always loved you."

Bella fidgeted with her hands. Such declarations made her uncomfortable.

Carrie elbowed her leg. "But you *do* remember them, don't you, Bella? Those arrogant princesses with their black Mastercards and their feather beds. Meanwhile—meanwhile—we had magazine ads decorating our walls and our late-night stashes were the cheapy instant ramens and Doritos."

"Yeah. It sucked." Bella pushed a few pebbles around with her sneaker and shivered. The sun had dipped behind the mountains while they were talking.

They had constantly complained about their classmates, but Bella knew, and she knew Carrie knew, that they would have traded in their "real" for the other girls' "fancy" in a second, and probably still would.

"You used to introduce yourself a little differently back in the day."

"Ha! Right. Something like, *Hi! I'm Carrie, like a fairy!* I know." She shook her head. "So stupid." She finished peeling her orange and offered Bella a section.

"No, it made me laugh!" She glanced at the orange. "No thank you."

"Well, you were the only one, I think. Sort of innocent, both of us."

"Yeah."

Carrie bit her lip. She watched Bella move pebbles around with her sneaker. "I'm sorry. I shouldn't have said that. I hate that word, *innocent*. It's a stupid, stupid word."

"No, it's true. We were so, so innocent. Especially me."

"So—how are you now? Were you ever able to get over that . . . whole . . . episode? God, I'm sorry, I'm not sure what to call it."

Bella smiled. "Oh yeah, of course. I'm good now. I mean, pretty good. You know, life isn't perfect but I can't complain. I've just followed my interests and they've led me here. I do massage and write poetry. It's a weird, lonely life, but I like it. It suits me."

"Well, good. Your face filled out some. I hope that's okay for me to say that."

"Of course, and I know. I used to have such a tiny little face and body! What did the senior girls used to call me? Baby doll?"

Carrie nodded. "Sounds right."

"You were the pretty one and I was the baby doll that followed you around and got into bad things with you."

"Like stealing the wine for Mass."

Bella smiled. "Like stealing the wine for Mass. I've been stuffing myself with sugar lately 'cause I quit drinking and smoking pot." She shrugged. "Partying can only numb so much."

Carrie leaned forward in her chair, suddenly more inter-ested. "So so true. I should know of all people." She took Bel-la's hands and got a serious look in her eye. "When I was eleven, my father's father lost his land. It was land from the part of his family from Spain and so he was sad, like deeply, almost-go-crazy sad, and my grandmother got that way too. Then all of it spilled down to my father and mother and both their siblings, and it was happening to all kinds of other folks in Española who had also lost their family's lands. Fucking US government. The sadness took everyone. It took and it took and everyone was chasing the numb." She shrugged. "And it had already gotten their souls." She brushed the white skin of the orange off her jeans. "But before all that taking and chas-ing, taking and chasing, it was just the sadness."

Bella pulled her hands back to her lap and noticed they were cold and trembling. "I don't know, Carrie. All I know is that I feel dry. Like bone-dust dry and I might disappear. Fly away or something. I don't want to fly away like some plastic bag."

"No, but think about it. What's the worst thing that could happen?"

Bella looked around at the rusted patio chairs and the rotted-out firewood and ax by a pile of stones. "I'd disappear."

"So disappear then, Bella. See what it's like. Might not be as bad as you think."

Bella got to her feet. "Look. Sorry if this is rude, but I didn't come here for advice. I just wanted to catch up, espe-cially if we'll be working together. I didn't plan—"

Carrie tugged at Bella's sleeve. "Shhhhhhh, okay, okay, I'm sorry, sit down, I'm sorry. I didn't mean to pry or push. You're perfect. Sit down."

"Can we change the subject?"

"Of course."

* * *

Three months passed before Bella found herself free from cravings and feeling more upbeat than she had in a long time. She had moved in with Carrie shortly after their reunion, and living together felt natural. During those months, Bella was experiencing all kinds of déja vu. At fourteen, Bella had always wanted to be more like Carrie, and she was finding years later that she felt that way again. Carrie was brave and strange and blunt and she cursed and spoke about menstruation and masturbation like they were completely normal things to bring up in small talk. And this delighted Bella.

Carrie also wore tight black outfits and different-colored scarves around her neck every day, which Bella found sophisticated and different, especially in Santa Fe, where people mostly wore ugly shapeless dresses and Birkenstocks. She figured Carrie must have a thing for Audrey Hepburn, like Bella's mother who used to watch *Breakfast at Tiffany's* obsessively when she was a young girl growing up in Korea. Charming girls had a thing for other charming girls, as if recognizing their gift to entice. Carrie's swearing and her humor and her bright-orange and blue and green scarves were all so very charming. To Bella, at least, who preferred wearing neutral colors and always thought long and hard about what she said before she said it. But like most things in life, the moment usually passed and her chance disappeared. She wanted to sparkle too, but she drew into herself like introverts usually do, and she just watched for the shine in others.

At the very least she knew she felt at home with Carrie and up at the spa. The walls and slanted ceilings of the rooms at Ten Thousand Waves were covered in honey-colored wood, and like the rest of the natural desert landscape and the adobe architecture in New Mexico, the wood relaxed Bella's body and made her feel at ease. Protected. Even the ancient samurai sword and the changing display of fine silk kimono robes by the lobby gave Bella some feeling of old world beauty and order, which she needed, what with all the moving that was going on inside of her. Shortly after she first laid eyes on the sword in its silk-lined case in Sakura, Bella watched a documentary about samurai sword-making and how putting the blade repeatedly in fire and folding the metal thousands of times upon itself drove carbon into the belly of the steel, and gave the sword its notorious power and strength. Their sword in particular was rumored to have killed ten thousand soldiers in one day and had gone on to protect the Emperor from the dead soldiers' and their families' vengeful spirits.

Perhaps most fascinating of all, Bella heard from the other therapists about a little girl ghost who lived in Sakura, and though people said she wasn't bad or mean, Bella knew somehow she was a revenge ghost, the kind that her parents spoke of when she was young, stuck between earth and the afterlife because of some grave injustice done to her. "This type of ghost is the most sad and angry," her mother had explained when Bella was five. "They have holes deep inside that can only get filled by getting their revenge." Dead flowers had been disappearing and reappearing in the bathtub of their hallway bathroom. "My younger sister fell down a well when she was three and drowned. She never got to live the life she was supposed to live, and she's angry for that. I don't blame her. I was supposed to watch her. I didn't." When her mother hit a deer on 495 outside of Boston and died shortly after the crash, neither Bella nor her father asked to see the deer's body or had any questions for the police officers. They knew some circle had completed in the universe. They had both been waiting.

Whenever Bella was assigned to Sakura, especially on nights when darkness began swallowing the pine trees and small waterfalls outside and the windows reflected only her faint image back to her, arms outstretched, back sloped over the table, she kept quiet watch. She thought at any moment she might see black smoke or steam floating up from under the massage table, perhaps some ugly green thing coming out of one of the vents. But she never saw anything. A few times at the end of the month when she was menstruating, she thought she felt a warm breath on her neck, but she would turn and there would be nothing. She figured it must be the hormones moving inside her, but she never thought about all that blood slicking down her insides. Carrie had only mentioned the ghost one time, saying she didn't know much about her, only that she had heard she showed up through blood.

Bella's shift on Easter Sunday was booked solid with eighty-minute massages, salt scrubs, and *yasuragi* head and neck treatments. By seven, Bella's joints ached and she felt lightheaded from not having eaten enough before the shift. She quickly ate two apples and a handful of nuts before splashing some water on her face.

The sun was shining a strange gold light through the branches of the pine trees and the waiting room danced with light and dark shapes.

A handsome man in his forties was sitting by the fireplace, sipping from a white paper cup.

The spa hostess introduced the two of them to each other before bowing to the guest and then bowing to Bella.

Bella smiled as she always did during the ritual, thinking the whole affair of white people bowing to each other was sort of ridiculous.

"I'm Chris," he said, extending his hand. He had a friendly smile but his eyes were wet and unfocused and he stank of alcohol.

As soon as they touched, Bella saw bright red. She felt a stinging in her right temple.

"I'm also drunk," he said, kicking one of his blue slippers off his foot.

Mary, the spa hostess, immediately picked it up with both hands, bowed, and placed it before the man's bare foot.

"Your restaurant has the best sakes outside of Japan. It's true! I tried them all."

Bella motioned him to the double doors. "We're upstairs in Sakura. Follow me."

It was an unusually warm night outside. The two climbed the wood staircase, then headed past the communal tub and down a long hallway. When they reached the blue tapestry with the image of a moon and two red-eyed cranes on it, Bella was still wondering where she had seen this man before. Something familiar was circling around her. Something evil.

"Don't I know you? You look so familiar." She closed the door behind them and locked it. She pointed to the black hook on the wall, then raised the edge of the sheet and towel off the massage table, and looked away. "Go ahead and hang your kimono up on that hook and then lie facedown. We can adjust the face cradle if it's uncomfortable."

The man got on the table and Bella immediately covered him.

"Did you go to college out east?" Chris asked.

"No, west. UCLA."

"I see. Class of '99?"

"Yeah that's right. '99."

Bella dropped the towel and sheet over the naked man's

body and folded the sheet back up around his back and legs. She walked around the perimeter of the table and smoothed out all the wrinkles. She undraped the man's back, squirted some lotion and warm oil into her hands, and worked her forearm and elbow over a dozen points along his spine.

"Oh, that's amazing. Like you know exactly where to go."

Bella kept working, trying to concentrate on just the skin and the muscles and the tendons of the man, not on the man himself. Not the red she was seeing or the stinging in her head that was getting stronger by the minute. She closed her eyes and said her usual prayer: *Help me give this person what he needs.* But the man's energy felt dark, like oil and thick poison beneath her hands; she could feel it trying to move up into her insides and she trembled, then stepped away.

Chris raised his head suddenly. "Wait a second, I remember! You were one of the bad girls at St. John's Academy, weren't you? You and that funny friend of yours, Carrie. You guys used to steal the wine for Sunday Mass and get drunk in your dorm rooms!"

Her back stiffened. "Ooh, that's right. That *was* me"

"Like the boys, that's right. Man! We were all such bad seeds back then, weren't we?"

"I think we were just being kids." Things were getting blurry and a few tears rolled down her cheeks. The pain at her temple was getting unbearable. She would do anything for a drink.

"God, it was a crazy time, wasn't it? All that pressure for Harvard, the all-nighters with Jolt and Ritalin—but I do! I remember your face! Didn't we party together or something?"

Bella quietly wept into the back of her hand and leaned back onto the wood table holding the scented sprays. She wiped the wet snot from her mouth and chin. *Do you also remember taking turns with all the other boys and being so fucking polite to each other while you were being so hard to me and to my insides that now I can't even grow a baby even if I want to? Do you remember your parents paying off my parents to take me out of school nice and quiet like nothing had even happened?* Her lips were curling and uncurling and her mouth was starting to ache from gritting her teeth so hard. It felt like her skull might explode from all that pressure.

He chuckled. "That's right, you were better than the other girls? More sincere. Less makeup." His voice was much higher back then and his hands were different, not soft and conditioned by the tub and rich hand creams from the spa. They were cold and sticky fourteen-year-old hands that he had put all over her after he yanked off her tights and underwear at the railroad tracks. She had fought them off, hadn't she? Kicked mud into his face, into all four boys' faces, put up a fight before they pushed her so hard into the mud that she thought she heard something go crack in her back, but then her face went smack into the mud too, cold and nasty and full of shit smells. And then someone flipped up her skirt and Chris was the first to get his cold little hands all over her before he was shouting, *I'm inside! I'm inside!* And then after the burning from him, there was another burning, another, and then another. Bella had been touched all over by four boys' grimy hands and their sweaty hips and thighs and blood-thick genitals, but all Bella could think about with each turn was how different each boy's hands felt as he used her body to push and pull up against. And then after the high fives and the zipping up of pants and a pat on her bare butt, there was nothing. She was alone. The sun had gone down, leaving her freezing cold with just her tunnels of air in the mud.

"So—are we getting a massage here or what?"

"Oh, I was just going to say it's time to scoot down a few inches and turn over."

Bella removed the face cradle and went to place the foam bolster under his knees. She placed her hands on both of his shoulders and tried to ignore his erection.

"You have the most amazing touch, you know that?"

Don't do it, don't. Please don't. Bella wanted with all her might to disappear herself or the man. Either would be fine.

"Say, would you, you know . . . touch me?"

Bella glanced over at the crockpot set on high heat, and could see herself pouring the hot water onto the man's disgusting face. His shit-talking face. It would melt his face like crayon.

"You know—I remember you too. I remember the last time I saw you; we were at the railyard tracks and there was a lot of rain and mud. Remember that?"

Chris's lips twitched.

"I remember wearing a new green skirt but it was cold and none of you offered your varsity coats." She suspended her hands over Chris's chest and up around his neck and face. Energy work, she was telling herself. It might help move all that darkness and poison out of his system, regenerate him into something better than his past.

Chris smiled. "I do remember us having some fun at the railyard once." He began rubbing his palms against his chest in slow circles and curling and relaxing his toes. His hands stopped. "What the—"

He batted away the rice bag from his eyes and blinked. But the blood had already started. The whites of his eyes were filling with dark red and blood streaked down the sides of his face. It dribbled out of the nostrils, the ears. The sheet bloomed deep crimson beneath his head.

"What's happening? What's happening?"

Bella stood up and screamed. Bright red veins covered both her feet, and she pulled up the hem of her pants to see tiny red lines going up over her ankle bones and branching up over her calf muscles. In shock, she looked down at her arms and her hands and they were covered as well. In the mirror across the room, her veiny face was almost unrecognizable.

Red was ballooning onto the white linens and Chris shook his head and cried. The blood ran in all directions down his face. "Why can't I move? What's going on? Help me! Jesus, help me, will you?"

Bella felt a weight on her thigh. She glanced down. The prized samurai sword, suddenly so much larger than inside its demure glass case on the wall, leaned up against her leg. It was surrounded by a halo of red light. Something in her stomach started to rise, and the rising moved up into her armpits and up her arms until they started to move with the rising. Bella watched her arms float up, and the outline of the sword in its soft veil of red appeared inside her hands. Suddenly the dark red lines all over her arms turned into a blinding white, like electricity, as if thunder and not blood was shooting through her.

The blade came down fast and made a wet sucking sound as it passed through the man's neck. At once, the top of the massage table came loose and was now hanging by a piece of yellow foam and green pleather, and there was a soft thump as Chris's head fell on the floor and rolled toward the stool. Thick blood pumped out of the decapitated head on the floor and the body on the table. Bella found large portions of her body slick and warm with it. Something broke inside, some root of her, and a warm flush began to spread and move up until she couldn't stop it and it was now in her throat and she had to open her mouth to make space for it all. "NO!"

She collapsed onto the floor and put her hands into all the blood puddled there. It was warm and thick. It felt good. She moved her hands around like she was a baby playing in rain for the first time; like she was four and trying to find matching images in a deck of cards; like she was fourteen at railroad tracks in New Hampshire, bleeding from the front and from behind. She was smelling all that new blood from her own body, metal smells mixed in with dank shit smells. Dirt and mud and dead semen.

And then everything was quiet and she felt a movement in her chest. It wasn't pounding in her ears, or grinding in her mouth and skull. It was soft, steady. A heartbeat, quiet and good.

Things were already vanishing by the time she opened her eyes. Particles of red were turning clear. Outlines of the puddles and foam table and sword were all disappearing; objects were returning back to where they had been. Within moments, the grain inside the wood floor came into clear view again; the stickiness and warmth of the blood evaporated and Bella could see her skin once again. There were details there, tiny details like brown freckles and moles all along her arms that she had never noticed before.

When she got up, there was nothing to clean. No blood or guts or even a man's headless body. Instead, there was just a clean white sheet and the towel and face cradle, exactly where they should be. The table was ready for a new body. She climbed onto it and spread her arms and legs out. Even the stinging in her temple was gone.

The moonlight streamed through the windows. She let it soak into every part of her until she felt something inside beginning to fill. Her entire body started to swell as her heartbeat grew strong and her long, deep breaths moved clean air through her throat and chest.

So much beauty, so much light.

THE NIGHT OF THE FLOOD

BY ANA JUNE

Casa Solana

I'm going on thirty-six hours at the blackjack table counting cards and watching my chips pile up when Russell, the night manager, tells me I got a call.

"Tina, it's your sister," he says, and I shrug him off because I already told him I'm not to be disturbed. Throws off my rhythm, and I lose track of what I'm doing.

"Tell her I'm not here," I bark over my shoulder.

But of course I'm on the phone with my sister after my next hand because she tells Russell she'll just keep calling and doesn't mind tying up the phone lines. It's a small casino, and my sister knows me too well.

"Aunt Mimi died," my sister says without so much as a hello.

I don't even pause. "Why are you calling me *here* to tell me that?" I hiss into the phone.

People have called me cruel but I think they just don't understand me. Those people are fully irritating. It's been fifteen years since I've seen my Aunt Mimi. Fifteen years since the summer I spent at her hippie, armpit-smelling house in Santa Fe "drying out and finding my mystery again." Bunch of hippie bullshit, really, that involved doing yoga with her students daily (skinny white women, mostly, with veiny arms who twittered to each other about balancing their constitutions) and eating plants. But I was seventeen then, and I'd crumpled the family station wagon around a light pole when I was on a bender. Internment at Aunt Mimi's seemed preferable to the other choice my parents offered: rehab.

Little did I know . . .

"I told you, I'm in Los Angeles all week," my sister snaps. "Go check on Mom. See how she's holding up, for fuck's sake. She's been trying to contact you too, and frankly, you're just lucky I didn't tell her where you are." She pauses, then goes for the jugular: "Katrina." My sister knows how much I hate my full name, so our conversation is over. I slam down the phone.

I'm outside next, squinting at the skyline, all neon and amber glow against the clouds. I pull a cigarette from my purse. Try to feel something for my Aunt Mimi, but fail. She meant well, but there's literally nothing about her that evokes anything like grief in me. I try, honest I do, as I smoke my cigarette to the filter and flick it toward a puddle a few feet away. The orange tracer lingers in the night; I turn, go back inside, and lose all my money.

A month later, I get a card in the mail and nearly drop it when I see who it's from. Aunt Mimi's full name, *Mildred Grant*, and her Santa Fe address are etched across the upper left corner in her unmistakable script. The envelope is postmarked three days earlier, as though Aunt Mimi's ghost is trying to catch up on things left undone.

I mean, probably someone found it and popped it in the mail, right? I rip it open.

Dearest Katrina, it begins, *if you're reading this, I'm dead.*

In her handwriting, reminiscent of my mother's family cookbook, Aunt Mimi tells me from beyond the grave that she enjoyed having me live with her, despite everything, and was proud of how I tried to redeem myself in the end. I bristle at the mention of redemption. I always just knew how to play the game, 'cause that's how you get what you want in the end, you know? Redemption is all sorts of brainwashy, so fuck that.

The note continues with an apology for labeling me a failure, something she barked at me when I didn't pass a drug test in the second month of my internment at her house. Up to that point I'd earned freedom by degrees, over some very painful weeks of yoga and vegetarianism, and when I met Tic on the plaza one night, while I was lurking around Häagen-Dazs scoping the party scene, I was smitten immediately. He was a beautiful human being. He parted his hair on one side, and dyed the tips blue, plus he was taller than me, which was no small feat given that I'm six three. He wore black rubber bracelets stacked up one arm and all I could imagine was that he'd give me a bracelet or two after kissing me. And then he'd kiss me again for good measure. He also had the best weed, so there was that.

Anyway, in the card, Aunt Mimi writes that she wants to make it up to me for calling me a failure. She finishes her missive with a hope that her death will help me "sort out my karma," and says that her lawyer will be in touch soon.

I can't help speculating that maybe she was a millionaire and made plans to leave me her fortune. It makes sense, after all. My mom kept me updated on Aunt Mimi's life after the summer I spent in Santa Fe, as though I cared. Apparently, Aunt Mimi's business in natural healing books and paraphernalia was thriving, so she traveled around a lot.

"She's in Europe this week," Mom would say, or, "Aunt Mimi is spending Christmas in Hawaii this year, isn't that great?"

I remember Mom hesitating then, after she told me

about Hawaii. She looked at me over her knitting, and said, "Wouldn't that be a nice thing to do, Katrina?"

That was code for *Get your shit together so you too can go to the beach.* Joke's on her though: I don't even like puddles. There is nothing whatsoever I like about being in or even around a body of water—flowing, stagnant, whatever.

Not after what happened toward the end of my stay in Santa Fe that long-ago summer.

It was the evening before the Santa Fe Fiestas; the burning of Zozobra. Tic and his friend Rachel told me about it, describing it as a local ritual of symbolically burning away people's "gloom." More importantly, the party on the plaza after the burning was the best of the year.

"It's kinda like New Year's in summer, drunken Santa Fe style," Rachel said.

Even though I'd lost most of my privileges for flunking the drug test, Aunt Mimi let me go and I didn't even have to beg.

"Zozobra is something everyone should see," she told me, all matter-of-fact, when I asked. Then she looked at me over her glasses, thin readers with paisley frames that sat atop her head on her wild gray hair when they weren't on her face. "You can go, but on one condition."

"What?" I asked, crossing my fingers behind my back.

"Pee in a cup tomorrow," she said, then added, "and be home by eleven thirty."

"That's two conditions," I replied.

"Well, you don't have to do either," she said, turning back to her book. "We could just stay in and read."

"Fine," I conceded, and turned to go.

"That's eleven thirty *p.m.*, young lady," she called after me.

* * *

An hour later, just outside the Fort Marcy baseball field where the burning would take place, Tic offered me a hit of acid with what looked like a Looney Tunes graphic on it. I asked him if LSD would show up on a drug screen.

"Nah," he said, smiling. He licked the tip of his finger, stuck it to the hit, and raised it to my lips. Our eyes locked and I took his finger in my mouth, all of it. He tasted like salt and chocolate and everything I wanted but didn't know I wanted until that very moment.

As we crossed the bridge over the arroyo and entered the park, Tic ran his hand up under the back of my shirt. It was all I could do to keep myself from dragging him down into the shadow of the bridge and ripping his clothes off with my teeth.

Zozobra blew my fucking mind—a fifty-foot marionette that moaned and rolled his paper-plate eyeballs while the crowd chanted, *Burn him! Burn him!* I yelled along with them, keeping one finger curled through Tic's belt loop so we didn't lose each other. The crowd pressed against us from all sides, the fever of thousands of people straining to see, yelling and pushing, like some massive animal wanting blood. The sun disappeared on the far horizon, casting a long red glow that foretold the spectacle we were about to witness, and then the lights in the park went out.

The fire dancer and the Glooms—local kids dressed in sheets, Tic explained ("I was a Gloom one year," he boasted)—made their way down the stairs. The Glooms waved their arms all ghostlike as they walked. Fireworks exploded, reflecting off my body, Tic's body, everyone's body. Over the mountains, lightning cut the sky into jagged shards. The crowd pushed and roared, and I could still taste Tic on my tongue.

Then, Zozobra caught fire. A falling arc from one cherry-red firework rained on his orange tissue-paper hair, melting and lifting it into a flame toupee. Pushed on by a rising wind, the flames licked across Zozobra's ear and wrapped around his face. That's when it hit me, the acid . . . the world suddenly sparked and animated. I was transfixed by the flames. Watched as they became spirits and animals and, for a split second, the falling face of my dead father.

Zozobra was fully aflame when the sky overhead split in two with lightning. Then the rain came. First it was a thin drizzle, then a downpour with fat raindrops I hadn't imagined in the desert. Tic hugged me close as though to keep me dry, and the rain washed through my eyes, distorting the already distorted world. The lights came up; raindrops buzzed through the beams, as smoke rose from the blackening mess that was Zozobra. Pushed by the crowd, we started toward the exit, and when we left the pool of lights over the baseball field, the rest of the evening snapped into pieces. It's broken, in my head. The memories are like snapshots laid out on a table, each image dim and smoky.

I lost Tic for a moment as the crowd surged; then I saw him, but from a distance. He was walking rapidly away from the plaza, where I thought we were headed, hunched against the rain. I rushed to catch him, wondering what he had in mind and trying to focus my eyes against the acid and the rain as the night pulsed and swelled.

I called out once, and Tic turned around in a pool of light from a lamppost. His face swam in my view, his features crawling . . . he didn't look like himself . . . suddenly he'd acquired a cap. *Where did you get the cap?* I think I asked or yelled, or maybe I just thought it, and then Tic turned and jogged away. I tried to call to him, *Wait up,* but the night split with lightning again and an instant crack of thunder. My words were lost.

Then I was falling down an embankment, sinking to my ankles in sand, losing my shoes. I was in an arroyo, and everything was so black. The air pulsed with visions of demons, monsters . . . dinosaurs? I thought I saw one and rushed up to it, ignoring whatever scrap of reason was still lingering at the edge of my brain. It was a tree, the most beautiful tree, and it seemed to glow from within. I stopped to feel its branches, distracted in a second, and then I saw Tic off to one side in the shadows. I went up to him and wrapped my arms around his waist.

I think I spoke his name. Over and over, shaping it in my mouth. I could taste the letters . . . I had never tasted letters before. But Tic wriggled free and grabbed me by my upper arm, pushed me away. Looked into my face. He was in shadow beneath the cap he wore, and I think I asked him again where he got it. Then I reached for it; pulled it down on my own head.

This is where I'm still very confused. I saw it with my own eyes, but what did I see? Long dark hair fell to Tic's shoulders from beneath the cap, and then his face morphed into something unrecognizable. He grabbed my other arm too, and gripped until both arms were on fire and I couldn't get loose. *Stop!* I wanted to scream, and maybe I did, but Tic just stood there . . . he wasn't Tic but he also *was*, both at the same time. It looked like he was trying to say something, but I couldn't hear anything over the roar of . . . at first I didn't know what it was. Thunder? The rain?

More lightning and I saw movement to my left. Something coming. Tic tried to drag me away from the tree and into the middle of the arroyo, the sand sinking beneath us, but he fell and pulled me down with him. I was so fucked up, my head imagining people in the dark, and then I saw the water.

It was a trickle, but the roar was getting louder. Tic scrambled up and something about his movements frightened me and, freed from his grip, I jumped back. He lunged, tried to grab my arms again, but I ran. All my energy, despite the world looking like it was being painted into existence before my very eyes as I moved, propelled me through the sand both sodden and sharp, until I reached the embankment.

Tic's hand was on my shoulder then, and my arm. And with the last bit of my strength, I shrugged him off and spun. Pushed him backward, then scrambled up the lip of the arroyo.

I looked back just in time to see what I can only describe as a monster filled with rocks and trees and trash roll the space where Tic should be, but he was gone. Vanished.

It was as though he'd evaporated.

So, here's where I lost my shit. I was standing on the edge of the arroyo watching it chew through itself, basically. The tumbling of rocks and debris sounding like a freight train. I screamed at least once, paced the crumbling edge, and stumbled toward a nearby street. I stood on the sidewalk, barefoot and dripping, screaming my fool head off, when a car rolled up to a stop. Its lights on my body made the world drop away and I felt suddenly so alone. Alone like I'd never felt before.

Then Tic was there; the car door slammed and he ran up to me, pulled me into his arms, and I knew it was him. He was alive!

I explained everything to Tic that night and he said it sounded like some grand-scale hallucination, with sensory experiences and everything, but the next morning, when I took off my clothes to get in the shower, I saw what looked like a handprint of bruises on my left bicep. A ring around my arm . . . a palm and five fingerprints.

What the fuck what the fuck what the fuck . . . I said to my reflection.

I didn't see Tic again until the following week, on my last night in Santa Fe. I'd passed the pee-in-a-cup test Aunt Mimi set as a condition of my Zozobra night, and she must have decided not to say much about the state of my clothes and hair and face when I woke up the next morning, because, well, she didn't say anything.

I mean, I guess she knew it had rained all night, and I was out in it.

Anyway, I covered up my arms so she wouldn't ask about the bruising, and I almost didn't show Tic either, because what could you possibly say to that? Bruising is not the same as a hallucination, and I was petrified that whomever it was I had encountered in the arroyo that night was a living, breathing human being.

A living . . . breathing . . . human . . . being.

Was a living, breathing human being.

Fuck, I thought, *what if I killed someone?* Or at least directly contributed to a person's death?

Tic laughed when I showed him the bruises.

"Look," I said, "it's . . . a handprint." I couldn't keep the fear out of my voice.

"Oh my God," he said dramatically. He poked the bruises with his index finger and laughed.

"What?" I said.

"I know who you saw in the arroyo," he told me, and winked.

"Who?"

"La Llorona," he said, his voice sinister.

I'd heard of La Llorona, the Wailing Woman who, in Mexican folklore, drowned her children after being spurned by her lover—her husband?—and then wandered the riverbanks wailing and grabbing feckless children who were out after dark. Drowning them. I'd heard she haunted Santa Fe arroyos.

But in what version of the tale does La Llorona herself drown?

I asked Tic that, and he laughed.

"Nah," he said, "she didn't drown. She'll appear somewhere else, someday. In the meantime . . . she branded you."

"Branded me? Is that something she . . . does?"

Tic laughed and poked my bruises again. "These will never go away," he said, "and she'll always be able to find you."

"Look," I said, annoyed by his laughter, "whoever it was, that person looked so much like you."

Of course, the long hair that fell from beneath the cap didn't fit—Tic's was longish on one side, but short on the other. The person I had seen in the arroyo had long hair that fell past his . . . her? . . . shoulders.

Rachel was sitting nearby, eavesdropping, and said, in all seriousness, "La Llorona can shape-shift, you know."

Tic, who had just stopped laughing, guffawed again.

"She can!" Rachel insisted. "She can look like somebody else . . . like an old dude or something, or even Tic!"

"People always tell me I look just like La Llorona," Tic said, giggling, "and what better way to lure you into the arroyo?" He struck a pose, then doubled over in more laughter.

"What the fuck, you guys?" I said, looking from Tic to Rachel and back again. They were fucking with me and I didn't like it. "La Llorona's just a folktale. A fucking myth. A fucking, I dunno, lie when you think about it. Designed to scare kids."

Rachel went straight-faced and looked me square in the eye. "Don't say that. Don't fuck with La Llorona, or she'll fuck you right back." She lifted a pipe to her lips and took a long drag, held it, exhaled, then leveled her dark eyes at me once again. "And I don't mean the good kind of fucking."

Tic collected himself and wiped a tear from his eye. He put his hand on the side of my face, and smiled at me. "Tina, Tina, Tina . . ." he said. "You fell down in that arroyo, what, three times?"

I nodded.

"I mean, what better way to get some bruises?"

I shrugged. Looked at my arm.

"We're just fucking with you," he said, and kissed my cheek. "You're so easy to fuck . . ." he paused, dragged out a long silence, "with."

I left Santa Fe after that. Went back home, across the country where rain meant green hills and trees, not flash floods, and on my twenty-first birthday I got a wild idea. I sketched up an image of whomever it was I saw in the arroyo, cap on and hair down, smudged it with charcoal (the one class I excelled in through high school: visual arts), added some deep black outlines, and then walked into a tattoo parlor.

Had that visage engraved into my upper left arm.

There's not much you need to know about my life from then until right now, except that I've always been shit-ass broke and in debt. So when Aunt Mimi's Santa Fe lawyer calls to tell me that I need to come to Santa Fe for a reading of the will in one week's time, I don't hesitate to sell a few things so I can afford the airfare. I can go back to counting cards again, 'cause I am pretty good at it, and maybe even borrow money from my mom, but I've got it in my head that I won't be needing much from my current life after this. My hopes for the future are pinned on that phone call, that trip, to a place I hated, mostly, but where I also found love for a moment or two.

I think about looking for Tic when I get there, but I'm not even sure where to start. Perhaps for now it's sufficient to just go and claim what Aunt Mimi wanted me to have so I can reckon with my karma, or some shit, and get on with my life. Say adiós to my shitty job, my crappy-ass efficiency apartment with rats in the walls, my beater car pockmarked with Bondo and held together, in several places, with baling wire. And maybe, once the dust settles and I have my inheritance in hand, I'll go to Hawaii just to spite my mother. Take a picture with a view of the beach. Send it to her.

Wouldn't this be nice, Mom? Signed, *Tina.*

I get into Santa Fe an hour before the reading of the will. The office is near the plaza so I walk around a bit, killing time. Grab ice cream from Häagen-Dazs and scrutinize faces for something familiar.

At the lawyer's office, I'm alone. A sole heir? I wonder, as I settle into a leather chair and prepare to hear my fate.

"To my niece I leave the key to my house, within which she will find more information about what is to be rightfully hers," the lawyer reads. She pushes a single key across the desk to me, and I pick it up. Turn it over in my palm.

"So, she's leaving me her . . . house?" I ask.

"Officially, she's leaving you the key to her house," the lawyer responds. "That's all it says here, so I suppose you'll need to go look for yourself."

"But . . ."

"Katrina, I suppose it's possible she signed the house over to you and left the deed for you there," the lawyer says, and shuffles a stack of papers. "I suggest you go look."

* * *

It's just like Aunt Mimi to set up hurdles for me to leap over even after she's departed this world and really shouldn't care anymore. Of course I go to the house. I use the key to unlock the big wooden door and step inside to a smell of musty feet and stale food. The refrigerator is still packed full of perishables, all, sadly, perished. Worse: the front toilet bowl still has piss in it. *"If it's yellow let it mellow . . ."* Aunt Mimi used to sing, because save the water or some shit. Now it's anything but mellow . . . it's fucking rank. I wonder why nobody bothered to clean shit up before I came.

"Isn't that what a lawyer or whatever is supposed to do?" I mutter to myself.

I have my hands full, clearly, but I'm not too disappointed. Real estate prices in Santa Fe are astronomical. At the very least, I can sell the house and make a kick-ass profit.

That's when I notice a padlocked wooden box sitting smack in the middle of the dining table, and there's a card with my name on it pinned to the top of a wire stand, like the type you put place cards in for fancy dinner events. Not that I've been to a fancy dinner event . . . yet. I open the card, hold it into the light from the dining room window, and read.

Welcome back, Katrina. I'm sure you're a little confused by all of this, so allow me to shed some light on things. I could think of nobody more worthy of this final task than you, so please follow these simple instructions. Before anything else happens, the box on the table needs to go to its rightful owner. Please walk it over to the house on the corner—you know the one. With the blue shutters and broken front walk. Ring the doorbell and give the box to Mrs. Santo. Do you remember meeting her? Her father, a Japanese American, was captured and interned in the prison camp set up by the government during World War II right here in what's now this neighborhood. Anyway, she'll open the box while you're there so that you'll know what happens next. She's expecting you.

Please give your mother and sister my love.
Aunt Mimi

I sigh. More hurdles to leap, and no, I don't remember Mrs. Santo. Maybe she was one of my aunt's yoga students? I grab the box off the table—it's not as heavy as it looks—and walk down to the corner. Ring the doorbell. *Let's get this over with,* I think.

A very old woman opens the door and looks at me. Her dark hair is streaked with a flash of white like lightning and it falls past her shoulders. Her face is a network of wrinkles, like riverbeds running from the corners of her eyes down over the curve of her jaw. Yes, I realize, when she pushes the screen door open and gestures for me to come inside, she was one of my aunt's yoga students. She doesn't smile; says nothing. I go inside and hold the box out to her.

"I'm Tina," I say. "My aunt died and she wanted me to bring this to you."

Mrs. Santo nods and takes the box from my hands, places it on the table. She walks away then, down a hallway, and I'm left standing in her darkened living room alone. *What the actual fuck is going on?*

She's back a moment later, and hands me something. It's the cap. The cap I took off the head of the person I thought was Tic. I hadn't seen it since that night—it vanished, much like the ghost in the arroyo.

"Where did you get this?" I ask, incredulous, and suddenly everything goes downhill.

"So, you recognize it," Mrs. Santo says, and pulls open the living room drapes. The room floods with light, and I turn the cap over in my hand. How does this relate to the box? To my aunt's death? To . . . anything at all?

I shrug. "I mean, yeah, I do. But—"

She nods and claps her hands. "But nothing," she snaps.

That's when I hear it, a high-pitched whine and the crunch of plastic—a sound I recall from my childhood, when my grandfather lived with us. He used a wheelchair in his final days, and my mom put down thick plastic runners over the hallway carpeting to make it easier for him to get around. I'd know that sound anywhere.

I turn and there he is. Unmistakable. The spirit . . . the person . . . from the arroyo. His dark hair still falls past his shoulders, and in his face I see what I saw that night, but without the distortion from the acid. He looks like Tic, but not, and he's in a fully motorized wheelchair. His limbs are Velcroed to the chair, a tube runs from the front of his throat. Only his eyes move.

And all I can do is look from him to the cap and back again.

Mrs. Santo walks over to the man in the wheelchair, and puts her hand on his. "This is my son," she says to me, then to him she asks, "Is this her?"

The dark night after Zozobra rushes back in fragments, and I'm rooted there, staring at the man's face, as his eyes travel the length of my body. They stop, then, on my upper arm.

He pushes his lips out, and his mother follows the gesture. Sees my arm too. Walks over and grabs it to look.

"Why do you have a tattoo of my son on your arm?" she asks.

I pull my arm away; her fingers burn. "It's not . . . him," I answer, tipping my chin at the man who clearly resembles my tat.

"It most certainly is," she says, and looks back at her son. He blinks once, and I realize that means yes.

"You're the one who was in the arroyo that night, aren't you?" Mrs. Santo says. "You're the one who pushed my son down as he tried to get away from the flash flood."

"That's not . . ." I stammer. "I didn't mean to . . ."

"You didn't mean to push my son into the flood?" Mrs. Santo says, her voice rising.

"It was an accident," I implore. "He grabbed my arms and—"

"You didn't report the incident."

I stand there, my legs rooted to the spot. A rush of anger burns my face. "It wasn't my fault! I was high . . . tripping . . . and I thought . . ." I gesture at the man in the chair. I'm about to say that I thought maybe he was just a hallucination . . . maybe even that he was La Llorona. But I stop. I can hear how ridiculous I sound.

"You thought nothing," Mrs. Santo says. "You are the reason he's in this chair, and worse, he was only trying to help *you* get away before the flood hit."

That snapshot image comes back to me: him pulling me, then falling, then lunging for my arm.

"I was scared, I didn't know—" I try, but Mrs. Santo cuts me off with a wave of her hand.

"Enough," she says. She swipes the cap out of my hand, and gently places it on her son's head. Then she walks over to the box.

"Your aunt found my son's cap in your closet when she cleaned up the room where you lived that summer," she explains, pulling a small key from her back pocket. "She saw his name written in it, so naturally she walked over to give it to me."

She sticks the key in the tiny padlock. Twists.

"She didn't know then that my son was gravely injured in that flash flood, and all because of someone who had pursued him to that arroyo, through the night, then assaulted him as he tried to avoid detection."

The lock springs.

"And even after being assaulted, he tried to help his assailant." Shaking her head in disgust, she lifts the box lid.

I can't see what's inside, but whatever it is, Mrs. Santo seems satisfied.

"Your aunt wanted you to work out your karma, as I think you know," she says then.

"That's, yes . . . what she wrote . . ." I have visions of being pushed in front of a flash flood wave—an eye for an eye. Absent that, a train? Truck? Bus? What's even happening?

"Well, this should suffice." Mrs. Santo closes the lid, walks over to her son, and places the box on his lap. "Had you only *found* my son's cap on the ground while walking home, I would be handing *you* this box. But in light of the truth of what happened that night, your aunt wished for my son to have it. Everything she left behind."

"Everything . . . ?" I can't form sentences. What's she talking about?

"Yes. Everything. Her house, her bank accounts, her home in Hawaii. All of it."

Rage rushes through me. "What?! It was an accident! I didn't mean to push you into the flood!" I'm yelling, looking from Mrs. Santo to her son. "I didn't mean for you to get hurt! I just—" I stop, try to catch my breath. *What's happening?*

"You just *what?*" Mrs. Santo asks, stone-faced.

"I thought *he* was trying to attack *me*," I screech.

"Nonsense," Mrs. Santo says, "you pursued *him*."

"I thought he was somebody else!" I can't breathe. My heart is racing and my face burns with anger. "He bruised my arms when he grabbed me, and I—"

"I've heard enough," she interrupts, her voice rising again. "If you need more proof of what's to happen, here's your aunt's statement."

She hands me a piece of paper in my aunt's hand, notarized on the bottom and dated more than twenty years prior— essentially a month after I left Santa Fe. In it, each detail Mrs. Santo just explained to me.

"I—" I start to protest, but stop. There's one stipulation at the very bottom that Mrs. Santo didn't mention: she'll seek criminal charges against me for attempted murder unless I agree to move in and care for her son in perpetuity.

"Take it or leave it," Mrs. Santo says to me, then pulls out a small recorder and places it on the table. She's been recording everything.

My anger turns to fear. I have nothing. I sold everything of value, not that I had much, and I only bought a one-way ticket to Santa Fe. Plus, I admitted to my involvement . . . *on tape.*

I may be good at counting cards, but I'm an expert at losing everything.

The paper slips from my fingers and flutters to the floor.

Mrs. Santo nods, and the room spins. All I can hear in my head is Rachel's warning to me years ago: *Don't fuck with La Llorona, or she'll fuck you right back.*

"Welcome home," says Mrs. Santo.

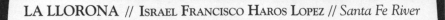

My name is La Llorona. We are many. People think we are just one.
We are born of the breath of Coyolxauhqui, Grandmother Moon.

We are born of
many other mothers,
fathers, beings
from the sky,
from the rivers,
from the oceans . . .

We are the weepers born of the moon

We are the weepers
crying for the children.

I've been wandering the roads of Santa Fe since 1598 when Don Juan de Oñate came to colonize this region.

I cry for our children, and when enough people cry for our children,

another Llorona is born.

I cried tears of fear and joy in 1680 when Popay led a revolt.

In 2007 I cried for this so-called Santa Fe River, in the so-called American Rivers. I cried that year because this river I've wandered for so long became one of the most endangered rivers of this so-called America.

AGUA FRIA ST.

SANTA FE RIVER

I say *so-called* America because this Turtle Island was home to us before this name. We've been crying and living and healing this land for thousands and thousands of years.

PART III

What It Feels Like to Be Haunted

CLOSE QUARTERS

BY JIMMY SANTIAGO BACA

Drury Plaza Hotel

Mysticism, of one sort or another, abounds in New Mexico. You've got a mountain of it, but since I've got a pretty good handle on my way (indigenous) of communing with the spirits, I wasn't expecting to run smack dab into that mountain recently.

When I'm not writing poetry or burying my head so deep in a novel I wonder what world I'm in, I'm giving lectures, keynoting a conference, running a writing workshop, fishing, hunting, or learning the ABCs on proper and healthy living from my twelve-year-old daughter. (I purposely left out raging at Trumpian Shit Eaters, those loathsome creatures that occupy our cherished democratic nest in DC.)

In this case, I find myself on I-25, driving to Santa Fe to give a keynote at the Santa Fe Drury Plaza Hotel. Didn't take me long to find.

It was one of those beautiful winter days, and I couldn't have been feeling any better had you given me Hawaiian dancers and an ounce of cocaine and put me out on an island where I win a lottery ticket every day. No, this was a perfect setting for my soul to join my ancestors and feel that extreme sensation we call . . . elation? No . . . nirvana? Maybe, but One With God will suffice in my case for this story.

There I am, I park, the bellman carries in two boxes of my latest books I plan on giving out for free to the graduates. I hit the front desk, check-in goes smoothly. No time for a quick nap (how I wish!). Up to my room to freshen up and then to the ballroom for the talk. I walk in and the kids are everywhere, my eyes travel over the faces and heads of hundreds of beautiful and brilliant DACA students.

They're typical in all ways except one: they represent the very core of what our democracy means. Most of us are inclined to take our most treasured values for granted—when was the last time you marched for justice? Against police brutality? Environmental justice? Chicanos get beat and jailed every day and most of them are guilty of only one thing: they're poor, have no money for big-time lawyers (who know how corruption works and can grease its wheels and turn the screws so the wheel of fate turns in their favor—happens every day, we hardly bat an eyelid at it).

They were not all DACA students, but I sure felt honored to be asked to speak by people who fought so hard for the American Dream, and so I gave the best talk of my life, I think. If one is to measure it by the fifteen-minute standing applause they gave me, some leaping up and down whooping as if they were at a rodeo, others whistling and so forth—can't stand the prim applause of trust-funders, give me the autobahn over the go-cart track any day. After giving away a hundred signed books, I took a group picture, shook hands, and encouraged them to go and enjoy the City Different, see Santa Fe—after all, their ancestors built this city—and continue to maintain it for the pleasure of tourists and the hordes of newcomers.

I skipped the banquet, went right up to my room, looking forward to a good night's rest. The second I walked in, I felt movement to my right and I looked at the sofa, the area by the wet bar, the fireplace, and attributed my overly sensitive state to exhaustion. My doctor had warned me to slow it down (but whoever listens? If you do, you're not living).

I wash up in the bathroom and I hear a baby crying in the other room. Again, I go into the entrance room and look around and think the cries are coming from the next room or hallway. I draw the sheets back, grab the remote (I use TV to fall asleep), hit the sack, and before long I'm asleep, when I start hearing and seeing weird stuff in my dreaming and I wake up. I sit up in bed for a bit wondering what is going on and then step to the window and look down at the parking lot and a vague sense comes over me as if I've been here before. I hear the crying again and a woman gasping for air and I turn quickly and hurry to the other room and stand in the middle, still as I can, and listen more.

Yes, I hear it again. It's dark but lit enough to see by the light coming from the other room. I slowly turn and I see her. Them. *Man, am I tired,* I think, and I run a bath, sink my whole body in until my head is under water, when I hear banging pots and pans in the sink; someone slams a coffee cup down when interrupted in the middle of a sentence; he kicks the chair when she says something dumb; she slams doors and leaves the house. And he yells behind her, "Stop asking me questions when I'm on the phone!"

I surge out of the water, search the bathroom, the other room, the bedroom and parking lot. Has to be the next room or hallways, I think. None of this makes sense—fuck, all that partying in my younger days is finally catching up.

I dry off, put some boxers on, grab a book (Roy's latest), and read until I fall asleep and hear the faintest murmurs coming from the main room as if a ghost is there. A shadow crosses my bedroom doorway. I get up to adjust the thermostat and find the wall-grill covering on the floor. I hear a pinging and I check the rooms again. On the bathroom counter, decorative glistening pebbles are piled into a pyramid. The mirror is cracked. At different moments, an audible buzzing compresses the space inside and there's no oxygen and I find it hard to breathe. I hear a woman's voice whisper my name in the darkness and when I turn to locate the face, the air around my bed makes a sucking sound, as if a presence has slipped away, rattling the glass panes at the window looking out on the parking lot, the panes flung ajar.

I get up to close it (who opened it?) and that's when I see my grandpa, walking across what was the parking lot but is now an open field. He walks in the dark to the fields to work. From the fields, he goes to the school across the street (the arts academy now) and cleans the classrooms, empties trash cans, and dust-mops the halls. (He dreamed I'd learn to read and write, yet I don't think he ever believed I'd have dozens of books of poems and be here walking around with other literary types.) I imagine his calloused hands applaud and hear his voice in the lofty pines looming all about. *"Eso si mijito, eso si."* That's right, that's my boy.

It's dark in my hotel room and when I lock the window and close the curtains I hear sobbing from the other front room and, when I go to inspect it, I find a woman who looks as if she's stayed up all night, sitting on the floor, legs spread apart, blood all over her nightgown around her vagina, hair all messed up, wedding photos and letters scattered everywhere on the floor, the air thick with cigarette smoke, a glass of Seagram's next to an ashtray stuffed with Pall Mall cigarette butts. She doesn't look up, she just stares at the papers.

The hallucinations must cease. I don't know what to do. I get in bed and stare into the dark, hoping the room stops spinning, hoping the wooden floor stops shaking, I can feel it all over my body, hoping the footsteps I hear in the main room stop, and in bed I gaze to my right at the glistening frost on the window and see how the moon refracts in a million shards and thorns.

And then I remember: days and nights in close quarters and everywhere—floor, table, on the dirt outside, on the sink counter and stove, in the tub; clammy and sticky, sheets tousled, pillows on the floor, my parents' parents' clothes strewn over the house, her flesh constantly touching his, hair and juices and bones and teeth and tongues in his and over hers, cigarette smoke and gin and wine and the cool night air, the dense, earthy smelling, claustrophobic humidity, the howl of barking dogs in the foothills, a quick and violent flapping of owl wings—all of this around me as I feel a connection to this place, this hotel room, merging with it.

It's my first time hearing my mother and I can't explain any of it—as if my heart is a seashell and the roar inside is her voice, the sole sane element in my otherwise crazy life, and it grounds me as she rocks me back and forth in her arms, affirming my belief that there is hope beyond the Santa Fe streets, beyond the prairie that surrounds us, beyond the windmills and forest; there's the possibility of another existence out there, and it strikes me with such clarity and space and truth: this used to be St. Vincent Hospital, and this is the room in which I was born.

DIVINA: IN WHICH IS RELATED A GODDESS MADE FLESH

BY ANA CASTILLO

La Fonda on the Plaza Hotel

That evening at La Fonda Hotel, the two weary and wary housemates (one from a long day of court and dealing with clients, the other from just dealing with life) were enjoying appetizers and cocktails. In the case of one, it was a virgin Bloody Mary with a decidedly impoverished stalk of celery leaning against the inside of the glass. The other was having his usual end-of-the-day destresser martini made with both sweet and dry vermouth and garnished with two olives. They were about to order dinner when a young woman of no small stature approached the table.

"Eleven o'clock," Gordo muttered, his way of giving his cowboy housemate Hawk a signal as to which direction to look. "It's *Project Runway*," he whispered.

As she quickly approached they tried to take in the girl all at once. She was striking at the extremes of imagination—hair like an Olympic torch, piercings, brilliant gaze, and most striking, an outfit that seemed to come out of the wardrobe department for a remake of *20,000 Leagues under the Sea*. The black hair (as black as Hawk's had once been) was streaked with electric red and cobalt blue, and held at the base by a silk ribbon. The ponytail stood straight up about eight inches high in a swirl (surely by the use of an epoxy-like gel). A copper nose ring and a silver one on her left eyebrow indicated, to

Gordo's mind, a person of certain daring. The lobeless ears were virtual swirls of mother-of-pearl seashells punctuated with various gems. Because of her heritage and her mother's well-known devotion to the Virgin of Guadalupe, they might have expected a medal hanging from a chain around her delicate neck. Instead, there was a small tattoo of a black dove right above the jugular.

Hawk gulped. "My God," he mumbled, standing up to greet the tall girl, "it's the . . . g-goddess of death."

"Whoa," Gordo said. His housemate—Mr. Cool himself— was stuttering? "No, man," he whispered from the corner of his mouth, "that's none other than your long-lost daughter."

Hawk felt far from cool. He was aware of who the girl was, although he had not expected to see her there. He'd just received a letter from a relative in Mexico informing him of the child who'd been born two decades before. Hawk unglued his gaze and swigged down the martini on the table.

"Hey," his partner-in-crime protested, not wanting to be responsible for Hawk falling off the wagon.

The lucidity that came from not drinking anymore seemed to have accelerated a latent gift in Hawk, the don of clairvoyance. And right then, in fact, he was seeing *something* that was either there—or it wasn't. Behind the girl he beheld the presence of four million warriors—men and women. The number came right to his head. That was how he saw things and got messages, with a certain inexplicable precision.

As a medium, he had learned, you might see something that also spoke to *you* or was without sound (like now). Sometimes you received audio messages only. A curandera once told him that bad spirits misled people. They spoke to you in your left ear. Good spirits approached your right. Hawk, left-handed and politically left, if anything, objected to the left being associated with evil. He didn't pay attention to either ear. Instead, he checked with his third eye. (Someone might call it a gut feeling.) The third eye in his gut said the four million Indians were souls waiting for justice for the Conquest.

Another explanation for the vision, Hawk thought, might be what some folks called genetic memory. As an Indian, a Native American, he'd inherited the legacy: the arrival of white people five hundred years before and the travesties they committed remained traumatic. Something about Divina made him believe she related to that history too—not just because of her Mexican heritage vis-à-vis her mamá or even through him. She'd brought those four million souls with her. Had she come to reconnect him to his ancestry?

"Hello, Mr. Whitman," the girl said, offering a tentative smile. Her red lips seemed to be lacquered porcelain.

Gordo, having been responsible for uniting the pair and keeping the plan to himself, clapped his hands lightly. Then he and the girl gave each other a quick, almost bashful hug. They had only met before by text.

"Hawk will do," the other said. He was her father but the reality was seeping in very slowly. It hardly seemed appropriate for the strange girl to call him *Dad.*

"Fine," she said, "Hawk it is." She pulled out a chair to sit down and he quickly put up a hand to stop her: "Don't, please." Hawk could hardly look at the girl, afraid his eyes would give away what else was present. The four million souls behind her were very still; they seemed to be waiting to see what would transpire between the two.

Gordo, who was unaware of the reason for Hawk's hesitation, was confused by his friend's reaction to meeting his long-lost daughter. His morose companion was about to foul up what should have been by anyone's estimation a gladsome meeting.

"*Don't?*" Divina repeated in a melodic voice befitting her beauty. With a deep sigh and with a simple hand gesture, Hawk gave in and invited the girl to join them. Almost instantly, the souls faded. He dared to look at the girl directly for the first time. There she was—María—a near clone of her mother, the love of his life. More unsettling, however, there he was in her too.

Divina turned to Gordo and smiled.

"Ah! Miss Divina!" He kissed her caramel-hued hand. "Goddess of death—pshaw, Hawk," he said to his friend. "That was just mean to refer to this gorgeous creature so morbidly."

"I've heard worse," Divina said, nonplussed. She leaned over and gave Hawk a peck on the cheek. "So lovely to meet you, Papá."

Somewhat shyly, Hawk kissed her cheek too.

The waiter rushed over to set another place and fill a water glass. He handed the girl a menu and stood by until she gave her order.

"I totally get your ambivalence," the girl said to Hawk. "You know? In meeting up with me. It must've been a shock when you heard about me."

Hawk didn't respond. It wasn't ambivalence, he thought, but bewilderment. Beyond her near-mystic presence, the girl was astonishing to look at, to be sure. Divina removed her neo-Victorian, double-breasted satin jacket. A golden sash of sorts emphasized a long torso and a small waist. Her corset showed off overflowing breasts, which both men pretended not to notice. They were relieved when the waiter returned with the soup and they could focus on something else.

Meanwhile, Hawk gathered up his courage to inquire about her mother. Haltingly, he asked, "Where is María Villafuerte?"

Divina arched an eyebrow. The mention of María seemed to change her mood. Her brow furrowed as she looked at one man and then the other. "She left this earth only days after giving birth to me."

Gordo snuck a quick glance over at Hawk for his reaction. Divina had already told him how she'd been raised by her mother's family.

Hawk lowered his gaze. How had he not felt María's departure from this life and always hoped she'd return? When he looked up at Divina, their daughter, they were back—the four million strong.

This time, one stepped forward. His headdress, mostly of quetzal feathers, was spectacular. "We have sent you our daughter," he said to Hawk. "She has traveled many miles from what was our kingdom to your land, which was once also our place of origin. But she has also traveled across time upon our wishes. Rejoice, Hawk, in this reunion. She has much to share with you and will do so. Open your heart."

Hawk understood that for the prince or king warrior who had just spoken to him, *heart* meant his mind too. He gave Divina a sideways look as he took a spoonful of posole. Now he began to recognize her. She was not the goddess of death as he had initially proclaimed. (He might instead have picked up that at the moment that she was a *messenger* of death—relaying to him María's passing.)

And while she may well have been his biological offspring, she might have had other reasons to come up to New Mexico—Nuevo México, at one time part of Nueva España—from Mexico City, formerly the Great Empire of Tenochtitlán. Perhaps, as the warrior apparition told him, she had come to relay something very important. It was 2021, exactly five hundred long years since the Conquest of Mexico. Maybe the gods had decided to return. Or at least one of them had, in the form of a steampunk rocker.

Good Lord, he was in for a wild ride.

HUNGER

BY MIRIAM SAGAN

St. Catherine Indian School

L ife was just fine for Trevor until it took a bad turn on Tuesday. It was now Wednesday, and he still didn't know what to do. His older brother had given him a lot of advice about girls, but not about this.

"Avoid crazy girls," his bro had told him. "All girls are somewhat crazy, but, for example . . . don't let stoned girls sit in your car. It's hard to get them out." Trevor did not have a car, but he nodded. "Never never fuck a girl who is drunk. Always have . . ." his brother demonstrated with the foil packet, "a condom. Two or three. Personally, I wouldn't even fuck a girl who is crying hard. Be careful. A crazy girl may not be your fault, but she IS your problem."

Trevor nodded like a person who had options about when and who to fuck. It wasn't a complete disgrace being a virgin at fourteen, the time of his brother's lecture. But by the time he was fifteen and three months he definitely felt behind the curve. Then, enter Ava. She was small and bosomy, shy but chatty, and unremittingly sarcastic and bossy. As a second brother, Trevor was primed for sarcasm and direct orders. She was also really cute. She'd been kind of mousy in elementary school, and then she went to private school for middle, and something happened. When they met up again at a charter high school they were still vaguely friends, and she was armed with copy of *Our Bodies, Ourselves* and lube and Trevor realized why life was worth living in a way that had nothing to do with magic mushrooms. Everything was fine until yesterday.

"I'm your type," Ava had told him.

"What's my type?"

"Short brunette," she said.

The truth came to him—his type was a pretty girl who liked him. But he didn't share that. And she wasn't crazy. She had hypoglycemia and had to be fed regularly—but he'd had guinea pigs. Her mother was a bit spacey and was obsessed with her job at the opera. At first, Trevor, raised by his pioneer stock–type mom, was shocked there were no regular meals at Ava's. But there also was no parental supervision—and they could just lock the bedroom door.

Ava's friends were a bit annoying—they cut themselves with X-Acto blades and threw up from eating hash brownies— but they were no worse than anyone else. Until yesterday when one of them lent Ava Michael Pollan's book *The Omnivore's Dilemma*, which Ava devoured in a double period of Japanese. And she decided to stop eating. For good.

"I'm not going to eat anymore," Ava told Trevor.

"You've got anorexia?"

"Of course not. It's just that . . . food is really disgusting . . . sausage . . ."

"So don't eat sausage. Aren't you Jewish? Don't eat pork."

"Meat is disgusting."

"So be vegan," Trevor said.

"You think cabbages don't have feelings? Trees do! Maybe potatoes . . ." She looked stricken.

That was yesterday. Today she said she'd skipped dinner last night, and breakfast. Her mom didn't notice. He saw she ate no lunch.

"I think I'm going to faint," she said.

And he hoped she would. Then the nurse would know. But she didn't.

They went to his house after school. But there was nothing to do. His mom was home, so no closed door. Ava wouldn't eat, so no snacks. Usually he loved that she played video games and Dungeons & Dragons, but neither of them was in the mood.

"Let's go," he said. It was starting to feel like spring, but the sun was still going down pretty early.

"Be back by nine, it's a school night," his mom called. "And are you kids going to get something for dinner?"

"Yes, yes. Bye, Mom."

He hopped on his bike, and she on the bar. Was she lighter than yesterday? Was she going to die? He wished he could ask his brother, but his brother had gone to State and this seemed like an in-person question.

He turned off the suburban streets and onto the dirt track. It was overgrown with dry weeds. Some dead cottonwood leaves drifted down. In the distance, at the far edge of the houses, they could hear a weird howling sound.

"Is that a weredog or something?" Ava asked.

"Pit bulls?"

"It doesn't sound . . . normal . . . I bet it's a weredog with slobbering mouth and burning red eyes . . ."

"It's creepy," he agreed.

They climbed over the chain-link fence, left the bike, and walked the rest of the rutted path. The sun seemed to be sinking quickly, and it was colder.

The ruin of St. Catherine Indian School loomed up before them, familiar and yet foreboding.

"My mom always calls it St. Kate's," Ava said. "But we never do. We always use its full name."

"Out of respect, I guess," Trevor said.

"Respect for the ghosts?"

"Or, like, the past . . . It was a school, after all . . ."

"Full of oppressive nuns. They made the students get up at dawn and do all the chores. That's how they saved money. They made the students scrub the nun's floors. On their knees. With wax." Ava's expression suggested even the meanest nuns couldn't get her to do that.

"I'm gong to climb a little, boulder up the wall," he told her. "Want to come?"

"I'm feeling kinda weak," Ava said. "I'm going to sit and smoke."

"Watch out for the ghosts," Trevor said. Everyone always said that.

"Wretched students snatched from their culture to die of homesickness . . ." Ava said.

"No one has ever seen them. The ghost is a nun. The Gray Nun."

"Whatever. I think the ghosts are students. They cut their hair and took little kids away from their families . . . They hit them if they spoke their own language." Ava's eyes filled with tears that might have been due to low blood sugar. She sat on the wall. She clicked her lighter, lit a cigarette, watched the smoke curl in the dying sunset. Kicked her sneakers against the masonry. "You don't care about what happened," she said. "How would you like it if the government had taken you and your brother away from your mom?"

"I think St. Catherine's was private," he said. "Maybe people wanted to come here?"

"I totally doubt it," Ava said.

Trevor started climbing freehand. He knew the wall well, some grooves and curves familiar to his hands. It was lonely, though. He wished his friends were there—Mateo and Dylan and Jade, who was the best climber of the girls. He could hardly see Ava in the dim light, just the tip of her cigarette.

"Ava!" he shouted.

"What?"

"If you don't eat, I'm going to let go. Just let go, fall, and die." Well, maybe not die, but break an ankle. "There is a granola bar in my pack. Eat it. Now." He wanted to say—*Ava, I love you. I've loved you since fourth grade.* But it sounded too sappy. And besides, he'd hardly noticed her in fourth grade.

"Fuck that," she said. "I'm going inside."

They'd all been inside, but rarely, because it was boarded up pretty securely—trespassing was one thing; taking out a piece of a school something else.

But this evening the board wasn't there, just a gaping hole, and Ava walked in the gloom of the inner courtyard. Some taggers had written *WEST SIDE* over the door, but other than that it was undisturbed. People said a tagger had died out here, or maybe that was at the electrical transfer station.

The courtyard was open to the sky, and light from the east showed a full moon coming up. Ava clicked her lighter again a few times, but she couldn't see much, just the arches and masonry and an empty space.

And then the space was no longer empty.

The air felt cold and clammy, and then a young woman stood opposite Ava. She had long black hair down her back, and she was wrapped in a shawl. She was taller than Ava, and a few years older.

"Hello," she said. "I'm here to help you."

"Are you, like, a ghost? Of a student?"

The young woman shook her head. "No, I am not *like a ghost*. I am a spirit. The spirit of the earth. Well, not THE earth. *This* earth."

Ava stared at her. The spirit flickered a bit. She seemed to be wearing a necklace of large chunky turquoise stones, then a cross on a chain, and then . . . impossibly, a Hello Kitty sticker pasted to the base of her throat.

"Okay," said Ava.

"You need to eat." The spirit extended both hands toward Ava. She was carrying what looked like a bowl of blue corn posole. It smelled delicious.

"No thank you," Ava said politely.

"You need to eat. To live."

"Why live?"

"What would your grandmother say?" the spirit asked.

"She'd tell me, *Ava, we don't know why we were born, but it's our job to find out. Maybe it's to do someone else a favor . . . or to find out what we're good at. So, choose life, because . . .*"

"Because why?"

Ava shrugged.

"Because it's difficult," said the spirit. "Don't be a coward."

"I'm not . . ."

"Then eat. Maybe you'll live to do me a favor. Save this place from developers and being turned into condos. Make it a park or a garden."

"Nuh-uh," said Ava. "You know eating food from the spirit world could be a trap. I'm not in that world, how do I know the food won't enchant me, take me away, and . . . like, you know, have you ever seen the Japanese anime *Spirited Away*? Where the parents turn into pigs from greed? And the girl eats just a tiny bit of spirit food to keep up her strength?"

"I actually don't go to the movies," the spirit said. "But that seems like a good idea. Just take a tiny taste."

Ava leaned forward, stuck her pinky finger into the corn mush, and stuck it in her mouth. It didn't taste like much but she felt warmth flood her body, starting from her navel. She was hungry, ravenously hungry.

When she looked up, the spirit was gone.

"Trevor!" she shouted, and bolted back toward the opening. She dashed out. Suddenly, a shadow loomed over her and she screamed.

"Ava!" It was Trevor.

She kept screaming.

"Stop screaming. It's me. Ava, what the fuck? You look like you've seen a ghost."

"Trev, I'm just really . . . really hungry. Can I have that granola bar?"

She wolfed it down, and drained half his water bottle.

"I'm starving," she said. "Let's go back. It's getting creepy out here. Hey, let's go to Boxcar. They're still open. I'm going to order green-chile cheese fries and . . . a ginger ale? Nutella milkshake? Something. Come on. I gotta eat. I'm hypoglycemic."

Trevor restrained himself from suggesting a healthier choice. She was going to eat! And then . . . suddenly his heart constricted. One day they'd break up. She'd go to college, and he'd fall for someone else, and this moment that seemed perfect would be gone . . . gone like the nuns and the sad students and the bones rotting in the little graveyard out back.

He shuddered.

"You're cold, poor guy. Come on, dude," Ava said. "Let's get the bike. And, um, Trevor, have you got . . . money . . . for dinner? I don't have any on me. I'll pay you back."

"You never pay me back," he said.

"That's true," she said. "Try not to mind too much." And she took his hand as they turned toward town in the moonlight.

I BOYCOTT SANTA FE

BY TOMAS MONIZ

Rancho Viejo

When my father died—shit, that must've been over five years now—I flew from my home in Oakland to Albuquerque with my partner. I had to rent a car to drive to Las Vegas, New Mexico, an hour and half up the highway—but not just any car. Nah, I rented a red convertible Mustang that, when you opened the doors, I kid you not, a galloping horse appeared on the ground. Magical. Mystical. I made my partner watch me open and close the doors over and over, made them lie down on the ground with me taking selfie after selfie with that illuminated galloping horse.

Once we left the lights of Albuquerque behind, my partner placed their hand in my lap and cooed, "It's such a beautiful night. Look at that moon. Let's stop in Santa Fe on the way."

"Absolutely not. I boycott Santa Fe."

"You've got to be kidding me. How can you boycott a city?"

I didn't respond but just drove on. They could tell something was up so they kept eyeballing me like, *Don't make me ask you.* They possessed such an unwavering stare, I broke.

"Fine," I said. "It's like a joke. My dad said he only went there to pick up work or pick up white women."

"Um, that's gross."

"But sadly true. He met my mom there."

"Thankfully," my partner said, and grabbed the hair on the back of my head lovingly and hard. The moon was almost full and this blue light filled the car. Beautiful indeed, but eerie in a way.

I said, "I was born in Santa Fe. My mom lived with a bunch of other women in some collective house. She gave birth to me in the middle of the living room surrounded by her friends, with my dad outside drinking and grilling carne asada."

"That's sweet."

"Not really. She had kicked him out. Told him to leave. But he refused so he set up outside, with a couple of his homies, yelling every now and then to see if I was a boy or girl."

"That's kind of adorable. Little did he know, " they said, and tried to kiss my neck, but failed because the seat belt kind of choked them.

I snickered and said, "It was adorable until my mom had to call the cops on him because the party got outta hand when he found out I was a boy."

"So you really are from Santa Fe."

"I guess you can say it's my hometown." I stopped talking when I said that: *hometown*. I hadn't been back in years. But I've always felt a sense of pride about being from New Mexico. Or a sense of longing. Of wanting to be filled with something. Connected, maybe. I remembered my parents' relationship. It was manic. The fights they had. And the parties. Every memory accompanied by screaming and drinking or laughing and loud music. Just thinking about it, my body tensed, like preparing for a fight, like sensing a threat.

My partner asked, "So I take it your dad's family doesn't have a framed poster of O'Keeffe on the wall?"

"Never. I tell people there's more to New Mexico than Santa Fe and it's not all pretty flowers and blue skies. It's actually an ugly, conflicted place. My dad took me to the courthouse that Tijerina raided and occupied in the late sixties."

"Have no idea who that is, but cool."

"But we also went to the pueblo in Taos and the Chimayo weaving stores. Honestly, the only time I went to Santa Fe was during the summers I came back here to visit my father in like the early eighties. Every Sunday, we drove to visit my uncle Eddie in the penitentiary just to the south. We'd stop in Santa Fe to buy cigarettes to give the guards. My father had to bribe them so he could see his brother."

"Shut up. That can't be true. That's not how prison works."

"Spoken like someone who never visited anyone in jail."

"Ouch, but I can't argue with that."

"This is the prison where that riot happened in like 1980. They don't even know how many people died because it was so overcrowded and chaotic. Thirty-three, according to the state historian, but who knows."

We drove through the night. I imagined all those deaths, all this history of violence, spreading across the desert. The mesas. The arroyos. The stories of Natives resisting US soldiers, of Chicanos resisting ranchers and hippies, of women resisting machista men, of my father and my mother and all they showed me about loving and hating and surviving.

My partner said, "Okay, I'm totally fine with skipping Santa Fe. I understand. Is the jail still there?"

"It became a tourist attraction for a while. Not that the new maximum-security prison wasn't there too, on the same grounds as the tourist attraction."

"People are just sick." Then they said, "Are you okay talking about your father? I know parents come with such problems."

"I got no problems."

They laughed. "Says the person who rented a convertible Mustang to go to a funeral."

We drove on for about thirty miles until we came to San Felipe Travel Center, which I guess is called the Black Mesa Travel Center now—fancy names for a gas station with a casino and a diner. I always got the pork taco with green chile topped with shredded iceberg lettuce and pale diced tomatoes. But more importantly, the place served the best damn sopapillas anywhere, accompanied by that sticky plastic bear full of honey. I beep-beeped the alarm in this parking lot full of old trucks and beat-up sedans. My partner acted all suspect when we exited the car. I could tell by how they sauntered up to the whooshing sliding glass doors.

We ordered four sopapillas and two tacos. The diner served Pepsi in thirty-two-ounce cups, the red plastic kind, with free refills. The food arrived and we watched each other while we ate the tacos: the green chile hot as fuck, my partner's light skin flushed red, their eyes watered. Me, I let myself go, let the heat and that burn cause tear after tear to run down my face. I didn't wipe one away. After, we slathered the sopapillas in golden honey and licked our fingers clean like kids.

When we left, the moon hung high over the desert. Somber. Slightly spooky. Like something might jump out and scare you. I suddenly felt exhausted. Like in all this excitement of coming home and bringing my partner, I forgot that I was here to mourn, to deal with my family, the ghost of my father, all the stuff that haunted me.

My partner said as we approached Santa Fe, "Hey, a place called Rancho Viejo is coming up. It's on the outskirts of the city so it's not really like going to Santa Fe. Let's pull over and take a moonlight walk."

"You wanna hear something hella creepy?"

"Um. Yes. Of course."

"A part of me is buried in this area. We can even cruise by

the house that's been built on the site on Bosquecillo Street. My mom made placenta pills with half of the placenta but then she gave the rest to my father, who drove out here and buried it. It was just open desert then."

"Get the fuck outta here. Why would he do something like that?"

There was, of course, no way to answer that without sounding ridiculous. Instead, I exited the highway and turned left onto Dinosaur Trail Road and drove past a smattering of housing subdivisions and soft, undulating mounds covered in shimmering silvery foliage, maybe big sage or saltbush, I couldn't tell. The last time I drove on this road, I was with my father. He wanted to fuck with the people who lived in the house. He wanted to knock on the door and ask if they felt it was haunted, if they knew they bought a house that was built on a buried placenta. I refused to stop the car. Told him he was acting crazy. My father called me a fucking pussy and didn't say a word the rest of the way to Vegas.

I parked across the street from the house.

They said, "What do you want to do?"

I tried to pull my partner's body to mine but the Mustang's bucket seats prevented any kind of physical intimacy. I stepped out of car and walked around. I opened the door and saw the illuminated horse appear as if it were racing across the desert sand.

"Holy shit. That's got to be a sign," my partner said as they sprinted away from the car into the wide-open space across the other side of the street. I could see their body jumping this way and that. I could hear them calling: "Baby Chino. Come here, baby Chino. Where are you?"

I ran after them, loving the way the earth seemed to grab

onto every footstep, pulling me back, pulling me down. When I caught up, we were both huffing air. They looked at me in blue light and breathed heavy and hard. They put their finger to their lips: *Shush*. I held my breath and closed my eyes and could feel the pounding of my heart, hear the slight rustle of wind moving through the bushes.

My partner whispered, "My little baby Chino, I knew I'd find you."

They placed their hands on my face. Delicate. Tender.

Something made a noise and we both looked quickly. Then we laughed. We howled. We held hands and jumped up and down. The sand felt warm when I sat and pushed my fingers into it.

"Isn't this state called the Land of Enchantment?" my partner asked, and made a gesture with their arms like, *Look at all this world in front of us*.

"It is."

"I see why. I bet this is the best part of Santa Fe. Perhaps the state. Rancho Viejo. Away from everything. Maybe your father was right to bury the first part of you here. Maybe he did it so that you'd always come home."

"Or maybe so I could do this," I said, and pulled them to me. I tasted honey on their lips. I laughed because that's like the biggest cliché possible: honey lips. As if next, I would come across a running horse or the very spot my father buried the placenta.

They pulled away and said, "Do you believe in ghosts?"

I looked out at the world spreading away from us. I remembered the last time I saw my father. I had woken early in the morning to head out on the road. I entered his room while he slept. Already sick inside. Already dying. I didn't kiss him goodbye. But I placed my hand on his chest. The rattling breath. The slow beating heart. Proof of being alive, of a living body.

"No," I said, "I don't believe in ghosts, but I do believe things can haunt you."

We walked back to the car because we still had forty-five minutes more to drive, yet I wasn't ready to leave yet. I clenched my fists as we meandered across the sand. My jaw locked tight. I wanted to grab something, to take control of everything. I realized perhaps the question wasn't, *Do you believe in ghosts or things that can haunt you?* Perhaps the question was, *How do we get away, how do we free ourselves from something like legacy?*

I pushed my partner against the car.

They said, "You look scary. And sexy. But scary."

"You ever wanted something but don't know what it is?"

"Every day."

"You ever get angry enough you want to hurt something?"

They just stared at me. Unflinching, but waiting. Not challenging, just curious. I had that feeling of when you step up to someone too fast and they flinch, that sick feeling of scaring a woman by just being a man. I looked away.

They said, "It's okay to be full of anger."

I fell against them. Let myself drop to my knees wanting to be filled with anything other than all of these memories. Without rushing, I undid their belt and unzipped their pants. I took them into my mouth, so warm and soft and squishy. I craved that power to make something so defenseless into something rigid and unyielding, to feel a person become desperately alive. They made sounds guttural and full of surprise and pleasure. I looked up into their face and, to see such desire, let me tell you, it's like finally seeing the end of something and racing to it screaming: *Almost there, almost home!*

PART IV

WHAT WE DO WITH THE BODIES

BURIED TREASURE

BY KEVIN ATKINSON

Santa Fe National Forest

I like my job. Maybe it's not for everyone, but I don't mind being out there. Santa Fe National Forest, about 100,000 acres scattered across the mountains of northern New Mexico, with some choice skiing, hunting, and the most beautiful sunsets on the planet. Not a bad place to spend your days, but I hate getting these sorts of calls. The ones with, you know, the bodies?

It was around seven twenty in the morning when my radio crackled, and Alicia's voice came over. She's been a dispatcher with me for six years now. "Andy, you copy?"

"Apodaca here, I copy," I said back, trying to edge the truck over a rut in the road.

"Hey, firewatch twelve reports lights at Porvenir Campground. Mind checking it out?"

"On it," I told her, and clicked the radio back down. There was probably a solid five minutes before I could get turned around and back to the main forest road and head north toward El Porvenir. It's a small campground by Beaver Creek, decent fishing if we have enough snow in the snowpack. This is most of my job, honestly, going out to remind campers who got a little too drunk last night that they still need to put out their fires. If I'm lucky they'll be a little embarrassed and move on. The real annoying ones are those who get belligerent like I've never killed a weekend getting shitfaced in the woods and couldn't possibly relate.

I pulled my truck up to the campsite; there was a gray Toyota parked there already. I got out of the truck and stretched, trying to ease my back a little bit. I'm a big guy all around, but I'm not in the best shape anymore, and driving a government pickup with busted shocks wasn't doing my back any favors. The car was nice, real nice, with Utah plates, and some driving dust around the tires.

It was spring here, but there was something about the campground that felt off as I walked over. There's a tension the morning after a frost, and it felt stronger than normal. There was the campfire, almost all embers by now, contained in the fire ring. The tent that was pitched here had collapsed on itself, and there was a backpack and a couple jugs of water around the fire. I looked around and gave a small call: "Hello! Forest Service here! Come on out. I just wanna have a word."

Nothing.

I tried to listen. In chilled air, sound feels like it travels farther, but really your ear is just focused on getting ahold of any little thing out there: bugs crawling in the leaves, wind whistling through the trees . . . that was all here, but I didn't hear any footsteps or breathing. Nothing human. A crow, somewhere far above me, fluttered from tree to tree. *Okay, fine, I'll walk around.* If they abandoned their car, it was gonna be a long, chilly walk back to civilization.

It took me about ten minutes of circling the campsite before I found the body. The crow gave a couple of short caws and flew off, heavy wings echoing across the forest as far as I could hear. Between that and the long shadows that cut between me and the body, the day had taken a turn for the Fucked.

He was about my age, maybe a bit older, white, in camping clothes that he probably hadn't looked at for more than a minute before buying at REI. The brown insulated jacket was too thin, I could see that. If he'd been near his campfire, he'd probably have been fine, but we're at almost eight thousand feet out here. Temperatures can drop like crazy at night. He was still wearing hiking boots that had mud caked along the grooves of the sole, but other than that they looked too spotless and sterile to be used.

I went back to my truck and called it in. After Alicia confirmed that she was getting help out my way, I snapped on my nitrile gloves, headed back, and tried not to get too near the body. I didn't see blood anywhere. Maybe the guy had a heart condition and hadn't prepped for the elevation. I didn't bother to check for a pulse; the skin was that gray color bodies turn when left alone for a while. Also, I'm not a forensics guy, and touching the body would piss them off when they got here.

Probably I should have stopped there, but I have a curiosity problem, so I kept looking around. I figured the guy had a midlife crisis, decided to do some hiking and all of that after divorcing the wife, thought he had a handle on the rugged lifestyle, and didn't prep enough. It's sad, but stories like this are more common than people think. I haven't exactly come across a *lot* of bodies in the forest, but, you know, it happens. It took some careful stepping around, but I was able to look into the backpack, and that's when things settled into place.

There was a change of clothes, the plastic maps they sell down at the ranger station, and a copy of *Where Glory Waits* by Eric Katzenberg. *Shit. A treasure hunter.*

You know about Eric Katzenberg? Born in Florida, inherited a bunch of real estate money, lost a lot of it in the stock market, and went to jail for three years in the nineties for running a pyramid scheme. After he got out, he moved to New Mexico and bought a bunch of recently released federal property, old homestead stuff, down by Clovis. Ever since then, he'd been shoving his way into the amateur archaeologist scene, complete with a website where he sold artifacts that he discovered on his property.

Then he published his memoir. Most people would have skipped it, except the last chapter of the book held a sketch of a site with three aspen trees, a big boulder in the middle, and a creek running through it. The boulder has an X sketched on it, and in this chapter, Katzenberg claims to have buried a box of gold and silver worth $1.5 million—somewhere north of Santa Fe. And just like that, his book sold out, and we started getting a lot more activity in the forest. It's not really a bad thing, but you get a lot of folks who haven't been hiking in thirty years suddenly passing out as they rummage off the trails looking for these three trees. It was a real nuisance for a few years, before things slowed down.

This copy of the book was worn, and the owner had scribbled notes in the margins throughout. It looked like the book in the *Evil Dead* movies, although printed in paperback. The only page in the whole book that was pristine was the page with the infamous sketch. Most of the things scribbled on the page were this guy's thoughts, or references to other pages, but the last thing written in the book was an address on Canyon Road.

I put the book back in the bag and hefted it. It seemed a little heavier than it looked, so I dug into the bottom of it, and felt my hand brush cold metal. I grimaced as I pulled back his change of clothes and saw a 9mm Glock at the bottom of the pack. At that point, I heard an engine coming up the road, and looked over to see the medevac crew out of Pecos coming for the body.

They cleaned him up, did their forensic analysis, and hauled him into the ambulance to get him down to the morgue. They told me the gun was loaded, and I let one of them pull out his wallet and hand me his ID; better if they mess something up moving the body than if I do. The ID read, *Charles Redmond*, and he was apparently from Blanding, Utah.

"Sorry, Charlie," I said under the deepening shade of the trees. "Rough luck."

Of course, I was done being out in the field for the day. Normally I'd put on some music and drive back to the ranger station, but this time, in silence, I hit the highway and headed toward Santa Fe. It felt good to get out of the forest and under the sun for a little bit. He wasn't the first body I'd found out here, but it had been awhile, and most times we were actively looking for one. Stumbling across the guy, about my age, stiff and blue in the face. . . well, it wasn't exactly how I wanted my week to start. I slugged some more coffee, and spent the next thirty-five minutes trying not to think about dying in the forest.

I was headed into the main office. I had paperwork to hand in and sign off on, a report to fill out, and it was often easier to do that in the city itself. Besides, their coffee's nicer than the pot we've had since the seventies in the Pecos ranger station. After I got my paperwork, I sat down in the break room and started to work on the report. My curiosity got the better of me after a couple of minutes, though. It happens. I get an idea on loop in my head, and there's not much I can do other than scratch that itch. So I pulled out my phone and spent a few minutes searching for that address on Canyon Road.

It pulled up an old listing on a realty website—$2.8 million price tag—but it had apparently been sold. The realty website was last updated in 2015, though there was a website that listed it as the address for Heron Ridge Dealers, an online Indian artwork and artifacts operation . . . run by Mary O'Shaughnessy née Katzenberg.

The treasure-planter's sister was in the body's book. That was weird. Weird enough that I stuck the report in my mailbox and grabbed my keys to go for a drive.

Technically speaking, I was supposed to leave it alone and wait for a cop to take over the investigation, but I knew this wasn't going to get a lot of attention. *Old dude dies in the woods.* Unless they found out that the body was poisoned or something, they were going to write it off and not pursue anything, no matter how much I pestered them about it. I figured it was worth at least checking to see if this woman knew anything before handing it over.

Canyon Road starts right off of Paseo de Peralta, and it's as ritzy as you get in Santa Fe. Most of the lower road is lined with the kind of modern-art galleries that sell a few million worth of art a year. People say Santa Fe is the second best city for art, but they usually leave out the "for its size" part of that ranking. In any case, that's where a lot of the city's money comes from. If you go farther north, there are some homes up there that are the most expensive in the city limits. Some are historic, some are glitzed up, but all of them have the feel of rustic hospitality, combined with more money than I'd made in twenty-nine years.

I parked my truck down the road where I'd be able to get it out when I was done here, and hoofed it up to the address. There was a flagstone path that led up the hill to the house; it wasn't big, but the stucco on the wall at the outside was impeccably maintained, and the garden path to the door was lush and green, despite the fact that we hadn't had rain in three weeks. Standing in between two vines that crawled up the wall and pressed in over me, I knocked on the door.

It opened on a woman in her midfifties, in a tight blue tank top and yoga pants. Her hair was held in a slightly messy bun, her skin well-tanned, and she was very clearly in the middle of a workout.

Part of me wanted to suck in my gut, but man, it was too late. I'm not exactly a cougar hunter, but she looked damn good. I put on my best "Officer of the Law" voice. "Mrs. O'Shaughnessy?"

"That's me. Are you with the police?" she asked, head cocked to one side, evaluating me. She knew I wasn't, but I do have a badge.

"Forest Service, ma'am," I said, "may I come in? I have a few questions about a Mr. Charles Redmond."

She stared at me as I tried to read her face. She clearly recognized the name, yet she took a second to think before saying, "Sure, come on in," and turning and walking away. "Can I get you something to drink?"

"A coffee would be nice, if you have it," I said, following her inside. The walls were perfectly white, sealed, with rugs hanging in strategic locations. They made the eye follow into the spacious living room, where a series of dusty pots, baskets, and a glass case with fragments and arrowheads stood against the far wall.

She turned and gave me an apologetic look. "I'm sorry, tea is all I have. Most of my clients prefer it, it settles the nerves." She hit the switch on an electric kettle next to a selection of bags with bright colors and a few small steel pitchers; various creams, I presumed.

"That's fine then," I said. "So, about Mr. Redmond, did you know him?"

"Briefly. He was a fan of my brother's work," she said, making her own mug of tea.

I stood next to the case, trying not to stare at her, so I opted to stare at the case instead. It was neatly organized and curated, with small plaques explaining each item: Diné pottery, arrowheads found at the Katzenberg property in Clovis, etc. Each artifact looked to be the sort of thing that could fetch several thousand at the right auction—maybe more. It wasn't my field.

"Have you seen him recently?" I continued.

She turned, the mug steaming in her hands, and leaned back against the shelving unit, her green eyes studying me, her face serious. "He was here a few days ago. Annoying, really; he was interrogating me regarding the treasure. What was in it, how it was buried, did Eric ever mention anything to me . . ."

"You must get those sorts of questions a lot," I said, taking out a notepad to write down important details.

She raised an eyebrow. "Well, less now," she said, "but it's always a topic of conversation. I generally just tell people that Eric didn't confide anything in me, unfortunately." She sipped from her tea, and smiled. "Have you drank much tea in your life, Mr. . . . ?"

"Apodaca. And not really. I'm more of a coffee guy."

"Fair trade?" she said, and it took me a moment to realize she was asking about the coffee.

"Folgers," I replied, trying to get back on course.

"Oh my God, you have to stop. It's impossible, the way they treat their workers. Pennies a day, in conditions that would disgust you. I can't imagine choosing to support such an unethical company." Her voice was hard and tight, and I could tell she was legitimately offended.

"I'll keep that in mind. Did Mr. Redmond say anything to you about *looking* for the treasure?"

"Oh, it was all he could talk about! He was going on and on about some breakthrough he'd had, and he wanted verification. I couldn't give it to him, of course."

There was an awkward pause as I tried to figure out what to ask her next. It felt stupid to have driven an hour and change to come in and ask very basic questions. "So . . . business has been good?" I pointed at the case.

She smiled, apparently happy to talk about her work. "Well, it's been profitable, and I like to think that I'm doing some good with my success. Twenty-five percent of our proceeds go to the O'Shaughnessy grants program, where we fund indigenous history programs in the public schools."

"How do you get all of these?" I asked, that curiosity catching up with me. "They couldn't all come from the Katzenberg property . . ."

"Well, some do. More than you'd expect, actually, it's been quite the boon for poor Eric. The rest are donations from old collectors, or sold, or purchased at auction. We've had some good luck the last few years."

"And that's the sort of thing that's in the Katzenberg treasure?"

"That's not particularly amusing, Mr. Apodaca," she said, although she couldn't help smiling, "but yes. According to Eric, it's a collection of artifacts similar to these, with the addition of some old family heirlooms." She grimaced. "Father had some old Spanish doubloons, and Eric had some replicas cast as well, which would only be worth the gold content. He loved the idea of people seeing actual coins in the chest."

"Huh," I said.

"Why are you asking me these questions?" She finished her cup of tea. "I'm afraid I do have appointments and need to clean up a bit before they arrive." She gestured to the spotless seating area.

I'd probably get in trouble for it, but decided to go with

the truth: "Mr. Redmond was found dead in the forest this morning, and he had a copy of your brother's book with your address in it. I thought I should check and see if he'd mentioned anything to you."

She nodded, her face a little sad. "I was worried you were going to say that. He seemed to be struggling to keep his breath, and when he said that he was going into the woods . . . well, I warned him that he should spend another few days acclimating before trying anything. It's so important to take care of yourself as you age, and it was clear he hadn't."

I thought about the paunch that Redmond had around his stomach, and how it was smaller than my own. "Yeah," I muttered. "Listen, here's my card; if you think of anything, feel free to call. Thanks for your time."

"Of course."

I walked to the door, but she said something to my back as I opened it: "You don't think it's out there, do you? You think my brother's a liar?"

I had to sigh. I'd been asked this question (minus the liar part) more times than I cared to count. "Ma'am, I think the only way to keep people from finding treasure is if there's no treasure out there."

I spent the rest of the day finishing the report, and going through Redmond's copy of *Where Glory Waits*. Most of it was references that might be clues to the location of the treasure. Apparently Redmond was quite the amateur archaeologist. He talked about other digs he'd done, and things he found, but his notes rambled, as if he didn't really know what he was talking about. He mentioned arrowheads that belonged to the Anasazi or Clovis culture, but up in Utah? He went on about his bitch of an ex-wife—his words, not mine—and had a lot of questions about "F-ton," which seemed kind of panicked.

There were doodles and notes, and he had a weird habit of circling some of his page numbers and squaring others.

The book messed me up, to be honest. I'd never bothered to sit down and read it, but here was Katzenberg painting himself as some kind of heroic man of the west, yet he'd never really lived here. You live on a compound with forty acres around you, and who can say that you actually know any of the people you're making money off? Moreover, with the notes that Redmond had written in here . . . Redmond had worshipped the guy. Talked a lot of trash about the idiots who didn't see things like he did, who didn't see the value in the arrowheads and the pots . . . Well, Mary O'Shaughnessy did. Hell, she saw so much value in them, she made a couple million a year on them.

That's probably why I drove off into the forest that night. I was thinking a lot, and wanted to get a little air. The whole damn thing had messed me up and so I headed out to El Porvenir. Maybe doing a little nighttime vigil would help me think it through. The camp was closed, of course, but it's not like the tape could keep me out and, according to my voice mail, the forensics crew had finished their sweep earlier.

Which was why I felt goose bumps rise on my arms when I pulled up. There were three pickups there, two sort of older and beat up, one more pristine. Also, Redmond's window had been smashed in. I called in to Alicia that we had some people breaking the tape at the site, and slipped the latch on my holster. She might think it was weird I was out there at that hour, but I'd blow it off somehow.

"What the hell is going on out here?" I muttered as I opened my door carefully, my lights off. I didn't want to startle anyone, so I rolled down my window and tried to listen. I could see flashlights swinging around in the trees out near where Redmond had been found. My gun was in my hand as I approached, and my Maglite in the other, although it was off. I figured I'd get close, listen in, and then startle them off.

They were a crew of kids. Not little kids but, you know, guys in their twenties. They were wearing jackets to deal with the cold, though you could see that some of them were wearing very little underneath, and they all looked pretty grubby. It was hard to get a good view of them, but one of them was standing still while the others were hunched over, searching around the campsite and the trees in the grove.

"There's nothing fucking here," one of them said, frustrated. It was dark, but I could see that he was skinny, almost skin and bones, and he scratched at his face as he spoke. *Aw shit*, I thought, *meth heads*.

There were four of them looking around, while the fifth one stood there on his phone, texting someone, the blue light illuminating his face as he stared intensely down at it. His fingers were flying over the screen. "It's gotta be here somewhere! They said he hid it in the forest, and this is where he died. It's gotta be here!"

"Probably stashed it in a fuckin bank or some shit," one of the other ones muttered, a woman. Something shifted near me, and I had to glance over to the left, making sure it wasn't some meth head sneaking up on me. It was a jackrabbit, holding still, its nose twitching and its breathing heavy.

I let out a small breath of relief. That's when the rock cracked across the right side of my face.

One of them didn't have a flashlight. He'd been hiding in the woods, I guess, keeping a lookout for, well, someone like me. The world went white for a second as I hit the ground, and my gun scattered out of my hands. With the sound of a scuffle, the meth heads started to panic, hollering and clumping up in the clearing. The one with the rock kicked me in the side, before crawling on top of me and lifting the rock over his head. He wasn't huge, though his eyes were wide and blank.

I reached for my gun, but couldn't get it in time. Instead I pressed the button on my Maglite and swung the beam up into the kid's face.

He was missing some teeth. He hissed, the light blinding him. I swung my Maglite up again and clocked him in the face, getting him off me.

"Nick, what the fuck is going on?"

"Forest Service, get down on the ground!" I barked, a little more thickly than I liked, reaching around for my gun as Nick moaned on the ground, holding his face. I fired it into the air.

Unfortunately, this didn't get them down on the ground; instead, they booked it toward their cars. I could hear their engines going by the time I staggered up and cursed, grabbing Nick. At least one of them wouldn't get away.

A few hours later, I was discharged from the hospital and got a ride to my sister Dolores's place. She works for the state, and has a house in Santa Fe. My side hurt as I walked, and I had a bandage over my head. The scalp had bled like a stuck pig. The doctors said I wasn't concussed, which was a blessing. I still dropped into sleep like a cliff rock into the Coyote Creek.

The next morning, late, I woke to a call from my boss telling me to check my e-mail. The cops had gotten an autopsy done on Redmond, and they wanted some insight. When I read through the report, Dolores's coffee in hand, things clicked together, and I knew I had to get moving— and quick. I grabbed the book out of my truck; Alicia had been nice enough to send two other rangers to grab it for me.

I sat down at the table and flipped around, making notes on a pink Post-It. The circled page numbers. The squared page numbers. Circles latitude, squares longitude. GPS coordinates. Redmond hadn't been out looking for the Katzenberg treasure—he'd been burying treasure of his own.

It can take awhile to get something like this done officially, so I called it in to the other law enforcement officials in the field to go out and see if they could find anything at those coordinates. Then I went off to talk to Mary O'Shaughnessy.

When I pulled up in front of the $2 million house, she was getting into a black Audi, a leather satchel in the front seat.

"Going for a trip, Mrs. O'Shaughnessy?" I asked, getting out of my truck. I still had my bandage on and didn't look or feel great.

"Mr. Apodaca!" She forced a smile. "I was thinking of visiting Eric, after our conversation yesterday . . ."

"Without your buddy Nick? Did they mention to you that we grabbed him?" I said. Not subtle, maybe, but my head hurt, and I was ready to get this weird-ass situation done.

"I don't know . . ."

"Come off it, O'Shaughnessy," I said, trying not to let too much anger show. "You had some contacts of yours go out looking for something at Redmond's death site last night. Meth heads, probably the sort of people who come out of Farmington, cutting petroglyphs out of the Bisti Badlands, so you can sell them out of your collection? But Redmond had something you wanted, something he wasn't selling to you . . . but he gave you a look, a tease. And here you are, all the money you'd ever want, and he's keeping something from you. And it made you mad, so maybe your Farmington boys drop by his hotel to make a suggestion. That spooks him, and he runs off to the forest. That's where you met up with him again."

Mary was hard to read when she was in her own gallery with her tea and cream. Now, she was almost shaking as I laid out my story.

"That's the last thing I can't figure out. Why'd he meet with you again? Did you tell him you had the cash? Or did you offer him the Katzenberg treasure?"

Her lip was trembling. "Mr. Apodaca, I don't know what—"

"Regardless of how you did it, you got close, and in the cold, you offered him some tea. The toxicology report noted the presence of Doxylamine succinate in Redmond's blood-stream. I happen to know that one by heart; I use sleeping pills sometimes and that was one that I'd had to stop because my job puts me at high elevations. Did you mean to kill him, Mary? Or was that just a happy side effect?"

Her eyes blazed at me, suddenly, and I thought about the movies. This was where the gumshoe gets shot, right, or there's some sort of dramatic confession. Instead, she just said, "Well, I've never been so insulted. Really, the nerve! Accusing me of drugging some lunatic? You'll hear from my lawyer tomorrow, Mr. Apodaca, and I hope you've enjoyed your career, because I'm sure you won't have a job this time next week."

"Your wheels are a little dirty, Mrs. O'Shaughnessy. Same kinda red dirt out at El Porvenir."

She turned and went to get into her car, and that's when she saw the cop car down the road.

"As a federal official, I do have to make reports to local authorities regarding investigations. You understand," I said, as the officer walked over, a pair of handcuffs in hand.

That was three days ago. I hear she's already out on bail. Apparently the FBI has some questions regarding how she acquired some of her rarer items, so that has complicated things for her at least, but Katzenberg is already on the warpath about how things have "been handled." I'm off the case, since I'm not a cop, but I'll probably have to testify, if that's worth anything.

As for the Redmond treasure, the boys brought it to me to look at. It was an arrowhead and, according to the notes Redmond had in his book, he thought it was a Clovis-era artifact. The last auction for one of those guys hit $138,000, so it wasn't nothing he got killed over.

I took the arrowhead down to my buddy Laura at the Indian arts college. She's out of the Tesuque Pueblo, but majored in anthropology before taking up sculpture. She's one of the experts in identifying archaeological artifacts in New Mexico, according to the Internet. News to me; my sister met her at a party awhile back, they're pretty close.

Anyways, I knocked on her door and walked into her office. She's a little younger than me, with long black hair. She was dressed nice, in a gray suit jacket and sensible pants and shoes. She looked up and gasped; I guess the bandage on the head shocked her a little bit. "Holy shit, Andy!" she let out, which made me smile. It was pretty funny to catch her off guard this time.

It took a bit of explaining to finish the whole story for her. I guess it must have been pretty interesting, because she made me wait while she ran out and brought back two Styrofoam cups of coffee. At the end of it, I pulled out the plastic baggie with the arrowhead in it and gave it to her. She huffed a little at it being handled this way, but put on her own gloves and took it out, giving it a thorough examination. She even used a magnifying glass. I didn't know those were a real thing.

At the end, though, she grimaced. "Andy, I hate to say it, but this is a fake," she said.

"Yeah?"

"Yeah. It's a pretty good one, but the chipping is a little too regular along this edge, and it's worn with patterns reminiscent of a small buffing tool . . . We'd have to do some radiometric dating to be positive, but yeah, I don't think it's legitimate. Sorry." She frowned slightly.

I knew the feeling. I thought about Charles Redmond, dying in the cold out at the campground. Did he know? Was he the forger, or was he just some guy stuck with something he and everyone else thought was going to make him rich? Did he think he'd stumbled on the stuff dreams are made of?

"So what now?" she asked, after I'd apparently let the silence sit too long.

"FBI takes over. Probably nothing happens to O'Shaughnessy. She's got a lot of money for lawyers. Katzenberg's sure to sell a lot more books."

"No, Andy," she said, still frowning. "What about *you* now?"

I thought about my answer long and hard. "I think," I said, curious about how things would turn out, and especially when the meth heads would show up, "that I'm gonna take a nap."

NIGHTSHADE

BY ARIEL GORE
Santa Fe Railyard

She stood behind her table at the farmers market holding a rose-colored heirloom tomato in her clean hands like a beloved.

I licked my lips, savored the cold breeze on my cheeks.

"You must be Juliet," she said softly.

And I gotta say, this was a fantasy so wholesome I'd never allowed myself anything like it: I mean, she grew tomatoes with those clean hands.

"I am," I whispered, trying to match her cadence. "I'm Juliet."

Her cheeks dimpled, just a little, when she smiled. "Try a slice?"

I wanted to see her fingernails pierce the skin of that tomato, but I knew she was too careful for that. "I'd love to try a slice."

She lowered her gaze to my tits. "I'm Molly," she said.

Have I only been out of prison forty-eight hours?

Molly set the whole tomato on a live-edged cutting board and she knifed through it, letting the juice and seeds gush onto her hand. "I noticed from your paperwork that you don't have any gardening experience," she said, "but I appreciated where you said you'd make up for it with passion."

My chest felt tingly.

Molly tilted her cutting board toward me and I took a slice

between my thumb and index fingers, brought it to my lips.

I can make up for it with passion, all right.

Molly didn't ask me why I'd skipped the prison gardening program. It would have been a valid question. I knew girls who dreaded parole they were so into that goddamn organic program.

Honestly, I'm not sure what I'd have said if she'd asked.

Truth is, dirt reminded me of burial. Reminded me of San Lorenzo Park and the Willamette River. I needed to put all that behind me now.

Molly didn't ask me what I did with my time inside instead of the gardening, either. I liked that she didn't need to pry, but I wanted to tell Molly things about my life. *Is that weird? You ever want to tell somebody all about yourself? Give them some reason to think you're special?*

I read a lot of Murakami in prison, that's what I would have told her if she'd asked. The truth. I had this idea to start telling the truth more often. Murakami. And I went to the pagan women's circle on Friday afternoons. Maybe nothing you'd ever get invited to give a TED Talk about, but it was a life.

I liked the way anything could happen in a Murakami novel: fish fall from the sky, a psychic hooker starts calling you out of the blue, you find your lost cat. All this crazy shit could happen and in the end it was like nothing happened. You go on with your life. You look up at the sky.

I liked the way the witch lady who ran the pagan group made you feel that way too—only different. Her name was Star. When she first introduced herself, I thought she said *Scar*. I said, "Scar? That's kind of tough."

"No," she laughed. "*Star*. But you can call me Scar if you want to."

We were both sitting on plastic chairs with steel legs bolted to the floor. It's like you're always in an airport but you can't go anywhere.

"And you are?" She hesitated for my answer.

I said the first thing that popped into my head: "Juliet." Then I worried that sounded stupid.

Scar had to know what name I was in there under, I realized that. But I like a girl who understands that not everybody wants to be called by the name they're in under. She had a hole in her nostril where a nose ring should go, but no nose ring. She said she was a witch, had a PhD in witchcraft or something because I guess you can get those now? Like, it's late-stage feminism or something since I've been inside. Anyway, on Fridays we sat on those plastic chairs with steel legs bolted and sometimes I was the only one there besides Scar and sometimes a few other girls, and either way, Scar would lead us in these meditations, instructing us to visualize roots coming out of our feet. Like actual plant roots, right? She said, "Visualization is the most powerful tool I've ever found to reclaim my own agency."

And I liked the sound of that. I had some agency I wanted to reclaim. Yes, I did. So I showed up in that fluorescent-lit room every Friday afternoon and I imagined roots coming out of my feet.

Sometimes I asked myself, *Where does magical thinking end and schizophrenia begin?* But I never did have an answer for that, so I put the question out of my mind.

Scar said, "Do you have a mantra, Juliet?"

And I didn't want to *not* have a mantra so I made one up right then and there. I said, "Yeah, I got a mantra. It goes, *Outta here outta here outta here.*"

Scar's teeth stuck out when she grinned. "I like that," she

said, "and I want to invite you to take it further. What if you imagined the life you desire, not just the escape?"

And that right there was pretty much a revelation. I'd never imagined anything *but* escape. Still, I didn't exactly know where or how to start. *Imagine the life you desire*, I told myself, but I didn't listen. I visualized roots and I chanted silently, *Outta here outta here outta here.*

Mostly I did that on Friday afternoons with Scar, but this one night, it's Thursday, right? And I'm as alone as I ever got in there and I'm reading Murakami and fish are falling from the sky and psychic hookers start calling out of the blue and you just *know* he's about to find his lost cat and I'm thinking, *I could write a book as good as this, easy*, and I get this idea to start visualizing roots, just like Scar taught us. So, the roots are growing out of my feet like bunions. They're clawing out through the skin of my soles and then through my mattress and down through the bottom of my bunk and into the cement and my roots penetrate the ground and that's when I realized I can tunnel down with my roots, right? I'm getting crazy into this visualization and I'm sure I'm gonna open my eyes and I'll have tunneled right out and into Our Table Co-op to buy myself a bag of squash, and I'm picturing everything—vivid, like *outta here*—but when I open my eyes I'm still in my cell. And that's when I think, *Well, shit. Scar's bullshit doesn't work.*

But the next day it's Friday, so I show up at the pagan group, trying to decide whether to tell Scar I think her visualization doesn't work, and I'm the only one there, which honestly isn't that unusual, and out of the blue like a call from a psychic hooker, Scar says she has a lead on this work-release program in Santa Fe, New Mexico. And usually they just take women from the gardening program, right? But Scar's got a lead like she knows someone, like it's just a matter of paperwork.

And I say, "Scar, that's the craziest thing because last night I was doing the root visualization and I thought for sure I'd tunneled outta here with my pagan Jedi mind power and then I opened my eyes and I accepted failure and now today I come in here and you're maybe handing me this tunnel out?"

And Scar says, "You know what, Juliet? *That's* the difference between crazy and magic. Crazy doesn't leave room for doubt. Magic always leaves a little room for doubt. And coincidence."

I closed my eyes and I saw a coyote and a cactus and from there it's just paperwork and interviews with this officer Jim I've never met before and more paperwork and a cold van in the dead of night and a Greyhound station like I'm a free woman. And I don't want to go down through California 'cause I don't wanna have to worry about memories, so I head inland.

You ever think about how many places there are out there? Well, for one thing there's plenty of Eastern Oregon. There's a little bit of Idaho out there. And let me tell you, there's a whole lot of Utah. And then if you cross the border into Colorado, even just a few miles, you can buy marijuana like it's just a cigarette or a candy bar. I keep reminding myself to do like Scar said, just believe in the energy. *The energy's gonna take me where I need to be when I need to be there.* And then next thing I'm here. In the desert. And it is fucking cold.

Like, I thought I was coming to the goddamn desert and they were gonna have cactuses and palm trees, but apparently I was visualizing Arizona. Or some LA movie set that passed for Arizona. Not to complain. I check into the Motel 6 because they're the closest place to the railyard that'll take my voucher. I mean, you ever just go outside in the dark and listen?

The first night I stepped outside on my own watch and

just listened and I knew I was outta there. I said to myself, *I am never gonna take the sound of the night for granted again*. But you know what happened? I swear, it was like the very next night and colder than a walk-in freezer and already I could give a shit about the sound of the night. You get used to upgrades in life a lot quicker than you get used to downgrades. I've learned that much.

All this to say, Santa Fe was definitely an upgrade.

The dry air smelled musty and fresh at the same time, like green chile on charcoal.

Molly picked up another slice of the tomato and I closed my eyes and opened my mouth and let her feed it to me and I said to myself, *Don't lick her fingers*, and for once in my life I listened.

The tomato tasted tart and earthy, like blood.

"You like?" Molly whispered.

"It's incredible," I whispered back.

She smiled and made her cheeks dimple again. "Our tomatoes win all the awards year round. Anyone can grow a tomato in summertime, Juliet, but I'm the only one yielding orbs like this in the middle of winter." Molly stroked one of her orbs. "I love them so much," she whispered. "Sometimes it hurts my heart to imagine them being eaten."

Looking at all the tomatoes in her basket, I wanted to know her secret, but I needed to pace myself. She hadn't asked me too many questions. I wouldn't ask too many, either.

Molly blushed, just a little.

Did she blush?

She said, "Well, Juliet, you can start by focusing your passion and packing the rest of the boxes out of the truck . . . *gently*. The regulars flood in right at eight a.m. and clean us out."

I glanced up at the sign behind her: *The Tomato Guru*.
Yes, I believe I can make a clean start here.

As I set down the last box of tomatoes, Molly says, "Juliet? Do you want to know my secret?" like she psychically knew I wanted to ask.

And I do. I want to know all her secrets.

And she whispers even though no one else is around, she says, "My secret is my compost." And she nods to this plastic box full of dirt she's got, and she says, "Put your hands in it, Juliet."

And I sink my hands into her dirt and I try not to think of the bodies I've buried.

She says, "Juliet?"

And I say, "Yes, Molly?"

And she says, "Women's prisons? Are they as hot as they seem on TV?"

And I can't help but blush at that. Because the answer is no. At least not for me. But I want her to associate me with things she thinks are hot, so I say, "Oh yeah."

Twelve hours later I'm moving into the little brown-and-white travel trailer behind the greenhouses in Molly's back-yard off Baca Street. Compost piles line the back fence and Molly points to a red-painted shed in the far corner before the coyote fence and she tells me the composting toilet's in there and I nod, all casual, like that's not the most disgusting thing I have ever heard in my life, because, not to sound like a gun-jumper or anything, but I think things might be getting kind of serious between me and Molly. I mean, nothing's happened, but I wonder what it would look like to visualize it. I wonder what that would lead to.

* * *

So it's weird the next day when I open the door to her green-house and she's got her back to me and I guess she's on the phone because I swear I hear her say, "They're *prisoners*, Jim. They're not *people*." And I step back real fast when I hear that. I close the door. And I wait a beat and then another beat, watching her through the glass until she clicks her phone off, and then I open the door—more dramatically this time—and I announce myself with a "Hey!"

And Molly says, "Hey, Juliet," like everything's fine and normal-like, so I decide maybe I misheard her, right? *They're prisoners, Jim. They're not people.* What would that even mean?

And that's when it occurs to me that maybe this work-release thing isn't on the up-and-up. And I think, *But I visualized it.* Like I've just got to trust the magic, and then I remember that I really didn't visualize anything but roots and *outta here.*

And I try to remember what happened to the women I knew who were actually in the gardening program, and I gotta say, I don't remember any work-release program in Santa Fe. I think *work-release* means you gotta go back inside at night or check in with your officer every now and again, and nobody said anything like that to me when they were hustling me out of there like it was some kinda heist.

And I look at Molly and I think, *I could kill her.* There's no doubt about that in my mind. But I probably misheard her.

I could make her love me.

She looks at me almost shyly. She says, "Don't you want to try a tomato, Juliet?"

And I want to try one very badly.

She holds the whole tomato up in her clean hand. She says, "It's a Juliet."

And I take it from her gently. It's very soft. I press it into my mouth, and bite down.

She says, "Juliets are my favorite."

That night in my trailer, I had a candle and I was trying to write. I wanted to write something like really fucking deep, you know? Like I wanted people to *get* me and maybe think I was special. But I couldn't stop thinking about the people I'd killed. And how everything would have been fine if they'd have just shut the fuck up. Some nights I get caught up on the past, and on all the places I've had to leave, but that night as soon as my thoughts started spinning, they slowed down.

I didn't feel so anxious.

The smell of tomatoes and compost held me.

Are Juliets really her favorite?

Outside my trailer window, it had started to snow. I opened my flimsy metal door and stepped out into the cold and upgraded night.

I looked to the darkened windows of Molly's house.

A cat leaped down from a low roof, ran ahead, and then turned back to me in the moonlight. I wanted fish to fall from the sky, but the snow felt like a fair substitute.

At the back of Molly's yard, I pressed my hands into her compost, and I swear I had the worst *Holy shit, I am hallucinating with all of my senses* moment right then, because it was a goddamn fucking human arm.

I know what cold skin feels like.

I know what a goddamn human arm feels like. A decomposing fucking arm.

I buried it deeper, rushed to the next compost heap like a crazy person, and I started digging.

I uncovered a whole body—unrecognizable, but all of it.

Then just a skull.

I kept tunneling down and it was historical trauma and bones, flesh becoming roots.

And I gotta get outta here.

When I finally tunnel up, I'm at the bar at Tomasita's waiting for my carne adovada and I'm nursing a Negro Modelo and this old man with a gray beard and a Panama hat offers to buy me a drink. I'm writing. He interrupts my writing to offer me the drink, right? And he says, "Do you know this used to be the old Santa Fe train station? Built in 1904. Denver and Rio Grande Western Railroad. Called it the Chili Line." And that's pretty fucking obvious with the brick walls and brick arches. And normally I'd say, *Listen, pal, you can take your drink and shove it up your ass*, but I'm still trying to be a better person—or a person who does right even if she's thinking wrong. The old man wants to know what I'm writing—like poetry or fiction or memoir or what? He says, "I want to write. I could write a book someday. But everybody's got to die first." And he laughs at that.

And right then the bartender puts the beer in front of me and right then, too, it occurs to me that maybe that's why I kill people. Or why I killed people—past tense.

So I could write.

I mean, is that fucked up?

Maybe everybody's gotta be dead, like the old man says.

You ever strangle somebody just to get them to shut the fuck up?

And it occurs to me that I miss the hell out of Scar.

I wonder what she'd say if I told her that—that I realized maybe I killed people so I could make art. So I could write.

And it occurs to me maybe that's what Molly's doing. *Is she gonna kill me and compost me?* Like maybe she doesn't see it as immoral any more than I do. She does it for the tomatoes. Like she's got a higher calling.

I bet Scar would *get* that, even if she thought it was fucked up.

Should I kill Molly first?

My order comes, garnished with shredded iceberg lettuce and pale pink diced tomatoes.

Maybe she would be right to compost me. Turn me into an heirloom she can hold in her clean hands.

You know, I once said to her, "Scar, I've gotten to a place in my life where I'm pretty sure the bad thing inside me isn't gonna get any better."

And I swear she didn't even blink at that. I think she *got* that.

And she didn't even seem to think it was that big of a deal.

She said, "Juliet?" She said, "You don't have to be right in your heart to act right—any more than you had to be *wrong* in your heart to act wrong."

And that kind of blew my mind.

She said, "I want you to entertain the possibility that good and bad are a false binary."

And that right there *seriously* blew my mind.

Like everything is crime and everything is punishment.

And suddenly it hits me like a call from a psychic hooker that maybe Scar is in on this whole prisoner-to-compost thing.

And that right there completed the blowing of my mind.

Visualize roots, my ass.

Maybe I just need a little bit of goddamn peace.

As I leave the bar, a train is pulling out of the depot. I stand in the gravel parking lot a long time, just looking up at the stars. *I never been to a place with so many goddamn stars.*

BEHIND THE TORTILLA CURTAIN

BY BARBARA ROBIDOUX

Southside

Ramona is a dreamer. She has recurrent dreams that often foretell the future. As a child she foresaw the death of her father when he wrapped his pickup around a tall pine tree on his way back from a fishing trip to Pecos. She asked to go with him but her father liked to fish alone in Holy Ghost Canyon. As much as Ramona and her brother Tony had begged to go, he insisted, "No, this one's for me." Another fisherman came upon the wreck but it was too late. Her father was dead.

Now sideways snow with 50 mph winds. Ramona knows better than to take the treacherous road to town but, stubborn as she is, she heads out anyway. It's the third day of the blizzard and she's been housebound too long. Cabin fever has her pacing and, anyway, she has laundry to do. She pulls a woolen peacoat on over her red flannel shirt and jeans, covers her head with a black beret, and walks out into the storm. Her '88 Chevy coughs and sputters but miraculously starts. Once Ramona hits the road, she drives slowly to town.

At the intersection of Cerrillos and Airport Road, she turns left and passes behind the "tortilla curtain" and into the Mexican part of town. Everything you could ever want or need waits at the Chamisa Center, a one-block stretch of stores: Lil' Dragon Pizza, Subway, La Cocina de Doña Clara, Dollar

Mart, the Bridal Boutique, Nail Time, Boost Mobile, a Mexican grocery store, and several places to get checks cashed. Ramona is in heaven. At the end of the block: a Laundromat.

Ramona's got a bag of dirty laundry in the backseat, so she hits the Laundromat first.

Hot air blasts her face when she opens the door; it feels good against the cold. She needs change so she drops her laundry near a washer and walks to the back and approaches a round, middle-aged Mexican lady who is glued to a small color TV set on the counter. It's telenovela time: *Abrázame Muy Fuerte* has the woman totally absorbed.

"Excuse me," Ramona says politely, "could I get some change?"

"Un minuto," the fat lady whispers, not taking her eyes off the TV screen.

Ramona waits, wondering how long until a commercial might break the woman's trance. She thinks maybe she should just go next door to the pizzeria, order something to go, and get her own change. Pizza is her favorite comfort food and she's hungry.

Tension mounts on the television screen. A very handsome but irate young man—naked to the waist—points a pistol at a beautiful young woman (presumably his girlfriend). She begs him to "cálmate" but he shouts what sounds like obscenities at her. Ramona is not fluent in Spanish but she does understand "puta."

The fat lady changemaker refuses to make change.

Ramona puts her clothes in a washer and is about to walk over to the pizzeria when she notices a young man with a long braid two washers down from hers.

The man removes layers of clothing. He takes off a filthy jean jacket with a skull and crossbones appliqued on the back and shoves it into the machine. Then he takes off a black Harley Davidson T-shirt and throws that in. Next he peels off his black turtleneck jersey and in it goes.

Ramona is transfixed. She can't take her eyes off the guy.

On his very white chest, he's got a tattoo of the Virgen of Guadalupe, roses included. The Virgen vibrates in all her splendor as the young man strips. Now he unzips his worn and dirty blue jeans and in they go. This guy is down to his boxers and white socks. He looks like he's considering removing his socks, but decides against it.

The floor of the Laundromat is cold.

The man feels Ramona's eyes on him and looks her way. "What?"

"Oh, I need some change," Ramona tells him as she walks toward the door.

At Lil' Dragon, Ramona orders a small pepperoni pizza, pays, and gets her change. "I'll be right back," she tells the pizza guy, and walks back to the Laundromat to start her wash. *Very convenient to have a pizzeria next to a Laundromat*, she thinks. She expects to see the half-naked guy with the long braid standing by his washer when she gets back, but he has disappeared.

Back for the pizza, she decides to eat it there. The booths are clean and comfortable—much better than eating in the Laundromat. The pizza is good—hot, spicy, and greasy, with a soft crust. Ramona thinks this might be a good place to work. Maybe she'd get free pizza too. Her unemployment is about to run out and she'll need a job. But not now.

It's snowing again, softening the sharp edges of this small city. Ramona returns to the Laundromat to dry her clothes. The place is now filled with young Latino women and children. *Good thing the stripper left*, she thinks. The kids run around playing games. The mothers wash and dry and fold, wash and dry and fold. *I never want to go there*, Ramona tells herself. She drops quarters into a dryer and takes a seat by the window. She's leafing through the *Rio Grande Sun* when her cell phone rings. It's her mother calling.

"Hello, Mom."

"Mija, where are you?"

"I'm at the Laundromat."

"In town?"

"Yeah, just a few blocks away from you."

"Can you come over, mija? I need your help."

"Okay, Mom, but my clothes just went in the dryer."

"When they are done, then."

"Okay." Ramona hangs up.

She wonders what kind of help her mother needs. She could have called her brother Tony. *Why me?* She waits for the clothes to dry then stuffs them back into her laundry bag. *I'll fold them later*, she tells herself. Tony's a coward. Maybe their mother needs something only Ramona can manage.

Her mother lives alone in a trailer at the Cottonwood Village Mobile Home Park off Agua Fria. After Ramona's dad died in the car wreck when Ramona was twelve, her mother never remarried. Just had a series of boyfriends. Some were good and she let them live with her; others were bad, like her most recent "old man." Juan's a mean drunk. One night when he was drinking, he busted up the trailer. He threw furniture around and broke an antique clock that had belonged to Ramona's grandmother. He said he'd burn the place down. He tried to attack Ramona's mother, but she threatened to cut his balls off with a kitchen knife and he backed off.

Her mom is a tough cookie. She called the cops and they

hauled Juan's ass off to jail. Turns out he was in the country illegally and so they deported him back to Mexico.

So Ramona knows it's not Juan her mother needs help with.

Snow keeps falling. They don't plow the roads on the Southside. It's the Eastside and downtown where the rich people live that this city takes care of—forget the people behind the tortilla curtain.

Ramona pulls her Chevy into her mother's driveway. So much snow, she thinks she might get stuck here for the night. She slides to a stop, feeling the ice under the snow.

The stairs leading to her mother's double-wide are ice-covered and slippery. She opens the door and walks in, then stops to take off her snow boots. The smell of beans and chile lures her into the kitchen where she finds her mother making tortillas. Even though she isn't hungry after her pizza, her mouth waters.

Ramona walks over to greet her mother and gives her a quick hug. *Must be Friday*, she thinks. Her mother's long gray hair is damp and smells of rosemary. Like clockwork, her mother always washes her hair on Fridays. In a room adjoining the kitchen, a fire blazes in the fireplace and the smell of piñon and cedar draws her in. The fire's heat feels good on her cold hands and feet.

Ramona grew up in this trailer. She remembers how much her dad loved the fireplace. He'd go to the mountains and cut wood every fall. Most times, the whole family piled into his old Ford pickup to go with him. Her mom packed homemade tortillas, fried chicken, and beans. Ramona's dad had special places where he cut his wood and everyone was sworn to secrecy. He'd find dead pine and piñon and his chainsaw would take them down then cut them into fireplace-sized logs. Tony, Ramona, and their mom loaded the wood into the bed of the truck. Now that he's gone, Ramona's mother has to buy firewood.

"Where'd you get this wood?" Ramona eyes the split wood on either side of the fireplace.

"Oh, from los Martinez up on Acequia Madre. They give me a good deal and the wood is nice and dry this year."

"So what's up, Mom? You said you needed help."

"I'm almost done with these tortillas; then we'll talk, mija."

Ramona pulls her chair closer to the fire. Cedar pops and crackles—the fire's soothing song. After a few minutes, her mother pulls up a chair next to her. They sit warming by the fire for a long time. Ramona hasn't visited her mother in a few weeks. She hasn't watched her mother lose her glow as her olive skin begins to gray. She hasn't noticed her mother losing weight. She hasn't seen the blood seeping from her.

Ramona faces her mother now and suddenly sees the changes. All at once, like a flower that's been hit by frost, her vibrant mother is fading.

"I'm dying, mija, and I need you to help me through it."

Outside, the blizzard is passing, but an arctic cold bears down from the mountains and freezes the land. Nothing moves. Everything is held in place. No snow melts, but the indomitable New Mexican sunshine returns.

Ramona's mother reluctantly tells the story of her progressing illness. At first she had thought it was a flu that had taken her energy. "You know I'm never sick," she says. "Strong as a mule. But everything changed and I was tired all of the time. Then the bleeding started. Just a little at first, so I ignored it. But it got worse and I finally called Dr. Maez. She told me to come right in and that I shouldn't be bleeding after ten years of menopause. So I went for the tests and now they want to operate, then maybe radiation or chemo."

Ramona feels fear enter her bones. She tastes the bitterness of grief. She tries to swallow, but can't. Instead, she goes to the bathroom and vomits into the toilet. But the grief won't leave. Her mother, her rock, the anchor that held her close in every storm, will maybe leave her. She can't shake the terrible taste of terror.

Ramona returns to the fire and sits at her mother's knees. She lays her head in her mother's lap and lets her run her fingers through her long hair. Maybe her mother can comb away the terrors that tangle in her thoughts. Ramona is overcome by the terrible desire to weep. And she does.

Ramona spends two days and nights with her mother, then she needs to clear her head. They have talked it all out: the visit to the doctor, the diagnosis, the blood work results, even alternatives to surgery. Now it all needs to settle in. Ramona needs to absorb her mother's words: "Mija, I am dying."

Ramona drives into the sun, and when she approaches a hairpin turn in the road, she thinks: *I'm dying too; everyone's dying after all*. Maybe her mother is overreacting. But Ramona knows by the sight of her mother that she is sick. Maybe it won't be fatal, though, maybe she got an STD from that no-good asshole Juan. Who knows? Maybe she should be tested for HIV. But Ramona knows that's her head talking. In her gut, she knows her mother is very, very sick.

She has a feeling that her mother is leaving her and she can do nothing to stop it. *Nothing* is a word Ramona rarely uses. She's always found a way to do something. Even in the worst times of her life, doing nothing was never an option.

* * *

The sun feels good on Ramona's face; it warms her but more than that it gives her energy. She knows she could never live without it. She drives out of town along the winding road to the little adobe house she's rented. A willow is growing in the roadside ditch. Leafless now, it will soon turn a vibrant red. Overhead, a red-tailed hawk hunts along the acequia, which runs parallel to the road. Generations back, this area was cultivated by Hispanic farmers who used the water from the acequia for irrigation. Now the ditch rarely carries water. The city holds it back for the rich side of town.

Weeks pass and Ramona's mother does not get better. She gets worse. Ramona decides to move back into the trailer to take care of her.

The first night she sleeps at her mother's trailer, the old dreams return. She was afraid this would happen, but ignored her fears in the face of her mother's need.

She dreams of that asshole Juan sucking the life from her mother like a vampire.

Everyone knew Ramona was a dreamer, but she was always too afraid to tell anyone about her premonitions. When she moved out of her mother's trailer as a teenager, the dreams stopped. Now that she has returned, the dreams have returned too.

She sees red-tailed hawks soaring above the Caja del Rio.

Ramona still needs to find a job, at least part time. So when she sees the *Help Wanted* sign at Jumbo Wash, she decides to apply.

It's a busy morning at the Laundromat. All the washers are occupied with the dirty clothes of the neighborhood. The air is thick with the sounds of Spanish and English married out of necessity into Spanglish. As she enters, Ramona notices two women leaning over a newspaper folded on top of a washer. They're involved in a highly agitated conversation regarding the news.

"That Chavez hombre es loco." The first woman points to a mug shot of a middle-aged man on the front page of the paper.

"Sí, he thought he could get away with murder. Maybe alla en Mexico but not here en el norte, no way," the second woman responds.

Ramona wonders if it's true that it's harder to get away with murder some places.

"Mira, look at this!" The first woman points to the newspaper. "It says he's trying to get off because his lawyer says he's *bipolo* and he didn't know what he was doing."

"Chingado, el Chavez shot his girlfriend in cold blood, sin verguenza."

"And she was the mother of his son, pobrecita, she didn't have a chance."

"Ay, we mujeres don't ever have a chance. La chota don't care, especially when it's a Mexican woman."

Ramona thinks they are right to feel oppressed. She walks to the back of the Laundromat where the so-called "office" is located. She wants to fill out a job application, but two women block her way in the aisle of washers. Kids are running everywhere and others hang on their mothers' legs. All eyes watch two other women.

Lola Chavez and Rosa Martinez are fighting over an empty washer. Lola put her hands and her laundry basket on the washer first, but Rosa had been eyeing it. She was wheeling her laundry in one of those wire baskets on wheels when Lola snatched the washer. So Rosa continued wheeling and ran right over Lola's left foot. The women stand face to face now, and Lola's foot hurts.

"¡Carajo!" Lola yells. "Are you trying to cripple me?"

Rosa, her dark eyes like poison arrows, looks straight at Lola and laughs. That's all it takes. Lola's on Rosa like a hawk on a rabbit. She slaps her hard across the face. She is not a pendeja. She has to fight for what is hers. She grabs Rosa's long black hair and drags her toward the door.

At that point, Maria Lopez pulls out her cell and dials 911. It takes the cops awhile, and the two women are outside in the parking lot, still fighting and spitting, when the chota get there.

Ramona needs a job, but she decides to look around, find someplace less rowdy. She walks out the door into the parking lot.

"Hey!"

Ramona turns to face the guy with the Guadalupe tattoo who stripped in the Laundromat a couple weeks ago.

He smiles at her. "Why'd you disappear the other night?"

"Disappear? I just did my wash and went home. You look different with your clothes on." Ramona steps back and eyeballs the guy.

"What's your name?"

"Ramona. Yours?"

"I'm Tino, as in Valentino."

Tino is flaco, as Ramona's mother would say—skinny. She watches him walk toward her and wonders if he does drugs. His long black braid trails him. He sports a thin mustache and a goatee. She might not have recognized him if he hadn't called out to her. He walks with a slight limp, something she wouldn't have noticed at the Laundromat, where he just stood in front of his washer and stripped. He wears tight jeans, a black hoodie, and pointed-toe cowboy boots with a high shine.

He steps toward Ramona and extends his hand. "I'm happy to see you again. Can we have lunch?"

Ramona takes a step back. "Not today, gotta get home to my mom, she's sick."

"Well, okay, then can I have your phone number?"

"Okay." Ramona rattles off the digits and Tino enters them into his cell phone.

"Want mine?" he asks.

"Later." Ramona gets in her car and drives away. En route to her mother's trailer, Ramona remembers last night's dream. In it, that slimebag Juan has come back from Mexico. After he was deported, he just spent the night in a motel and the next day walked back across the Arizona border. "Oh shit!" Ramona mutters aloud.

The trailer is warm and smells of beans and tortillas. A note scrawled on a Post-it stuck to the kitchen counter just says, *Taking a nap. Mom.*

Okay, I'll be quiet, Ramona thinks as she helps herself to a bowl of beans and pours herself a cup of coffee. *Maybe I shouldn't worry so much about Mom. When's her next doctor's appointment?*

Ramona walks into the living room and checks to see if there's firewood. She opens the glass doors of the fireplace to build a bed of newspapers and kindling and notices three cigarette butts, no filters, on the bricks of the fireplace floor. *My mother doesn't smoke,* she tells herself. She lights the fire and sits quietly as the cedar and piñon warm her.

In a few minutes, Ramona's mother joins her by the fire. "Feels good, the warmth of the wood." Her mother sighs.

"I didn't mean to wake you, Mom. How're you feeling?"

"Not bad today, just tired, mija. I've been thinking."

"Thinking what?"

"Like, what will happen when I'm gone." She pulls her chair closer to the fire.

"Don't think like that, Mom. You aren't going anyplace, you're going to get better." Ramona adds another log to the fire.

"Well, I want you to know where I keep the guns."

"What guns?"

"Your father's pistola and his deer rifle. You never know when you might need to protect yourself. They're right over there in the broom closet. The pistola is loaded." She points to the broom closet.

"Protect? Protect from who?" Ramona clears her throat.

"It's not like it used to be around here when you were growing up. We hardly ever locked our doors. But now I lock the doors sometimes even when I'm home. It's different."

Ramona listens and remembers the old days growing up when the Southside was considered the countryside. Open lots everywhere, even corn and bean fields. Now that open land has been turned into developments of Centex homes and apartment buildings.

Ramona's cell phone rings. She doesn't recognize the number but answers anyhow.

"Hi, Ramona, it's Tino. Remember me, the Laundromat stripper?"

"Oh yeah, what's up?"

"Want to have lunch tomorrow, my treat?"

"Okay. Where?"

"How about the Plaza Café Southside?"

"Perfect. I've been meaning to stop by there to see if they're hiring."

"Good. I'll meet you there around eleven thirty before the lunch rush."

"Who was that?" Ramona's mother asks.

"Oh, just some guy I met in the Laundromat," Ramona chuckles.

At the Plaza Café Southside, Ramona finds Tino in a booth.

When he sees her, he stands up and waves. "How's it goin?" he asks.

"Goin." She slides into the booth.

"Hungry?" Tino asks.

"Starving. I want a stack of blue corn piñon pancakes and a side of bacon."

"Got it." Tino waves to the waitress to take their order, then looks back at Ramona. "So what's up?"

"Oh, my mother is sick. I'm just worried about her."

"Sick with what?"

"Cancer."

Tino lowers his eyes. "Sorry."

"Yeah, just when she kicks some slimebag boyfriend out of her life, she finds out she's sick." Ramona can't shake the image of Juan sucking the life from her mother.

Tino sips his coffee.

"Yeah, and now I'm afraid he's back. He's Mexican, got deported, but you know how those guys just turn around and walk back across the border the next day."

"How do you know he's back?"

"I found three fresh cigarette butts of his in our fireplace when I made a fire last night. My mom doesn't smoke." Ramona is close to tears, but when the waitress presents her with her pancakes, she perks up.

Tino picks up his green-chile cheeseburger and takes a big bite.

"So how long you been in Santa Fe?" Ramona asks.

"All my life. You?"

"Same, born and raised, Santafesiño all the way. Funny, I've never seen you around before the Laundromat."

"Oh, I went away to the Marines right after high school. Then Afghanistan. Deployed three times, that's how I got this limp." Tino taps his left thigh. "But I'm okay now. Got a disability check. I live with my mom too."

"How's the burger?"

"Excellent!" Tino offers a thumbs-up.

The café fills with lunch customers and the noise level rises. Ramona and Tino finish their food.

"Let's get out of here." Tino motions to the door. "I'll pay up."

In the parking lot, they make small talk. Ramona thanks him for lunch and he tells her he'll call. "Maybe we can take in a movie. I hear there are some dope films at Regal 14 now."

"Okay. Call me." Ramona gets in her car and leaves Tino standing in the parking lot.

Ramona knows that slimebag is in the house as soon as she walks in. She breathes him with her first breath. She doesn't see him or hear his voice but she smells him as she walks into her mother's kitchen. She sees his half-empty plate on the kitchen table. Beans half eaten, a piece of tortilla left with the rice. Salsa jar left open.

"Where is he?" Ramona demands.

"Who, mija?"

Ramona points with her chin at the beans and rice. "Him! That asshole."

"I'm eatin' that food, mija, what are you talkin' about? There's no one here but me and you." Her mother sits at the table and starts eating the food.

"How can you eat his food and lie to me? I know he's here." Ramona walks to the broom closet where her mother keeps her father's guns.

"I'll kill the bastard." She pushes past her mother, who stands up to stop her.

"Mija, no. I'll call the cops, they'll take him away."

"That doesn't work! He just comes back." Ramona stares at her mother. "Look at you." She points to her mother's neck. "That bastard's been sucking on you again. You have the hickeys to prove it." Ramona will not be stopped. Her mother asked her to take care of her and she *will* take care of her. She holds the pistol and remembers her mother told her it was loaded. *No need to find bullets.* Her father taught her how to handle the gun when she was a little girl. They used to target practice together in the Caja del Rio.

By now Ramona's mother is crying, desperate to keep her daughter from shooting Juan.

"Come out! You son of a bitch!" Ramona yells toward the pantry just off the kitchen. She pulls open the pantry door and sees Juan crouched under a shelf of canned tomatoes, gallon jars of rice and beans. He holds a twenty-pound bag of flour to hide his face.

"Get up, you bastard!" Ramona points the gun at him.

"No! Don't shoot. Your mother loves me and she's not sick. We just made love."

"You son of a bitch!" Ramona screams. "Go to hell where you belong!" She points the gun at Juan and fires three rounds.

Juan lies dead on the pantry floor, white flour covering his face. The blood from his chest wounds mixes with the flour, creating a pink paste encasing him.

"Oh my god, mija, you killed him!" Ramona's mother

pulls Juan's still-warm body out of the pantry to the kitchen floor. "Now what?"

Caja del Rio is an 84,000-acre expanse of volcanic plateau five miles from Ramona's mother's trailer. Two abandoned thirteenth-century pueblos lie within the Caja. It's an area of piñon and juniper, big sagebush and chamisas. The roads in and out of the Caja are rough dirt roads not well maintained by the Bureau of Land Management or the US Forest Service, which oversee them.

Ancient petroglyphs carved into basalt cliffs and outcroppings watch what occurs in the Caja. It's home to coyotes, bobcats, mountain lions, and grazing cattle. Nopales turn red in the January sun.

In Tino's battered Ford pickup, Ramona and he take Juan's bloodied body, shrouded in an old blue tarp, up into the Caja.

They drive to the edge of a steep cliff and push the body off into a deep ravine.

Two red-tailed hawks soar overhead. Ramona looks out over the Caja where the sky is more than half the world. One-hundred-year-old junipers dot the red earth.

"I wonder if we really do return to the stars when we die." Ramona remembers her father telling her stories of the Milky Way and how in death we live there again. *Will even that bastard Juan make that journey?*

She steps back from the edge of the cliff. "I never thought I'd turn out to be a murderer." She faces Tino, and thinks about the first time she saw him, stripping at the Laundromat before she even knew her mother was sick. "You had to do it," Tino says. "That's it." He wipes his hands on his jeans. "Let's get out of here."

ME AND SAY DOG

BY JAMES REICH

Santa Fe Plaza

Against the mountains, a vast wave of blood broke and receded. Through the waxy aspens and bristling pines, over the crenels and ragged tracks, shucking the soil and switchbacks, it fell like a robe of red from the reclining rocks—Sangre de Cristo, the blood of Christ—beneath it all, Kuapoga—Santa Fe—where Tséh Dog drinks her martinis at Hotel La Fonda. I sit next to her at the bar. We come here all the time, like a dare, some affront, a double-dare. With the jut of her jaw and the wicked scrawl of her pomaded hair, her leather jacket, cuffed pants, and motorcycle boots, she is photogenic in her Brando drag. In the hotel it is permanent dusk, an antique light drips through the bar. We become flies in amber. The counter is curved, a scimitar shape. Beyond the square tables, margaritas, and menus, the bar is open to the arcade that rims the hotel, a series of fragrant tourist traps selling silver and leather, haute couture cowboy duds, pottery. There are crocodile-skin bags in striplit terrariums. Turquoise stares back from locked cabinets. Behind us, the sometime open-air restaurant with its central fountain hums and flashes—mole and squash blossom, poblanos and corn. The conversations are loud. It sounds like Texas.

"I think this is the hotel," Tséh Dog says, brandishing a ratty paperback, "from this book." The book is *Brave New World* by Aldous Huxley. "This is the hotel ahead of the 'savage reservation.' That's what they call it. Big men hunting from helicopters." She sips her drink, and pushes the book into her back pocket where the spine suffers. "I got us a room," she says, and there are no choices. Her smile is crooked. "Let's see if it has perfume faucets, like in the novel."

Rainbows caught in lemon bubbles—eyelashes—some bright glycerin reef, or a glossy discotheque, popping dreams glittering around Billy's asshole, a shiny penny encircled with soap. He was a dishwasher, and the hotel where we did this has been covered over with another. So it is with dreams. So it was with Billy. The last hotel is low in the rosy sediment, where the subterranean parking lot gouges like a gray goldmine. Everyone loves Billy, in the way that crows love their scarecrow. You know the sepia smut of his photograph, the stupid eyes, his rabbit teeth. I like to come to the new hotel and pretend. The scent of his groin like raw lamb, he shrugs through the furniture like a civet cat, drifts up through the floor. What was Garrett thinking with this feral boy?

We wake and it's not yet midnight, so go downstairs and walk the few yards to the plaza where the drivers of a pair of unmuffled lowriders, both sixties Impalas, one violet the other grasshopper green, are doing their slo-mo Ben Hur past the muted yellow windows of the Palace of the Governors—wolf-whistles—deferential applause—no one wins—and this is where the Indians sit in the day, surrounded by tourists who must look uncomfortably down upon them to see their jewelry laid out on black sheets. Tséh Dog doesn't sit on Indian row anymore. She struts and poses for photographs and tips. But mostly she's a pickpocket. Moonlight slips through the plaza's broad trees, strobes in the wind. Briefly, she engages with a man dressed in a quilted jacket, seated on a park bench, returns empty-handed. We're sitting on the stone steps of the bandstand, watching the past ripple across the facades of the expensive stores, where once there was a drugstore, a firing squad . . . Tséh Dog regards the gray light falling on the obelisk, *To the heroes who have fallen in various battles with —— Indians in the Territory of New Mexico.* The word *savage* was removed in 1974. She thinks of Huxley and his shining helicopters, of nerve gas falling on wolves, pueblos strafed by machine guns, and she thinks of American Spirit and Holly-wood, motorcycles and buffalo. Tséh Dog wants a Manhattan, so we go back.

The rugged, sandy-haired man in the bar says he's an astronaut. He is spending one night at La Fonda, and a night at the Sierra Grande Lodge down in Truth or Consequences, three hours south, before he is shuttled to the spaceport on the Jornada del Muerto. "Then what?" Tséh Dog asks. Mars, he tells her. The Agency's colonization project, he explains. She's imagining becoming an outlaw on another planet, a planet blushing with promise, taking a dune buggy, a motor-cycle, or a horse over the ancient curves of red sand. How old are you? he asks, and Tséh Dog says, "Old enough," and presses a cherry between her lips. He hooks it out with his tongue. Something goes wrong in the elevator to the floor where the room is, and when the guillotine doors open the astronaut is dead. "Get up," Tséh Dog insists, puts a motorcycle boot into his ribs. "Get up!" She is certain now, satisfied. The astronaut, a shriveled heap of plaid and denim, is still and silent, stiffen-ing in the gaping doorway.

He's the third. In the hotel room, he is arranged on the bed, and Tséh Dog stands over him, pulling a crease out of the blanket with its Navajo pattern. She is cool-nerved, contemptuous of the body, thumbing shut the eyes. She pulls his room key from his jeans, and $312 from his new snakeskin-embossed wallet. It has a receipt in it from one of the arcade stores off the lobby. His cell phone rings, and Tséh Dog rejects the call, thumbing that shut also. In the night, long before dawn, we'll use rope to saddle him up into the Sangre de Cristos—pinion—piñon—the astronaut will ride up there into the pines like the corpse of El Cid into battle. So much Christendom . . . Charlton Heston played Ben Hur and El Cid in the movies. "And Moses, and the astronaut Taylor in *Planet of the Apes*," Tséh Dog says. "He also played a rancher who hired Billy the Kid. And he played Andrew Jackson." That's something. His room is on the same floor. We make it with his key. There's a suitcase from the Agency and a packet of American Spirits, and a silver vinyl wash bag in the bathroom, but that's it. These things we take. The sandy-haired astronaut waits for us. Tséh Dog lies down next to him while I go through the suitcase and count the cigarettes. I'll show the stuff to Tséh Dog when she wakes up, in a few hours—rosary—book—silver flight suit, like the others . . . When the hotel is quiet, we will carry him with our shoulders like a crucified man pretending to be merely an alcoholic. Tséh Dog dreams of Billy riding on the red dunes, the plumes and plummets of their ghosts. I think of the fear and disgust rippling like heat haze through mission control as another astronaut goes missing. I open my eyes and the corpse is still there on the bed.

At another time, in slanted monochrome, Martin Richter would have been a Pinkerton man. Now he is an Agency man, paramilitary police for the Mars program, gaunt and moonlit, pulling on the dog end of his cigarette before striding toward his helicopter. It waits on the Kirtland tarmac, tense as a crouched grasshopper, a Huey UH-1, its skids pulsing and bracing outside the hangar. Lights blink on its green shell. It emits a high-pitched screaming over its rhythmic chop, before this becomes a thick percussive drone. The pilot works dispassionately through his checks as Richter climbs into the passenger compartment behind him, pulling his comm-link headset on, and crossing the belts over his flight suit. "Get us up." It should have been reported hours ago, when the biometric link ran flat, when he didn't answer his cell, or when they couldn't reach surveillance. A local cop found the watcher on the plaza, bloody quilting seeping from his jacket, around the horny grip of a bone knife. The thirty minutes to Santa Fe will pass slowly enough for him to slow his pulse, slipping it inside and under the rapid beat of the blades. Momentarily, he imagines himself on Mars, less vulnerable than these missing astronauts. There's a blank space in his consciousness where his wife and children might be. It would not be hard to leave. Martin Richter studies his phone for a moment, before addressing the pilot. "He's not at the hotel anymore. He's moving."

When we leave La Fonda, the plaza is taped off close to the obelisk. Yellow plastic flaps between the trees, sectioning the space where men scan their forensic grid for evidence. The body has been removed. Though the cops are engrossed, Tséh Dog works the throttle tenderly, and turns her black Thunderbird onto East Palace Avenue toward Paseo de Peralta. We pass the adobe-colored Basilica of Saint Francis of whom it is said that he pitied the wolf, and loved wild flowers, the vivid animals, and haunched mountains. The ropes hold the astronaut upright on the motorcycle, lashed around Tséh Dog's leather back, his rigorous arms pointing at the road, his head

encased, embalmed in a glittering silver helmet. She acceler-
ates toward a high abstraction in the mountain, chiseled by
old rain and old lightning. The road is empty and the sky is
full, the dark scattered with mica. The astronaut lolls slightly,
like a sailor bound to his wheel, or Ahab on the whale, as the
asphalt switches and undulates closer to the summit, and the
toe of her left boot works the gears. His ghost shivers under
the weight of his skin, the gravity of the speeding motorcycle.
When the time comes, Tséh Dog will stop, unfasten the knots
across her chest, and disentangle the astronaut from the cycle.
Heavy with himself, he will be carried into the pines as a deer
is carried, up the ragged slope, under the canopy of the forest.
Soon, we will stand together in the grove in the mountains
where the others are. The way is difficult. She sweats in the
darkness. Two bodies, strips of blackened flesh hanging from
grids of bone, cavities chewed from their torsos, are propped
against the rock when she brings the astronaut there, one in
the remains of his gray flight suit, one in bloodstained jeans
and a denim shirt. She places the third, wearing his helmet,
between them. The originals have been desecrated by animals, decomposed. They face west. The moon exposes them.
Here are the decaying orbits of the archangels. Here is the de-
cline of the overmen. Theirs is the madness that makes ours,
these hopeful men. Tséh Dog appears oblivious to their state,
accepting them, as she puts her weird trinity together. Whatever this is, it is her own. It has no past in her ancestors. There
is quiet fury in it, a waste of courage. It is sad to observe. The
hollows of bough and bone exchange absurdity and sorrow.
She cocks her head subtly, listening.

Like Say Dog? I had said, and she'd nodded that this was
close enough. I don't know how many years ago I met Tséh
Dog. She recognized me at Hotel La Fonda one night, the

place that sits like a ziggurat upon the crushed labyrinth of the old hotel, The Exchange, where I washed dishes. I heard her call my name. "Billy," she said, noting my shade crossing the bar, and I was brought up like a man called out on the street. My ghost is like shattered glass—some in Mesilla—Silver City—Fort Sumner—and she had one of me to scry with. She calls me Coyote, Fox-Boy, Rabbit, other things. Tséh Dog may be the future, earthbound, resistant to astronauts, protector of emptiness. "There's a chopper coming." She reaches into the leg pocket of the first corpse's flight suit.

If the others had subcutaneous trackers, we wouldn't have lost them. Yet, did it give the third a false sense of security, as if the Agency was a god to watch over him? Martin Richter studied his screen, the blue blip movement without biosignal. They were close, but both things could not be true, he thought. Perhaps the chip was damaged, reporting movement randomly, without cause, while the astronaut lay sleeping at the hotel; or perhaps he was moving, playing the tourist oblivious to the fact that his life signs were flat. Now, Richter felt a thin flush of embarrassment—better to have instructed the pilot to take him to the hotel first, to rule out catastrophe before assuming it? Now they were low over the pines, skimming the flanks of the Sangre de Cristos, closing in on a sparking microdot, their searchlight probing out ahead and below them, vicious white against the darkness. Taking the rifle from its rack, he opens the side door to a gale of freezing air, and the deafening beat of the rotors. "There!" The spotlight falls on the dead astronauts, a glitter-ball light blooming from the silver helmet of the third. The men seem to have spilled from space. The pilot's voice squelches over the comm-link, and the Huey jolts like a startled horse, as his shock translates through the stick.

Richter fires at the figure standing over the bodies. He hears the bullet ricochet from the rock. Struggling to aim again, he calls to the pilot, "Gas, now!" He sees her clearly for a moment. The hunting rifle feels good in his shoulder, riddled with cool rage. The pilot hovers the chopper over the scene. *Like shooting the wolf that took your lamb*, Richter tells himself. He fires again, and pulls on a mask as the spectral plume drifts below, but is taken by the wind, away from the grove with its terrible shrine. "Keep us still . . . Keep us—"

Tséh Dog curls her shoulder under another shot from the helicopter, like a boxer turning under a punch, raising the pistol she took from the flight-suited dead like an uppercut, fluid and fierce. She fires off-center from the spotlight, second-guessing the pilot. The second shot paints the cockpit with his larynx and milky studs of jawbone and tooth that drip down the curved glass. The chopper pitches and howls in the moonlight, the beam of the searchlight swiping over the deep trees, moving away, before it enters a terminal tilt and dives forward, as if into unconsciousness. The rotors are ripped from the fuselage and the tail breaks like a wishbone in the shredding boughs. Birds lift into the night. There are no flames. Soon there is silence. And we ride back to La Fonda.

The astronaut's possessions are in our room, like relics of the future. Tséh Dog doesn't think the Agency will send anyone here, not with one of their choppers lost up in the Sangres. Somehow, they knew we had taken him there. They will discover their crashed helicopter. Certainly, then, they will discover their dead astronauts arranged in the grove. The terror of it will hold them at bay for a time. The story will not get out, unless Tséh Dog tells it. We sleep like the dead, awaken shimmering with rude promise. "We should go down there," she says, "to the spaceport." I look at her funny. "Go to Mars in their place," she suggests. I'm not certain that she is kidding me. For the present, we ride the elevator down to get break-fast in the old Placita, now La Plazuela, the hotel dining room with its fountain. Her chromium reflection suggests that she is thinking about the third astronaut. How she killed him, I don't know. "Come on, Coyote. I'm hungry." The future is visible, like a movie, readable for those with eyes to see it.

After breakfast we walk the plaza; now the yellow police tape and forensics crew are gone. The sun is bright over the mountains. The air is crystalline, sharp with altitude. Tséh Dog has a hip flask of mezcal, and the taco carts are out. Gradually, slow in the glamour of our time, we turn the quadrants onto Indian row, where the vendors are out, cramped on their blan-kets and folding stools, with their silver, clay, and turquoise on black sheets before them. A sunburned child with a plas-tic raygun shoots sparks at the Indians from across the street. Tséh Dog combs her pompadour and gets five dollars from the parents for posing as a villain. Afterward, she curls her lip in disgust, but she does have the mother's wristwatch. It can be sold in a few days. The day goes like that. Later, we watch a Native kid skateboarding on the bandstand. The kid rumbles and scrapes in radical circles, and there are tears in Tséh Dog's eyes. She's happy. She has the bonfire taste of the mezcal in her mouth, and she's thinking about the ritual in the moun-tains. I can feel it. The pines redden at the close of day.

At La Fonda, there's a Western swing band playing in the arcade bar, and the tourists are dancing like rhinestone cow-boys and their booted cowgirls, so we take the elevator to the Bell Tower, to drink in the open air over the streets. It's quiet and the evening is glassy with stars. Lifting her martini, she points out the constellations as they emerge—Bear, Spider God, Elk Skin, Coyote, Two Dogs. Tséh Dog speaks: "*Why do we do this?* James Dean asks Bud before the chickie run in stolen cars toward the bluffs. *Why do we do this?* the boy asks his father under the spokes of the sundance tree where the hooks hang. *Why do we do this?* Jesus asks his father from the bloodstained cross. *You've gotta do something*, Bud says, and is crucified in his car. So say the fathers, but that's not it. Marlon Brando says, *What've you got?* Is it our fate to dash ourselves against the sky, to interrupt the stars with craziness?" I don't know what to say to her. By now she is soft and melancholy with the alcohol. She is out on some bough of self, and it bends under her weight. There is her gravity. There is the earth's gravity. There is Mars, and dead astronauts. She is on the rim of a red crater in being. Finally she says, "Fuck it. Let's go down and dance with the cowboys."

Unknown, I pass through the thick bodies as they two-step. They think it's the warp of their drinks working on them. No, that shiver is a ghost through your flesh, insisting, *Yes, yes, I'm here.* A guitar string twangs. The hi-hat ticks. The air is heavy with perfume, as if it runs from the faucets of the rooms. These people make me nervous, and soon I'm waiting at the edge, beneath the surface. Alone, Tséh Dog grooves and ruts between them, and a little space forms. But they can't get far from her. No one gets far, that's what I've learned since 1881. That's what it is to haunt and be haunted. A shadow is never merely a shadow, you can ask Pat Garrett. When the band takes a break, I sit beside Tséh Dog at the bar. She is panting. Sipping from her martini, she pulls out one of the relics of the third astronaut. Her smile is crooked. "I think this is the hotel," Tséh Dog says, brandishing a ratty paperback, "from this book."

Acknowledgments

As soon as I got this gig, I messaged Julia Goldberg, longtime editor of the *Santa Fe Reporter*. Yes, Julia would know where the bodies were buried. She climbed on as associate editor, and generously shared her vast experience as a journalist in this high desert town.

In addition to the talented team of *Santa Fe Noir* writers who went above and beyond their roles as contributors to share their secrets, I got early and invaluable input from the booksellers at Collected Works and op.cit.

Fellow noir editor Susie Bright consulted and cheered me on from Santa Cruz, and Akashic Books publisher Johnny Temple offered his understated advice and dark brilliance.

Thanks to Jess Clark, Cecile Lipworth, Maia Swift, Max Gore-Perez, China Martens, Rhea Wolf, Megan Moodie, Megan Kruse, Karin Spirn, and Michelle Cruz Gonzales, for your insights and support. And to my wife, Deena Chafetz, who makes the best red and green chile there is, for also keeping the wood-fired hot tub at a perfect 110 degrees.

—A.G.

ABOUT THE CONTRIBUTORS

BYRON F. ASPAAS is Táchii'nii born for Tódichii'nii. Born and raised in Dinétah, Byron now lives northeast of the Four Sacred Mountains. His life is filled with six dogs, three cats, and a wonderful partner named Seth Browder. He is currently working on a few projects—soon to be finished. He is Diné.

Evan Hubbard

KEVIN ATKINSON is a writer and performer in Santa Fe. A graduate of the College of Santa Fe, he was the recipient of the 2014 George R.R. Martin Screenwriting Grant.

JIMMY SANTIAGO BACA was born in Santa Fe and began writing as a young man in prison. He won a 1988 American Book Award for his semiautobiographical novel in verse, *Martin and Meditations on the South Valley*. He has also won a Pushcart Prize and the Hispanic Heritage Award for Literature. Recent books include the poetry collection *When I Walk Through That Door I Am . . .* and the writing textbook *Feeding the Roots of Self-Expression*.

Drew Stevens

ANA CASTILLO is a celebrated and distinguished poet, novelist, short story writer, essayist, editor, playwright, translator, and independent scholar. She is the author of *So Far From God* and *Sapogonia*, both *New York Times* Notable Books of the Year, as well as *The Guardians*, *Peel My Love Like an Onion*, and many others. Her latest, *Black Dove: Mamá, Mi'jo, and Me*, won an International Latino Book Award, a Lambda Literary Award, and a PEN Oakland Lifetime Achievement Award.

Ana June

ARIEL GORE has won a Lambda Literary Award, a New Mexico-Arizona Book Award, and an American Alternative Press Award. She's the author of eleven books, including *The Hip Mama Survival Guide*, *Atlas of the Human Heart*, *The End of Eve*, and *We Were Witches*. Her spell collection, *Hexing the Patriarchy*, is out now from Seal Press. She teaches online at literarykitchen.com.

KATIE JOHNSON leads by example with good glasses and excellent fashion. She originally hails from the California Bay Area, but has been haunting Santa Fe for many years. She earned her BA in creative writing and literature from the Santa Fe University of Art and Design. From redwoods to aspens, Katie has always been most at home in the forest.

ANA JUNE grew up in Santa Fe, swapping stories of La Llorona with her friends and partying after Zozobra. In 2017, she earned an MFA in creative writing from the University of New Mexico, where she still teaches English. Her work has appeared in the *Hip Mama* anthology *Breeder*, the *Rumpus*, and the *Santa Fe Literary Review*. She is currently at work on a memoir and a novel, and lives on a mini farm in Belen, New Mexico, with her family.

ELIZABETH LEE got her BA in English at Brown University and her MFA in creative writing at the Institute of American Indian Arts in Santa Fe. She's currently working on a novel about two sisters separated during the Japanese occupation in Korea, *Sunlight, Starlight*, and a memoir about trauma, womanhood, and infertility, *The Remembering Body*. She lives in Santa Fe with her husband and her beautiful pup Annie.

ISRAEL FRANCISCO HAROS LOPEZ was born and raised in East Los Angeles. He graduated from the University of California, Berkeley, with a degree in English and Chicana/o studies and California College of the Arts with an MFA. He brings firsthand knowledge of the realities of migration, US border policies, and life as a Mexican American to his work with families and youth as a mentor, educator, art instructor, ally, workshop facilitator, and activist in Santa Fe.

Zora Moniz

TOMAS MONIZ is an author of children's books and short stories, as well as the editor of the *Rad Dad* and *Rad Families* anthologies. He is the recipient of the 2016 Mary Tanenbaum Award and has participated in the 2016 Can Serrat, 2017 Caldera, and 2018 SPACE residency programs. His work has appeared in *Barrelhouse, Acentos Review,* and *PAL-ABRITAS*. He is at work on a forthcoming chapbook and his debut novel, *Big Familia*.

CORNELIA READ is the best-selling author of *Valley of Ashes*, *Invisible Boy*, and *The Crazy School*. Her first novel, *A Field of Darkness*, was nominated for an Edgar Award for Best First Novel. Her short story "Hungry Enough" won a Shamus Award for Best PI Story. A reformed debutante, she currently lives in New York City.

JAMES REICH is the author of five novels: *Soft Invasions*, *Mistah Kurtz! A Prelude to Heart of Darkness*, *Bombshell*, *I, Judas*, and *The Songs My Enemies Sing*. A regular contributor to *Deep Ends: The J.G. Ballard Anthology*, his work has also appeared in numerous international magazines. He is the founder and publishing editor of Stalking Horse Press, and a professor of philosophy and literature in Santa Fe. Born in England in 1971, he has been a resident of the US since 2009.

BARBARA ROBIDOUX is the author of the poetry collections *Waiting for Rain*, *Migrant Moon*, and *The Storm Left No Flowers*, the short story collection *Sweetgrass Burning: Stories from the Rez*, and the novella *The Legacy of Lucy Little Bear*. Her fiction has appeared in *Denver Quarterly*, *Santa Fe Literary Review*, and numerous anthologies. She holds an MFA in creative writing from the Institute of American Indian Arts. She lives in Santa Fe, where she is at work on a forthcoming book of poetry and stories.

MIRIAM SAGAN is the author of thirty published books including the noir novel *Black Rainbow* and *Geographic: A Memoir of Time and Space*, which won the 2016 New Mexico–Arizona Book Award in Poetry. She founded and headed the creative writing program at Santa Fe Community College until her retirement in 2016.

HIDA VILORIA is a first-generation Latinx writer, author, and vanguard intersex and non-binary activist. S/he is a frequent op-ed contributor (the *Daily Beast*, the *Huffington Post*, the *Advocate*, *Ms.*, CNN.com), consultant (Lambda Legal, UN, Williams Institute), and television and radio guest (NPR, BBC, *The Oprah Winfrey Show*, Al Jazeera, *20/20*). He/r first book, *Born Both: An Intersex Life*, was nominated for a 2018 Lambda Literary Award and has been translated into German.

Laura M. André

CANDACE WALSH is the author of the New Mexico–Arizona Book Award–winning *Licking the Spoon: A Memoir of Food, Family, and Identity*. She coedited *Dear John: I Love Jane: Women Write about Leaving Men for Women* and its sequel. She is the editor in chief of *El Palacio* magazine. Her essays have been published in *Cactus Heart*, *Into*, *CRAFT Literary*, and in various anthologies. She holds an MFA in fiction from Warren Wilson College.

AJ Goldman

DARRYL LORENZO WELLINGTON is a poet, essayist, journalist, and performance artist. He initially became engaged by the plight of the homeless while participating in the Occupy Wall Street movement. His poetry, fiction, essays, and news reports have appeared in the *Nation,* the *Washington Post,* the *Progressive,* the *Huffington Post,* and *Blood Tree Literature*. His poetry chapbook *Life's Prisoners* received the 2017 *Turtle Island Quarterly* Poetry Chapbook Award. He lives in Santa Fe.